THE VULGAR STREAK

By the same author

THE
VULGAR STREAK

By

WYNDHAM LEWIS

JUBILEE BOOKS, INC.
New York, N.Y. 10001
1973

PR6023
.E97V8

CONTENTS

PART I

VENICE

PART II

LONDON

08114

6   CONTENTS

PART III

ONE LAW FOR THE RICH

PART I

VENICE

CHAPTER I

TWO STROLLING MEN

A T the end of the Venetian street were the waters of the Grand Canal, graved with the denilunar wavelets of Venetian art. They were passing small shop-fronts as they talked. It was the morning and the September sun was hot. The taller of the two men was athletic, handsome and elegant; his companion on the other hand was a tweed-clad Briton with a Peterson pipe—of that "tweed and waterproof class," as registered by the eye of Concord.

"Venice g-g-grows on me," said the pipe-sucker, who cultivated a mild stammer. "I felt at first either something had happened to *it* or something had happened to *me*."

"To *you* probably." The tall one smiled indulgently down upon him. "Twenty years have passed. That's what's happened to you."

"I suppose so," said he of the pipe. "But don't you ever feel impelled . . . to do something about it! Der-der-don't you see a *décor* in a performance of the M-m-merchant of Venice."

"Do you know, that's the *last* thing I should think of here."

"I thought it might give you ideas for the Stage."

The stately Vincent shook his head.

"Lord no," he said.

"You've brought some artist's tack-tack-tackle with you, Vincent. You der-der-don't feel like doing a *sketch*."

"No desire whatever," Vincent laughed. "I hate sketching anyway."

"I just got a fer-fer-*frightfully* strong feeling . . . as if I wasn't . . . *paying attention enough*."

9

Vincent laughed.

"So you thought sketching was indicated, what! To keep you up to the mark."

"I suppose I thought that would help me to concentrate."

"Well, I'll tell you what. Let's do some sketching! How about this afternoon? Let's see if we can . . . concentrate. That would be fun."

They laughed together, in easy clubmanesque amusement, as they sauntered forward, at the idea of *concentrating*, the more prosaic of the two occasionally glancing up at his companion with quietly hero-worshipping eye.

"This afternoon?"

"Yes," said Vincent, "let us go into action this afternoon. Let's go out to the lagoons. The rite can be performed with greater privacy out there."

They came out upon the Piazza San Marco. The secret of this great open space, of course, is it's immunity from traffic. It belongs to man, it is not overrun by his machines. The two friends entered its sun-glazed expanse from the end opposite to its rhetorical basilica.

"I would stop here a week over my timetable, just in order to indulge in strolling! It *is* a luxury to stroll. It does my soul good." He, named Vincent, slowed down and gave a magnificent exhibition of fine leisurely strolling. "We are always scuttling to shelter, and *pushed* if we loiter, in the big cities."

"I a-agree. We should keep away from the cities. As far as p-possible."

They moved in from the centre towards the colonnades. Vincent was talking gaily, as a strolling-man, with no cares in the world, should talk. This was a most agreeable change, for since their arrival in Venice a week before he had been restless. They passed into the shadows of the shoplined cloisters.

"I shouldn't wonder if all our troubles come from the monster cities," meditated Vincent.

"Ser-ser-some of our troubles."

"Why can't we live outside them I should like to know?
Treating them as great concentration camps for the unintelli-
gent majority? Most people like them. Well, let them *have*
them."

"I certainly would endorse that," Martin agreed. "Vincent!" he exclaimed, "that's what you were looking for."

Martin stopped in front of a shop. Vincent had only half-
halted but his companion brought him to rest with an im-
perious stammer—"B-b-but *stop*! This is what you w-w-
wanted!"

In the shop window hung a large photogravure, in colour,
of a picture by Guardi. The picture represented a scene in
Venice when this extinct show-place—a godsend to Thomas
Cook—was alive with passion and intrigue. It revealed what
underlay the formal beauty, which to-day alone remains,
like a splendid ball-dress once worn by a mistress of great
princes.

A sinisterly darkened lofty apartment, into which a crowd
of small masked figures had just poured themselves, gathered
in a dark palaver. They had gone aside, into this empty
room in some tarnished palace, to set up a dark whisper.
Then later, when the maskers had dispersed, probably in a
moonlit salizzade or streetlet, a long dagger would flash, a
little masked figure would fall, crumpling up like a puppet.
Expectant and intent, they crowded their masked faces
together.

"A great swell, G-Guardi!" stammered Martin dully, his
eyes fixed in painful concentration upon the masterpiece.

But his tall friend eyed bleakly the painted scene: the only
sensation of which he was conscious was *fear*. He felt per-
sonally involved in the plots of these masked and nameless
beings of disintegrating pigment, as if they had been plotting
against him. His eyes dilated and a careworn expression
came into his face.

"Venice once was a hell of a place!" he observed glumly.
"I suppose one ought to hate its beauty."

"Oh, come! Does not that j-j-justify its crimes?"

"I wonder!" Vincent turned abruptly away from the shop. They proceeded along the arcade. They had only taken a few steps when Vincent plucked his ancient by the sleeve. His frown relaxed, Martin had a glimpse of an almost bucolically eye cocked to the left, and he knew instantly what to expect. He cursed under his breath.

"April!" Vincent breathed with a mock softness. "I must go and have speech with her! Go back to the Guardi. Go and mount guard over the Guardi, there's a good fellow. I will rejoin you anon."

"O-o-kay!" Martin gasped, in instant dull agreement, and turned upon his heel, moving towards the shop they had just left, without so much as a glance in the direction of the solitary figure of the girl seated at a cafe table beyond the pillars, towards whom his friend directed his steps. The world of girls was outside the orbit of this fat young bachelor, with his double chin so comfortably settled in his rather high collar, and his moist blue eye that kept itself to itself.

Chapter II

APRIL MALLOW

" Miss Mallow! Good morning!"

Raising his hat, Vincent Penhale stood in benign downward contemplation of April Mallow, who looked up from her Continental *Daily Mail*, pleasantly wincing, and with a pleased laugh at his presence.

"What is the news?" said he.

"The usual thing. Herr Hitler," she answered, laughing and shrugging.

As he stood there, gallant and smiling, there was something of the player about him. April was reminded of a scene upon a beach, at a south coast watering place, when she was a child. It was a beach minstrel, it amused her to realize, that had been brought to mind by this elegant young man. It must have been the way he was standing, she told herself—as if making his bow to an audience!

If Penhale's manner of presenting himself was exotic or exaggerated, reminiscent of the footlights, there was nothing in his way of dressing that departed so much as a fraction from the norm of English restraint. He was extremely elegant, but with that austere refusal to admit the claims of the imagination that distinguishes only the very best English tailor.

There was however, apart from his manner, something else, vaguely discordant: namely his face—his head. Its kind of beauty demanded the footlights perhaps and the accessories of a more picturesque epoch. And he held it, he held his head, just a shade too much like a courtier out of a coloured plate in a history-book. There was a smiling suavity that seemed to come out of a book, like a recipe for distinction.

13

"And what is the Führer doing? Is he *Fuhrious* as usual!'"

"Mr Penhale!" she screamed at him. "I wouldn't have believed you capable of that!"

Vincent laughed with gusto at his own gross verbal misdemeanour.

"Sorry!" he said, with graceful regret. "If the waiter who brought up my breakfast this morning had told me I should make a pun like that before the day was out, I should have knocked him down!"

"It was a pretty detestable one. I can understand that you would have been *furious* with him!"

Vincent dropped his arms upon the back of the next chair and gazed down at the newspaper, which Miss Mallow had pushed away. He had beneath him the banner-headlines:

PREMIER URGES CALM. HITLER SILENT
GENERAL SYROVY REPLACES HODZA

He did not read beyond them but looked up smiling.

"I consider punning," he said, "a mark of breeding, don't you? It is in the same order of things as snuff-taking, really."

"What an extraordinary idea!"

"How is it extraordinary, Miss Mallow? Reflect. The *poor* are unable to pun."

"They can't make puns?" she asked, confused.

"Constitutionally incapable of doing so," he said gravely.

"I suppose they are." She thought of the poor, and certainly she could not see them collectively engaged in punning —not in the same way that she could see them engaged in hop-picking.

"Oh, absolutely," he solemnly averred. "The only puns they make are involuntary."

"You mean . . . malaprops?" she enquired.

"Yes," he nodded, and as he did so dropped an eyelid, in a motion like a wink. "Probably they actually believe that the word *Führer* means somebody who is always *furious.*— As it does of course," he added with a laugh.

"I shouldn't be surprised if they did." She hoped he wasn't

being snobbish about the poor. She preferred the poor not to be referred to directly, anyway. She believed in letting sleeping dogs lie.

"The poor are afraid of words." He was again dogmatic. "There is that, too. It would never enter their heads to play with them. Not as we do: you and I, Miss Mallow."

She smiled blankly up at him at this. They were heading out into rather deep water.

As Vincent Penhale looked down upon the ash-blonde silk of her head, which rocked and nodded as she talked, he appeared to be weighing something coldly: a pro, and a con. The ayes had it, it seemed. April was twenty-nine—he gave her a year more in his secret computations. She had the nice face of a nice quiet twenty-nine year old girl. A big baby on the brink of thirty. As a dress-designer Penhale knew what the clothes she wore cost within a few shillings, and approved of their selection. A scheme of milky-brown and dull red russets, blended with the mind in her mild grey eyes. It was clever of her, Penhale reflected, to know the exact shade of her soul poor girl! A sad colour—such as a soul gets, thought he, after thirty solid years of babyhood, and still wide-eyed and ingenuously be-lashed.

She had a good body he could see, if a little on the heavy side. But he liked them heavy. What she did with her hips he did not know, but he saw they might need lacing—at thirty—though her waist was really small for a girl of her size. And the long wavering legs! He had enjoyed watching them stalking in and out of the table-d'hôte at the hotel, beneath the weight of those quite Venetian shoulders of hers. She was like a Titian Venus stilted up a foot or so and crowned with ashes instead of carroty gold. *And* it was an elegant stem upon which all her upper self swayed so gracefully.

His eyes had a soft look for a moment: they had relaxed. Vincent had come to a great decision.

"May I sit down?" he enquired, with a smiling elaborateness that looked ironic; as still smiling, as if to himself—in the fixed way a maître d'hôtel has of smiling—he seated himself in front of her.

"Have you decided, Miss Mallow, whether to stop on in Venice?"

She flung out a discouraged hand towards the newspaper with its giant headlines.

"I don't want to go just yet," she said. "But it depends . . . oh well, on *that*!"

He gravely inclined his head.

"Do you think there will be war?" she asked. He shrugged his shoulders, then shook his head.

"God knows!" he said. "I doubt if *God* knows." He laughed.

"What a bore it would be. Or don't you think so?" she glanced up, more than resigned to detect a blood-lusting glint in the grave eyes that were watching her. "That man at the hotel—you know that Frenchman who speaks English so well . . .?"

"I know, Monsieur Deutsch."

"Yes, Monsieur Deutsch. He told us this morning there would be war."

"Monsieur Deutsch has perhaps forgotten Mr Chamberlain."

"You think Mr Chamberlain . . .?"

Vincent Penhale nodded.

"He'll buy off Hitler," he said, looking very knowing and nodding his head emphatically.

April Mallow brightened up and frowned angrily at the same time.

"We all seem a little mad, if you ask me!" she exclaimed.

"I am completely batty!" he announced with disarming pleasantness, but with a vibration in the voice that caused her to look up rapidly to see what was wrong. "Meanwhile," he went on, in a voice below the normal pitch, "they ruin all of us. I don't see that war matters. I don't know why we should mind *that*!"

This speech, as the speaker saw, had had a painful effect.

April Mallow lowered her eyes upon the paper. She knew she was being mildly courted, and whoever yet went courting with the word *ruin* on his lips!

There was an ironic glitter as he carefully lidded his eyes and offered an explanation of his *faux pas*.

"All I mean is that we all live under a great shadow today," he said. "A *Last Judgment* like sort of a thing. Like a coming eclipse. An unhealthy sort of condition of course. War is only another shadow. I can't understand how anyone should worry about *war*. It might be the best thing for all of us."

"Do you think so?"

"We need a storm to clear the air. Anyway it would get rid of Hitler." With two long stalking fingers he twirled his hat upon the table. "I was too young to fight in the last war . . ."

"You would be, of course," she hastened to let him know that he must have been—it was obvious.

"All those of my generation feel that war is nothing. Older people take war much more seriously. Then they take everything much more seriously."

"How right you are!" she cried with great brightness. "Don't they just!"

"I have an uncle who would sooner die than go for a ride in a car. He thinks automobiles are dangerous," he gave a hearty laugh at his imaginary uncle, and she gladly joined him in this assault upon the older generation.

She had not been certain of this before, but it appeared that he quite welcomed the idea of war—horrible as it was of course. It was natural that a *man* should. She gave him a bright appraising look. His face was a soldier's, apart from his looking magnificently fit: he looked like an officer in one of those crack dago regiments, because he was so dark. But no antipathy to Mars was visible in any feature, from the brow, which frowned, to the small muscular jaw.

"Did you visit the Palazzo Pesaro after all?" she asked him.

"My god, yes!" he said. "I'd forgotten."

She laughed, very glad to have got this funny boy among things that didn't matter, like pictures.

"I gather you didn't like them!"

"No." He smiled at her—as a matter of fact he *leered* at her. For her benefit, he allowed such odds and ends of Screen star assets as he was aware of possessing—his teeth were good, and his eyes 'fine'—sociably to flower, upon the bronzed background of his face, and was gratified with the effect. She was certainly a responsive young woman.

"Why not?" asked she, gently amused.

"Oh, difficult to explain. When you listen to Sebastian Bach, would you go and waste your time with 'the Moderns'?"

"But there must *be* moderns mustn't there? We do not live in the time of Bach. *You* are a modern." She beamed at him in a youthful accolade.

"That makes no difference!" with a light hearted laugh he retorted quickly, as he stood up. "This is not a *time* at all. It is merely a gap."

"Oh!"

"However!—We're on our way to the Pizzake."

"Are you going to Lido?"

"Are you? No, I can see you're not."

"Not this morning." She shook her head.

"I shall take you to-morrow to Murano, don't forget. *Glass!*" He was moving off, calling back to her as he left.

"I shan't forget. That will be lovely."

"Also a magnificent church," he shouted.

"How lovely!" She smiled her adieu.

₁A newspaper seller rushed along the colonnade, making for the cafés, bellowing Czechoslovakia, Hitler, and Budapest. He must burst his lungs if he tried to add *Benesh*. He was intercepted by Martin, who appeared from between two columns, his pipe between his teeth.

"More trouble!" Vincent called back to April. He turned to summon Martin.

.   .   .   .   .

"News-hound!" Vincent Penhale whispered pleasantly to Martin Penny-Smythe. "Sensationalist!" he hissed in his ear. "Hysteric!"

"I jus-jus-just thought I would s-s-see," the latter apologized.

"There is nothing to see."

"We'd better step on it, Vincent."

"All right, old man."

The portly Martin set himself in cumbersome motion, with what alacrity his body could command: jumped to get into step, like a schoolboy out with the pater.

"The talks at Godesberg have been broken off . . ." Martin remarked tentatively, as they bowled along.

"That of course would happen," Vincent told him. "That doesn't mean a thing."

"B-b-but if Chamberlain flies back . . . without an agreement . . .?"

"What of it? . . . This is a game of poker, Martin. Why suppose it's anything else? It's just poker. Chamberlain and Hitler are bluffing us. They are buddies. You must see that. We should be very stupid to be taken in."

CHAPTER III

MRS MALLOW

Aᶠᵗᵉʳ Vincent Penhale had left, April sat looking at the newspaper, without reading it however. Her unseeing eye was beseiged by such vocables as *Hitler*, *Eger*, *Horace Wilson*, *Bad Godesburg*, *Theo Kordt*, and *Hore Belisha*.

This was a language with which she was perforce familiar. As when you are tired the brain will refuse to operate a foreign language which otherwise would trip off your tongue, so this portentous volapuc beat upon her sight but made no intelligible impression.

She had fallen into a day-dream upon a theme suggested by the word War. Dressed as a hospital nurse, she looked extremely attractive: and she was dressed as a nurse. To none was she more attractive than to a certain pallid and war-worn man, with a head bloody but unbowed, who was propped upon a nest of pillows in a hospital bed. Not an ordinary hospital, but a beautiful one run by the Duchess of Gloucester or the Duchess of Kent (in that order) in a delightful part of England; yes! not far from her home in Wiltshire, indeed conveniently close. Shocking things were happening up in London, bombs were raining down—the balloon barrage, as that Professor-man had foreseen, was entirely useless. But here all was peaceful and orderly . . . brutes as the Germans were they would hardly drop their bombs upon a hospital run by the Duchess of Gloucester (or even of Kent) and so these works of mercy might be performed without rumbustious distractions, by all these beautifully dressed Women of England, who hovered round the beds where the haggard young heroes lay, bringing grapes from the buttery for the more attractive, and often sitting down—between dressing wounds and trimly and smartly accompanying the doctor on his rounds—to have a cup of tea with the patient, who, poor boy, was anything but averse to a bit of female company.

Her mental cinema was abruptly terminated by the arrival of her mother: there was a rustle, a scraping, the unnatural sound of a human voice; disembodied at first, and then a little misty, there was Mrs Mallow, preparing to sit down.

"Darling, have you been here long?"

"No, not long, mother darling."

"Did you go to the post-office, dear, as you intended? They told me afterwards it was over at the Rialto. Quite a longish walk."

"I sent the chasseur instead. I felt a bit under the weather, so . . ."

"Much wiser. In this heat! Phew! What are those scarecrows of newsboys shouting about. This place is full of shouting from morning to night."

"I know."

"Europe is spoiled—it will never be the same again. I wish we'd never come to Italy. It's abominably hot—and now all this. It's ruined my holiday anyway." Protruding her head in the direction of the paper. "What do they say?"

"There's nothing very new."

"I suppose not."

"Hitler wants the whole of Czechoslovakia and, as far as I can gather, Poland as well. A slice out of Russia too. Oh, and he wants the Black Sea."

"Mr Chamberlain is arranging for that, of course?"

"Apparently."

There was a muffled exclamation, half facetious, half indignant from the older woman, who was placing a large pair of horn-rimmed spectacles upon her nose.

"Our wonderful prime minister. Terribly impressed with that awful crew at Godesberg."

April intercepted a yawn with her hand—she always yawned if she concentrated for long on European politics.

"That wretched little man will be crowned in Paris yet as the second Charlemagne, you see if he isn't," her mother nagged on, with historical relish. "The males of the species have made a jolly old mess of our planet!"

She delivered herself of the slangy expression with old-war-horse gusto. She was small, with a still handsome lively little yellow face, and, in odd contrast to her daughter, as dark as a Latin.

She began reading the *Daily Mail* with an ironic arching of her old black eyebrows. April lit a cigarette and returned to her old day-dream—though now, instead of the strident political volapuc which had danced blindly beneath her gaze before, her head was turned towards the cupolas of St Marks and her gaze mesmerized itself with the sleepy performances of a circus of pigeons, established in the ornate architectural cliffs which rose up in imitation of Constantinople, descending among the sightseers beneath for food.

The inner scene had shifted from Wiltshire to Venice: April was pondering Vincent. Mr Vincent Penhale was a dark horse. What did *Penhale* stand for? Was he this —was he that? Several things puzzled her very much. Mother, up to a point, approved. But then Mother was invariably wrong: Mother's standards were those of another day.

Mary Mallow had of course pondered this interesting young man too. She had remarked the budding interest her daughter was taking in him: she had noted the evidences as she thought of economic ease—the age of the "boy" in question (not much more than thirty-six though probably that) and for Mrs Mallow the man must not be too young— *the right side of forty* was the best as she saw it. She had appraised the resolute eye, if a thought ill-tempered. Self-confidence—he had that. Public-school backgrounds appeared indicated. Perhaps Oxford. Mr Penny-Smythe was Oxford. So that was all right. Mary Mallow had not regarded it as necessary to restrain the tendency to smile with welcoming lips, on the part of her daughter April, when a certain tall impeccably dressed fellow-guest at the hotel would draw near to them and bow, with a hint of un-English formality. (But Penhale was a Cornish name. And Cornishmen were Celts of course. Some were very odd-looking. Penhale, as a matter of fact, was the best-looking Cornishman she had ever seen).

So far so good; for all this April had, in her turn, noted. Vincent was among other things an exceptional conversationalist. But to be exceptional was not the first recommendation, it belonged to the order of dubious male assets. Next came his artist-status. When asked what he did, he said, "I am an artist." He seemed very knowledgeable about pictures. But she found it very difficult to arrive at a definition. He could not be a *professional* artist. Of that she felt sure.

He was a queer boy decidedly. But he was young, mused April—or at least *sufficiently young* so that his unorthodox views could be put down to youth. Or was youth too strong a term in this case? What was it that fell short of the attractiveness of youthful rebellion in some of his remarks? something that made him seem—yes, *older*, somehow? April frowned—he was certainly well provided with money. She could not help remarking how he had tipped the gondolier when he had met them at the Ca' d'Oro; it must have been twenty lire, the way the man bowed and scraped. No, he could not be a professional artist.

Vincent was *original*. Perhaps he was a genius. April was not sure whether she liked him well enough to be *quite certain* that he was a genius. But it was quite on the cards. And it did account for that slightly peculiar impression she had received once or twice. April Mallow sighed and moved lightly in her chair, coming out of her meditative trance. Her mother withdrew her face from the paper, and its expression was far from conciliatory.

"That dreadful blackmailing person has stolen a march on

our P.M. in his mountain lair at Berchtesgaden, or it looks uncommonly like it."

"They are somewhere else, now, mother darling. They're meeting at a Rhine town, aren't they?"

"Same thing! It would be just the same if they were in Downing Street. If it had been Lord Baldwin there'd have been a different tale to tell."

"He was a strong man . . . I think they call them. Wasn't he?"

"Best P.M. we've ever had. The only stupid thing he ever did was to retire. He was quite a young man, too, for a politician."

Mrs Mallow grunted darkly.

"He'd have settled Hitler's hash!"

April sighed. She was gazing at the mental picture of the little rotarian Napoleon, as popularized by Low, in her mind's-eye—standing at attention in the back of her consciousness, and slowly raising a jack-booted leg till it stuck out at the national-socialist salute.

CHAPTER IV

VINCENT'S CONFESSION

"IL pic-pic-picoli canale! S-s-sisi! Il picoli canale!"
Martin vociferated from his seat in the gondola, with
all the pomp of British aloofness from the foreignness of foreign tongues. And the gondolieri sang back—though a very
different boatman to the turcoman puppets of Canaletto—
that he would follow the small canals, he understood the
wishes of the signori.

Martin sat squarely, in frowning state, an expression of
almost official reserve upon his Bellocian features.

"You pocket Belloc!" Vincent had hissed, in the early
days of their association: "How on earth did you get to look
like that!" and Martin had blushed. For Martin knew how
uncannily he resembled—upon a smaller scale and allowance made for his great advantage in years—the celebrated
catholic.

Almost immediately the dongola had left the steps, Vincent had begun.

"You've never seen me at this before, have you Mart?"
he remarked offhandedly. He was stretched out in front of
the other, his face upturned, to catch the full impact of the
sun. He had a satchel, containing sketching material for
Martin and himself at his side. For they were ostensibly
in search of pictorial concentration.

"Seen you at wer-wer-what, Vincent?"

"Oh . . . don't you know what I mean? After a woman."
Martin frowned.

"Ner-ner-no. It is a novel spectacle."

"Well, I've always done it."

"Indeed! I was not aware . . ."

25

"Indeed yes! I started young. When I was just nineteen. I slept with the local Vicar's youngest daughter. She was a year older than I was. I must tell you about that some day."

"Yes do. I should l-l-love to hear about the Vicar's daughter."

"A jolly pretty girl. She was a Cavendish."

Such sixth-sense as their great intimacy gave him made it plain to Martin that what his friend was now talking about was very important to him, in spite of the casual manner. He was not enjoying this. He was not talking about his conquests *for pleasure*. There were many things about which Vincent was as close as an oyster. The oyster was opening up. The process threatened however to come to a stop, for Vincent remained silent and brooding.

Martin stirred himself and blurted out with a puzzled frown—

"A Cavendish!" He had been genuinely puzzled by this most irrelevant piece of information.

Vincent nodded in confirmation.

"She was a pukka little swell. It was my first taste of the women of the upper classes."

"Indeed!" Martin was still more bewildered.

"Yes. I like 'em. You'd never guess why Martin. Shall I tell you? But I do hope the whole subject does not revolt you too much?"

"Not in the least, my dear chap!" Martin fruitily lisped. "Why should it?"

Women as a subject was certainly not taboo for Martin. Prostitutes of course were a much less controversial subject than the other sort. A good straight tart was in an abstract category, disinfected of all hypocritical and horrid privacies, as full of fresh air as a public conveyance. His robust catholic heart went out to the tart. He would have highly approved a visit by Vincent to the local brothel. That was the correct, the classic, solution.

Martin was a catholic convert. That was why he had got to look like Mr Belloc, or, once established, that resemblance was why he had gone papist. Upon profane love he had views of a suitable orthodoxy. In his hearty, super-catholic, way he would abet, he would condone, anything that left the marriage-tie intact. But attacks upon such young ladies as Miss April Mallow were a different matter altogether. Here, too, his personal prejudices came into play. Miss Mallow as an object of desire frankly disquieted Martin. She was quite a nice girl, and certainly pretty—rather too pretty —but not a very interesting person. He had far too high an opinion of Vincent to suppose that he would fall for a pretty tennis-playing Miss. He snorted at the very thought.He had said to himself more than once in the last few days that should Vincent blossom out, beneath his eyes, as a lady-killer —in contradistinction to an honest whore-master—that would be a contretemps he declined to contemplate.

Miss Mallow and he eyed one another with a perfect understanding on both sides of how small the sympathy between them could ever be. Middle-class young women of the April type were to Martin's mind a scented and silken sect from which he did not exactly avert his eyes, but which he kept firmly at arm's length. If he tended to advertise himself as a member of "the tweed and waterproof class," it was partly with this end in view. There was nothing like a good big Peterson pipe for keeping a woman at a distance. That was one of the many uses of a pipe.

"Well, I will tell you, Martin, something that is a great secret." Vincent sat up and looked over at him brightly. "It is the skeleton in my cupboard. I am going to pull it out and show it you. I made up my mind to do so this morning and decided I might as well take this opportunity of *coming clean*, as they say in mystery stories. I said to myself: 'I will put my cards on the table.' And that is what I am about to do."

"This all sounds very por-por-portentous!" Martin gasped.

"You're going to have a big shock! You really are."

"I'll do my best to s-s-stand up to it!" the donnish voice purred and chuckled back.

"This is a *confession*, Martin—a very grave one I am afraid. I hope you will realize that. I am not about to ask you to accord me your apostolic blessing for a little mild seduction. It is far more serious than that."

"Well, let's have it. Let's hear, Vincent, wh-wh-what it's all about."

"Will you hear me at once, Mr Father-confessor?" Vincent humbly enquired.

"Proceed, my son!" Martin mumbled, settling his double chin in preparation for this séance he appeared to be in for.

"Thank you. I will prepare myself for confession."

Vincent folded his hands in his lap and smirked darkly for a moment, looking, as a fact, far more like a priest (on the point of being defrocked, but still most professionally levitic) than did his convert-confessor. "I fear that I have sinned. Please give me absolution."

Martin bowed his head, folded a fat leg, cast down an eye, prepared to do his stuff.

"It's difficult to start."

Martin appeared to doze. Vincent began, his eyes cast down, chanting his words a little, in an undertone, to imitate the conditions of the confessional.

"I am the son of a workman," he announced meekly. "Of a labourer. That is my major, that is my mortal, sin. It is for that I have above all else to petition for forgiveness."

He paused. His face had a painful contraction, like a child's who has swallowed a bitter medicine. Martin looked up in amazement, forgetting his part. What for mercy's sake was this act Vincent was putting on? Vincent the son of a labourer? What preposterous nonsense was this?

"All my other backslidings," Penhale went on, "emanate from that. They are effects of which that is the horrible cause. And if you protest that the word *horrible* overstates the case, then the full horror of the case must be hidden from you. You have no inkling of what it means to be born in the 'working-class' in a democracy of snobs—in Edwardian England.

"In that free land, to which we both belong, I was born unfree, because I was born of working people. I was born so that I could not lift up my eyes without circumspection to look in the face of a member of the master-class. That educational system, so cunningly devised for the underdog, saw to it that I should continue to speak with an accent that branded me as an inferior. As a man of *no class*—as a man of the 'lower class.' You on the other hand, issue from the ree—the 'monied'—classes. I issue from the ranks of the 'under-privileged.' Coming as I do from that great majority of Englishmen who are born beneath something like a feudal curse—or post-feudal, which perhaps is worse: who have to address as *sir*, as the stigma of their inferiority, all who are 'educated'—who are 'gentlemen,' as they are taught to think of them; I, coming from that dark and tongue-tied multitude, you coming from that privileged minority, I was obliged to *lie*, in order to gain your confidence. To make our friendship possible, upon terms that would preclude patronage, I was obliged to deceive you. For the 'classes do not mix,' is a good old English dictum, which I could not forget if I tried.

"So I misrepresented myself. I transformed my father into a prosperous solicitor. He is really a labouring man—an old evil-smelling, aitchless and g-less, serf; just as truly a slave as any negro sold in a Mississippi market before the emancipation. But I could not exactly *say* that, could I? Or do you think I could? Put yourself in my shoes, Mr Penny-Smythe."

Martin, his eyes cast down, shifted very uneasily indeed upon the cushion of his seat. This was truly awful! What was the fellow going to say next?

"Born in the gutter, as the expression goes (I was not romantically conceived at Tintagel, as I pretended, but pupped a few feet above one of the dirtiest gutters of Poplar), I taught myself to speak and act like this. As you see me doing, in this beautiful and polished way. *Now* I speak the same language as you. Once I spoke another tongue almost.

No mean feat, you must agree. To teach myself Sanscrit and Hebrew would not have been more labour.

"In my composition is a great deal of the actor, which was just as well. I possess also a singularly good ear. But still I am a sham person from head to foot. I feel empty sometimes, as if there were nothing inside me. I lied to you at once when I first met you. I began building up a false image of another man than myself. Of someone who was not there. For *I* am not here. It is not I who am here. And ever since in my intercourse with you I lived inside that empty shell that I began to manufacture . . . But of course at present it is second-nature until I hardly know which is the real man."

Penhale paused—as if searching in what he was laying bare for something he wanted to find. He seemed to abandon the search.

"What is more," he said, "something like the appetite of the artist for his clay, or for the colours he uses in his creations, supervened. Necessity having taught me to disregard the truth, I have developed a relish for all that is not true. If I am able to deceive people, that elates me. I get a big kick out of fooling them. (But quite *innocent* I promise you that!)

"I have not always been like this. Once I *confessed* to a man: just as I am doing to you now. He was horrified. He was nearly sick. I never made that mistake again.

"This confession goes against the grain. It is difficult for me to make it—because I am violating what has become second nature by this time. I am telling you the truth."

As this "confession" proceeded, the effect upon Martin Penny-Smythe was almost ludicrous. He was quite unable any longer to conceal his extreme discomfort.

He had, to start with, believed that Vincent was putting on an act. But after a very short period of stupefied uncertainty he was convinced that these were *facts* that he was hearing. Horrible facts! Not only ugly and squalid in themselves, but in the way they were being interpreted. Vincent's reaction to the facts he revealed was the worst part of the disclosure.

He gazed away in tremendous embarrassment. Painfully he unfolded his legs, allowing them to lie dejectedly side by side. The Bellocian personality suffered a disintegration. Some spring had been touched, as it were, and the whole set-up had begun to drop to pieces. The little imitation Belloc, as artificial in its way as the bogus Public schoolboy and Old Haileyburian, and all the other *personæ* in sight, began to come unstuck, in the insidious heat of this strange confessional.

This man was after all his best friend—indeed his only very close friend—who was unmasking himself in such an aggressive manner before him. For there was no question that aggression entered into it.

Never for a moment had it occurred to him that Penhale was not exactly what he represented himself to be, a gentleman, that is one who from birth had enjoyed the same social advantages as himself; except that Penhale had no private means, or had not until recently. Now he seemed to have money enough, though he had said very little about where it came from.

A sensible period elapsed before Martin regained his poise. He lay back, staring stupidly in front of him. But by shaking himself, as if to call upon his reserves of social aplomb, he got back sufficient to reconstitute the Bellocian exterior. Vincent, as he proceeded with his narrative, was watching him all the time, which did not improve matters. Martin had distinctly the feeling that *he* was being unmasked as well. There had after all been two actors upon the stage. If one insisted on stripping off his properties, that left the other in an invidious position.

"But Vincent, what about Hay-Hay-Haileybury!" the stammered. "How did you manage to get there? Or did-did-didn't you!"

Vincent smiled mournfully and shook his head.

"No, I didn't—not in the sense you mean. I was never at school there. My father had a job there once, as servant of the headmaster. He stood by as a bodyguard when boys were being birched. My, mother scrubbed the Head's study out, while my father put the rods in pickle."

Martin scratched his head.

"It's a rum go, isn't it!" laughed Vincent.

"It *is* a little rum," Martin ruefully agreed.

"*That's* an expression now—'rum go'—I was very proud of when I first acquired it. It came out of the *Magnet* as a matter of fact."

"Out of *what*?"

"The *Magnet*. A weekly magazine that is widely read by the children of the poor."

"Never heard of it."

"Never heard of the fat boy, Bunter? You should have a look at it. Very curious and instructive. It's all about Public School life. Pathetic isn't it?"

"It-it-it is . . . rather." Martin looked up uncertainly. "I don't know whether to ter-take all this *seriously* . . . or *not*. I der-der-don't believe it's *true*. Is it true? Or are you ragging me? You are not a trained actor for nothing."

"It is unfortunately true." Vincent leant over towards him and held out his hand. Martin shrank, grinning, from it, in great confusion. "Will you take my hand, Mr Penny-Smythe sir, and say you forgive me for deceiving you?"

"Don't be a fool, Vincent!" Martin Penny-Smythe protested testily. "Do stop playing the fool."

"You refuse to take the hand of the labourer's son . . . who rose from nothing into the ranks of Penny-Smithery!"

"Vincent! Will you per-per-please stop playing the fool!"

"How do you know, sir, that my name is Vincent?"

Martin was more shocked at this than by anything yet. Suppose Vincent were not Vincent? Suppose there were *no* Vincent, and this had been an illusion? Suppose he had to call this man Bill or Bob hereafter? He threw himself back in mute exasperation, pulling hard upon his pipe, which emitted a frustrated gurgle.

"It is Vincent however!" Vincent assured him. "I was given that first name, redolent of victory, no doubt in an ironical moment. No. The poor are incapable of irony. Perhaps it was in mockery. The poor are not strangers to that."

"Vincent! . . . listen . . ."

"Yes, sir! And as to my patronymic, that is quite o-kay. My forefathers were called Penhale right enough. You need feel no uneasiness regarding my names. No readjustments are necessary there."

"*Please* Vincent . . . der-der-don't be such a silly ass, if you can help it!"

Vincent laughed—a light and sceptic laugh.

"All right. I see you are getting over the first shock. Now I can go on with the story of my life. I am a Celt—I belong to the older, finer, race. That gave me an initial advantage. No Saxon could have done what I did. My father—who did, in fact, come from Cornwall, as I always told you— is a fine nervous man, who, apart from the shabby workman's clothes that his 'humble' station impose on him, looks far more the gentleman than most people who pass for that because they had 'people' with the necessary jack to send them to a 'good' school—where a hundred or a thousand other snobbish little brats confirm their worst characteristics."

"Don't rub it in, old man! I only went to wer-wer-Westminster. We had lots of p-p-proletarians there."

"Westminster and New College Oxford. The jack that's been spent on you first and last, to make you what you are!"

"Spare me, V-v-Vincent! Sp-spare me!"

"To proceed. He really looks quite an old swell at times, does my old dad. That gave me the first idea, perhaps. I must as a small boy have wondered why he smelled so musty, why he had that scarecrow outfit of the labouring poor—he who, had you dressed him up as a swell would certainly have looked the part. When later I came to understand the full reality of my unpleasant position, one of my first ideas was to get hold of *clothes*. Last of all I understood about my *voice*: that was the last and worst of my evil discoveries how the way in which I spoke my mother-tongue, however much I might disguise myself in beautiful clothes, would betray me. When I first understood *that*, I did see red. I could have bitten my tongue out when I realized that every time I opened my mouth I advertised my 'humble station.' But I set to work. I was helped a great deal by my elder sister."

"Was that . . . Victoria? The one in Canada?"

"That was Victoria, as you say. She had pulled herself out of the mess. And when she saw I had inclinations to do the same, she lent me a hand. It was she who introduced me to the Vicar's wife—whose daughter subsequently I got through . . . I mean I lay with. I beg your pardon."

"It's immaterial to *me*, Vincent, her-her-how many Vicar's daughters you corrupted. Why apologize to *me*."

"Right you are. I'll skip that next time. Now what I shall be saying next will disgust you rather. For I shall be talking about my *face*."

"Is *that* not your own then?"

"Oh, yes. That's genuine. But I will explain. When you are born so denuded of every advantage as I was, one seizes upon anything that can be turned to account. Just as much as does hunger, humiliation sharpens one's wits. Quite early on I became aware of that. I possessed an asset; of all unpleasant things, in my face. I had a well-shaped *face*. I had a gentleman's face."

And as he spoke, the *face* was there in front of Martin, smiling at him with a twisted Clark Gable sugary smile of such deliberate, almost sickly, pathos, that Martin hurriedly looked away. This was really getting too much of a good thing! But he could hardly stop Vincent and inform him that he was not interested in all these objectionable details. On these lines however, they might reach very embarrassing subjects at any moment. And sure enough at once they did.

"Don't you like my face eh, any longer?" Vincent softly jeered. "Well, I can understand that. You've never had to think about your personal appearance. If people didn't like your looks, well they could do the other thing. Not so with me. I have always been on show. Now you may, or may not, have observed how personal beauty functions. Should you not have given that matter your attention, I can illustrate it very easily. Take (if you don't object to that) our personal relations. I do what would be called 'dominate' you, to some extent, don't I? Well, leaving out of count all the other odds and ends that go to the making of *friendship* between two men, and of what gives one the mastery over the other, our relationship would have had quite a different pattern had I possessed a tubby, undistinguished presence, such as yours, and had you been tall and well-proportioned, possessed of the physical beauty that is undeniably mine. I should then have followed *you* as now you follow *me*."

Martin continued to avert his eyes from the face that was under discussion. His eye was upon a woman who was about to empty a pail of garbage into the waters of the canal. Where did it all go to anyway? She heaved it over with the rhythmical disinvolture of a figure of Tintoretto. The ritual of the cloaca. The Italians still had the repertory of gestures that made up the grand style. His eye ran down the vista of beautiful rose and russet dilapidation. Odd to have an architectural paradise established upon a sewage-farm. He sighed—it was a dismal wheeze. Nature made one pay for one's illusion! By associating beauty with bad smells. But Vincent's voice went on, gathering zest as his theme grew more (as it seemed to Martin) gruesome.

"My face plays a very important part, then, in this relationship of ours. Even my excellent muscular development counts. I could knock the guts out of you if we had a fight, couldn't I? Well, that goes for something. Anyway, I lead."

"I don't know why you're saying all this," Martin observed, looking at him with a touch of indignation. "Soon you will be producing in evidence your genitals."

Vincent laughed appreciatively. "It's all part of the story of my life. Aren't you forgetting your rôle of father-confessor! To get back to my face. As a youth, my face had character as well as beauty. (You can't help getting character into your face, if you're born in the walk of life I was). My face—and the rest of my physique, of course—has had a great influence upon my destiny. I realize that now, looking back. Perhaps it has not got me very far, but it has smoothed the way on numerous occasions. Very soon I shall be forty years old. It will not hold out much longer, I am afraid. I see signs of deterioration. So what . . . as my Canadian sister would say!"

As Vincent sat looking at him, and his flow of words appeared to have halted, Martin moved dispiritedly and spoke.

"You seem," he said, "to have had things all mapped out very carefully. The er-story of your ler-ler-life has been a remarkable one—if that is the end of it?"

"My dear man, I have not finished. But there is something that might give you an even greater shock: that I will reserve for another day—for we shall remain friends in spite of all this. I feel sure of that. But I have yet to make a few remarks about my amours. It seemed odd to you that so very conventional a girl as April Mallow should attract me? I an 'intellectual.' An artist. Well, after what I have told you perhaps you will dimly understand."

Martin shook his head as if to shoo away a tiresome fly.

"I suppose I see what you wish me to understand, Vincent." (He was stammering very much less. This his friend was quick to notice and a smile came to his lips as he listened. So he had cured Martin of his stylistic impediment *à la* Charles Lamb!) "But you dramatize this per-per-precious *humble origin* of yours as you describe it—if it's as you say it is—a little o-o-overmuch. Don't you?"

"Oh, I suppose I dramatize it yes. What else can one do with such a thing? A cripple or a deformed person can derive some comfort I suppose out of a little dramatics. People with unsightly physiques I have often thought enjoy alarming others with what otherwise would awaken pity or ridicule."

"There may be s-s-something in that. It seems to me however you get such a kick, as you say, out of exaggerating . . ."

"No. I'm not exaggerating. You cannot exaggerate the social handicap I have revealed. It lies like a blight upon three-quarters of England. I grew up in that poisonous air, of class-discrimination: of the superstition of *class* like a great halter round one's neck—in which my very tongue was branded as if I were a despised property. No overstatement is possible *there*. But that was a long time ago . . . Martin. (I shall still call you that, with your leave). The actor who plays all the time the Prince of Denmark, in the end is more Hamlet than anything else. I *am* by now what I *seem*. I am of course a snob—like you. I look at things with the same eyes as you do. I have made this confession. And there is the end of it. . . . We go on as before, Martin Penny-Smythe."

"Not quite," said Martin. "Let me say, Vincent, how t-t-terribly sorry I am that you have suffered ser-ser-ser-so much. I am more your friend if anything, now you have told me this, than before. I am . . . *ashamed*."

"That's jolly decent of you, Martin. You're a brick." Vincent said this without any apparent consciousness that 'brick' belonged to the *Magnet* vocabulary. It was Haileybury speaking—to a rather inferior school. (Westminster?) He was a great gentleman, putting at his ease some stammering subordinate. "But I'm pretty tough you know!" he added with an easy laugh. "Pity would be quite out of place."

Vincent lighted a cigarette, then smiled down at the glutinous water as he threw the match away.

"Confession, Martin, is a great sport," he said. "A great sport. How right you catholics are to keep it up!"

"Why did you suddenly experience the desire Vincent . . .?"

"To resort to confession?" Vincent laughed. "Ah, *that* would involve another confession." He stood up and pointed at a church, appearing upon a platform, surrounded by water. It was Sunday, a procession was issuing from its baroque portal. "Cameraman forward!"

Martin who had brought his camera with him soon had it against his stomach, as he sighted the church.

"Wh-why don't you get him to pull in, and sketch it? That's a bew-bew-beauty!" His stammer had returned—a sign that all was normal again.

Vincent shook his head quickly.

"No, I don't feel like any more performing just now."

"Not now?"

"Not just now. Let us get out to the lagoon and *bask*. I don't want to sketch, do you? I don't want to 'concentrate.' I feel I never want to concentrate again. Let's just bask— and sing."

He sang a few bars of a sugary American lullaby.

CHAPTER V

LIDO (THE NAVY FOR VINCENT)

THEY had been bathing from a boat. April was dragging her long flamingo legs on board, and Vincent was doing a last duck-dive, with all the upside-down aquatic intoxication of a temperamental Chinese water-owl. Again and again he dashed his heels into the air and his head into the Adriatic.

This was intended as a jubilant exhibition of mastery, on the part of the star-instructor. For it wound-up a period of intensive instruction, during which he had several times nearly drowned his attractive pupil, with a determined pedagogy that had left her without a breath in her body. Her feet had been more often in the air than her head. Half sobbing and water-logged, when she *was* right way up, she had been forcibly coaxed into another submarine somersault.

Now he followed her, dripping and with doggish grins, into the boat. His torso, basket-worked with exact muscles, did credit to the Riviera sun, where he had collected this athletic colouration.

"I'm through!" there was pathos in his gasp, disarming modesty in his words. "One has to be a youngster . . . to go on doing that!"

April had drawn the towel round her, offendedly it seemed; and her breast had a rise and fall, too, as she sat a little stiffly at rest; she was indignant as well as spent. As he referred to his years, however, the frown broke down. A smile began covertly to play about her lips—a reluctant smile of pathetic age—solidarity. She drawled at him demurely—

"Your years, you poor old man, do not seem to weigh so heavily on you as all that! I'm bound to say I didn't notice it at least. It would be better perhaps if they *did*, don't you think!"

She looked away as he sat down beside her blotting the water off his chest with a sun-scorched towel.

"No, but one has to be fit as a fiddle," he answered, "to keep that up. The years do tell!"

She turned and smiled banteringly at him, almost boldly. His judgment had been excellent he told himself—this subject drew her like a magnet. Good old *useful* Father Time.

"You didn't consider my years young man," she crossly purred, "when you were whirling me about like a top!"

He administered another turn of the screw, upon her melting vanity.

"On the contrary, my dear, I made allowance for *every single one* of your four and twenty summers. The immersions were timed to a second!"

She beamed silently in response. But as he only went on smiling at her, likewise in silence, she once more turned away her head. His steady smiling eyes told her something of which she had not been perfectly sure up till then. Her frown returned.

Whatever it might cost her she must make up her mind to it—for she already realised that there was a cost involved. This young man was among other things a cad. The sooner she realized that and took the necessary steps by terminating their acquaintanceship the better. Oh, how she wished she had understood this earlier!

They lay, still panting from their recent exertions, for a few minutes more. The Italian boatman smiled at her in sunny detachment, comparing this big splendid foreign girl with his dirty raucous garlic-tongued housewife, whose skin was the colour of dirty mustard and her little bony legs shrunken with child-bearing. He smiled in sunny detachment and left it at that. But she saw his eye, with the innocence of that of an animal, basking lazily upon her beauties. Of a sudden she felt isolated and nervous. At other times that would not have mattered. But there was another man here now, supposedly

of her own class and kind, who turned out (shockingly) to
be only another strange man—in the category of boatmen,
waiters, and game-keepers. Not as she had supposed a
gentleman.

The boatman's oily Latin face became suddenly offensive.
It had an insolent leer. There was nothing *sunny* about it!
The fact that the privileged man at her side had put himself
in the same category as this unnoticed underdog, gave the
latter an importance that otherwise he could not have had.
She flashed her eyes angrily at the harmlessly ecstatic
fisherman.

"I think we'd better go back," she said, as coldly as
possible to the smiling Vincent, looking at him under her
eyelashes, and then removing her gaze like a supercilious
lighthouse, transforming its unwinking beam from one part
of the ocean to the other.

"At once?"

"I think so."

"Yes, why not!" he agreed heartily. "When we're once
more clothed and in our right minds we can go to Farrario's
for lunch."

"I think I will go back to the hotel."

Miss Mallow did not return from the Lido to the hotel.
An hour later she and Vincent were sitting upon the terrace
at Farrario's beginning their lunch. He had persuaded her to
stop and she was glad now, as they sat so happily together
among the *fearfully* noisy smart holiday makers, the growl
of the swing music providing the correct undercurrent of
cosmopolitan hysteria.

He had been ever so gentle and sweet as if to make up for
it, she thought, and if he wanted to put out of her mind,
forever, that . . . Oh, did it matter? Why must she hark
back—it was she that was horrid. Men were queer . . . look
at the books they wrote like that horrid book Vincent had
lent her. They looked at things utterly differently from
women. Vincent too had lived a Bohemian life, where one

contracted habits that in another man would stamp him an outsider if not an out-and-out cad. Their way of thinking about things in Bohemian circles was awfully original. What, she wondered, would pompous little Major Hoskyns say if he could have heard the kind of conversation that they had just been having? She could just see his face! and poor old Jim Plomer although he was younger than she was would seem a perfect *old fogey* compared with the vivacious Vincent. What a nice name Vincent was! It meant *conqueror* and she had to confess that Vincent had made a conquest of *her* all right. She had never felt this way before, as if she could eat out of a young man's hand. But did he love her? She could not make up her mind. That was why she hated so much . . .! But she must not keep thinking about that. Besides, what had taken place in the water might well have been an accident, in that awful rough and tumble. It was she who was horrid. He had a beautiful body that you could put any clothes on to and they would look nice, though his clothes were smarter than any man's there. He must be as strong as a horse—but he told her he had been captain of the school Fifteen at Haileybury and she thought he had said he was a Swimming Blue too, but she was not sure.

As if he had read her thoughts he asked her if she had ever been to Haileybury. She said, *Yes, twice as a matter of fact.* He changed the subject and asked her suddenly what her father was.

"He is dead," she replied astonished, "but he was something *very* unromantic."

"Impossible!"

"He was a stockbroker."

"Stocks and shares are *too* romantic if anything," he replied, "that's what is the matter with them."

"What is yours?" she asked shyly.

"Dead too," he said, pulling a solemn face. "He was a diplomat. He *had* to be a diplomat as a matter of fact because all his family had been diplomats. However, he suffered from a lack of what *your* father dealt in!"

"Oh, no! Stocks do you mean? If they could have got together now!"

"I wish they could have!"

"Mine always said he *hated* stockbroking."

"Mine loathed diplomacy. Too much dissimulation necessary for *his* taste. He always wanted to be a painter."

"And what would you soonest be—if you had your choice? An art . . . I mean a painter?"

"Heavens, no. That entails *work*. That is, the great drawback of most of the arts."

Art entailed work? He was pulling her leg she thought, and smiled self-defensively.

"No. I should rather not be a man at all," he announced.

"Not a man . . .?"

"No. I should like to be an owl . . . and sit all day long asleep in a hollow tree. Then at night I should go *mousing*."

"How horrible! Aren't you afraid that your wish might be heard—and granted? I should be. Do you believe in . . . what is it 'transmigration'?"

"I should like that. What I should best of all like to be is *a parrot*."

"A parrot! Why *a parrot*?"

"A very intelligent one. One who was able to select his remarks, with deadly effect."

"That would be rather fun!"

If Major Hoskyns were listening-in to this, thought she; he would certainly conclude that they'd both gone batty! She smiled at the thought of the gallant major's face.

"Would you like to be a politician?" she asked. "My father always wanted to be a politician. And mother would have liked him to be that too. Have you ever wanted . . .?"

"No, that's never appealed to me."

"But you are interested in politics?"

She rather liked the idea of his being fond of politics. It implied a serious disposition. It implied the social bracket of Lord Baldwin or the Earl of Beaconsfield. It was the next thing after all to Royalty.

"What *are* politics, Miss Mallow? Can you tell me? I always think *everything* is politics. Why, *you* are politics!"

"I? Oh. How am I politics? I don't see how you make that out," she pouted and frowned.

"I'm afraid you are, all the same." He frowned back at her. "Not very good politics either," he added suddenly, as if to himself.

The puzzled face flushed, but she smiled, for she didn't mind much being bad *politics*.

"Must a girl be good politics? I don't mind however what I am *as politics*."

He leaned over towards her and placed his hand upon hers on the table.

"You are a nice girl aren't you, April? Perhaps a nice girl *cannot* be good politics. When you are no longer nice, then you may become quite respectable politically."

"Oh! I see."

"Politics are morals. See? Well, you don't want to be *moral* do you. Not just yet awhile."

"I don't want to be immoral," she protested, blushing, shaking her head and causing her ash-blonde cloud of hair to flash dully as it oscillated in arch negation. "But we are talking at cross purposes. I didn't mean politics in that way. Aren't you talking about religion? I meant hadn't you ever thought of standing for parliament? Becoming an M.P.?"

"As a matter of fact I *have* toyed with that thought," he told her, rather to her surprise. For she had never heard that M.P.'s were particularly *moral* and so it surprised her to hear that he had considered becoming an M.P. himself. But perhaps it was with a view to converting M.P.'s to a more moral way of life. And then she blushed. It struck her that this was rather absurd, for she was not quite sure that being *moral* was exactly his long suit.

"Oh, you have?" she said, rather lamely.

He nodded.

"Often thought about it," he said. "I should make a fine

speaker. I should be a great acquisition to the Conservative Party."

Her eyes lighted up.

"You *are* a conservative of course?" she asked.

"Of course. What did you suppose I was? A labourite?" He laughed derisively.

"Heaven forbid!" she exclaimed. Then the brightness left her face. "But I'm afraid that just *at present* . . . Do you really think there'll be a war? I asked you that before though."

Vincent levitated his shoulders and dropped them again with a discouraged bump, crushing his cigarette stub into his plate with his thumb afterwards.

"There *ought* to be," he answered. "But whether there will be . . ."

"Why *ought* to be? Oh, yes, I suppose . . ."

"That's it!" he said. "There ought to be."

"What would you do if there were a war?" she inquired, a little breathlessly. She could not stop herself from putting the question.

He returned her V.A.D. gaze with a comic tension, as if at any moment his solemn mask might break down and give way to unseemly mirth. He appeared about to say something: but instead he drew out his case and lighted a cigarette with aggressive slowness. Then he looked up and said—

"What should I do? I don't know."

"I mean . . ."

"Join an anti-aircraft unit probably."

Her face registered a slight disappointment.

"I should regard it merely as partridge-shooting." He shrugged. "That's what I probably should do. Plane-potting. Sky-sniping."

She turned this over in her mind for a moment or two. ("My husband is in the Anti-aircraft." Put in that way, it answered itself). She looked up and smiled. An R.N.V.R. uniform would suit him well. One of her old cousins had been in the Naval Reserve in the *old* war. Yes—the Navy.

But of course on shore. It was with a *Navy League* eye that she henceforth regarded him.

"At least," Vincent added meanwhile, "that's unless all my friends got there before me! There might be no vacancies for anti-aircraft!"

"You are not . . . oh, superior about war?" she asked him—for she thought she had better know the worst. "Some men are you know. I hate it of course. Then I'm a woman."

He shook his head.

"Dear me, no," he said. "There will always be wars. *Modern* war I feel a little superior to. It's not heroic enough for me."

"I suppose it isn't."

"I should like a war fit for heroes to fight in."

"But you would be a soldier?" she asked nervously. "I mean if there were a war."

"Yes, of course," he smiled. "Of course I should. No German should rape you except over my dead body, if that's what you mean."

She blushed and laughed awkwardly and he joined in her laughter very heartily indeed.

"No, that's not what I mean," she said. "I should never blame a man if he didn't want to fight."

Vincent flung himself forward, into a belligerent posture.

"But I do want to fight!" he exclaimed, looking round at the guests at the neighbouring tables challengingly. "My trouble is that there would be very little fighting to be done."

"There might be," she said grimly.

"I don't call machine-minding *fighting*! That's not good enough for me. My temperament inclines me to the use of spears and battle-axes."

April laughed, applauding his recent demonstration, and Vincent flung himself back, hooking his arm over the chair, in comic automatism as if returning the puppet to its original position.

"What do you *really* think. Shall we have war?"

He shook his head. "Put your trust in Herr Chamberlain!"

"Mother doesn't believe we shall have war."

"I and your mother see eye to eye. We have so far. Your mother is a most remarkable woman."

She had liked the way he had talked about the possibility of war. No heroics, such as some men she knew would have indulged in. He would regard it only as "partridge-shooting!" How much better that was, and more genuine, than false heroics! He would probably, for all his bored attitude about it, do much better, if it came to the point, than lots of those who were such fire-eaters to start with. The Navy would obviously suit him best. He would be among gentlemen there. And Navy men were more like *him* too, in their attitude. No heroics. Rather bored. Whereas, sometimes Army men . . . but the martial figure of Major Hoskyns promptly made its appearance out of the back of her mind, and she smiled to herself as she thought what *he* would be saying at this moment. There would be no "partridge-shooting" about him!

CHAPTER VI

THE MOTH'S KISS FIRST

THE gondola, that snail-like craft, in defiance of Time only pretended to move. It's glistening trail was only painted no more, upon the dark green waters. To April it seemed that *they* had been painted too. Vincent and she, as neither moved, their faces going dark like the faces in old pictures. The red mist of the defunct sunset impended above the ivy-green of the red-tipped waves. But Santa-Maria della Salute was there before them, not very far away, like an ineluctable guide. With the dusk the *fondamenta* began to be lamplit.

They had spent the latter part of the day upon a dilapidated island. Time had stood still there too. Time, rather, had *pretended* to stand still. Indeed Time had been stupidly pretending to stand still all day. But how absurd that was of Time, for as anyone could see, Time moved with a violent speed that took one's breath away. It was the modern age of course. It hadn't always. That was why one felt so old, although one was quite young.

This was Monday, and she had met Vincent for the first time last, last . . . when was it, Tuesday? And now they called each other by their first names and she felt she had known him the whole of her life. Just now when she had been talking about her childhood in Wiltshire she felt surprised suddenly that she had to explain something to him—about how a lane ran down behind Ringley Wood. It had seemed at first that he was pretending too. It seemed extremely odd that he should not know it. It *still* seemed odd even now, that Vincent had never been there! Never been there! He who had never been there might in a year be dead. If this war came many would soon die. She perhaps would be alive. She felt somehow that *she* would be alive, poor old She! That she felt would be to be alone with Ringley Wood.

Was it perhaps this terrible likelihood of war that made Time go so *particularly* quickly at that moment in her life? She thought it might be that, for certainly Time was just running away with all of them it seemed to her. Time was quite out of hand!

Quite out of hand! And a painted hand drifted over in the half-light and settled, no more heavily than a leaf the wind has abandoned, upon hers. Quietly it settled down upon hers. But the leaf was hot.

Her shoulders were slipping sideways and she drew them in to huddle them into a smaller compass since they were big shoulders, as if to go through a narrow opening—there was a hot breath; her cheek felt a pressure for a moment, and two living things were moving upon it, against each other, and then they were gone. But she was being drawn in, and softly and warmly battened down: hands were pressing her body against . . . oh, oh, she caught her breath, her mouth went slack, it faded away, she had no mouth, and all her body was dissolving into a fiery trance. As she clung tighter and tighter with her mouth to his, deep panting sighs escaped her. Her body was not in the same place any longer, it had been lifted up, it had been carried away into a new dimension. She was riding a muffled, a rhythmic sea, she was now face downwards; her whole body was clinging to his. When the kiss had lasted a long, a very long lifetime indeed, she shuddered and drew her mouth away; then she pressed it back again, then again she withdrew it: then she put it down beside his ear and whispered "darling!" and he whispered "darling!" back. Vincent and she were in love with each other. Now for the rest of time she should be his, only his! This was what life had been for.

When they went up the steps to their hotel after leaving the gondola, it was already dark. They held each other's hands, mounting the steps side by side. At the uppermost step Vincent gave her hand a farewell pressure, which she returned; they moved apart, and not many yards along the paved surface of the *campielli*, passed together into the hotel.

CHAPTER VII

THE ARREST

As Vincent and April entered the lounge it was empty except for Martin Penny-Smythe. He was the first person they saw, seated by himself in the farthest recess, a drink at his elbow, reading an English newspaper. But, undiscovered until Vincent and she had passed through the inner swing doors, stood two men.

April could not say why she should have at once become conscious of these two shabby, sullen-eyed individuals, discreetly withdrawn, half-concealed by a pillar. Perhaps it was because they had this furtive look—obviously not guests of the hotel, too: obviously waiting for somebody or something. Why they should have produced in her that surging fear, the moment she became aware of their presence, was even more difficult to decide. But she suddenly felt terrified.

It may be that that fear was communicated to her by Vincent. He had become so pale that his tan looked unreal of a sudden: a make-up upon the face of a corpse, or some ghastly sun-tan out of a bottle upon the face of a sick actor who has to play a hearty part.

Both stopped at the same time, by common consent. April felt she could not have taken another step. Side by side, as if halted by some word of command, a little foolishly, she and Vincent stood just within the entrance. Neither allowed their gaze to travel round to where the two unexplained strangers waited, half-concealed by the fussy mock byzantine pillar, without moving.

Vincent's eyes appeared enormous: they had a vicious warp as he stared ahead of him. But what in fact they were looking at was not the lounge of the hotel, and the puzzled

51

homely face of Martin Penny-Smythe in the background, but an ante-chamber in some tarnished palace into which, cloaked and masked a group of the dark little beings that belonged to Guardi and his times had moved, to engage in one of their sinister palavers—probably concerned with the destruction, in a treacherous ambuscade, of a friend. It was the print in the shop-window Martin had stopped him to look at, which had come down like a painted curtain, to intercept his gaze.

However, in the reception desk there were conspiratorial whispers too: the dark heads of the Latin clerks were close together. One of them signalled to the two strange men and nodded in the direction of Vincent and April. The two horrible little men who had been waiting stepped forward—April could see that though her head was rigidly averted. They appeared before Vincent and herself, placing themselves obtrusively in Vincent's path. They were addressing Vincent in Italian—they were savage little scowling figures: *her* they seemed to ignore.

Vincent waved his arm towards the reception desk. His Italian she knew was much the same as her own, a negligible quantity. They followed him—rather with the movement of well-trained dogs prepared to spring if the occasion arose. The three stood talking for a moment with the desk-clerk. Then Vincent turned on his heel. The two men appeared to close in on either side of him; and in that way the trio, Vincent in the centre, suspiciously like a person under arrest, went rapidly out of the hotel.

A state of suppressed excitement prevailed among the hotel personnel. The clerks left their cage-like office-quarters and hurried towards the entrance, intent obviously on following events outside. They too disappeared through the swing-doors.

April had remained where she was. As, on their way out, Vincent and the two strange men had approached her, she had moved away. She had looked at Vincent's face. It was calm and white, his lips drawn tightly together, but that he had forgotten her very existence was plain enough. Now she walked across the lounge until she reached the elevator, without looking to left or right.

The elevator was in the back of the hall, and there she came to a halt, but without pressing the bell. She stood staring into the dark and rather untidy shaft of the elevator through the plate-glass doors.

A voice stammered in her ear and she turned her head away from it.

"Wur-wur-what's hap-hap-happening? Wer-wer-what's the trouble?"

For a moment, Martin remained beside her, holding his newspaper in one hand, his pipe in the other. But seeing that she did not look at him or respond to his politely-stuttered enquiry, he took himself off. Her eyes again moved in the direction of the bell-push. She lifted her hand towards it, then rested it instead upon the iron-work of the grille. Why had Vincent lost colour in that extraordinary fashion and been put out of countenance? Why had he gone off with those two horrible little men? What could possibly be wrong? The voice of the reception-clerk recalled her sharply to the present.

"Does the elevator not come, Miss Mallow? Oh, I will ring. Allow me." The man pressed the bell and stood deferentially aside.

Arrived in her bedroom, April locked the door and lay down on the bed. Two thought-streams met head-on, as soon as she did that. There she lay battling with a great impulse on the one hand to give herself up to exultation, because she and Vincent were lovers, and on the other hand an equally powerful impulse to despair, because, under circumstances of unusual oddity, her lover had been snatched away, or rather marched off between two odious little men.

She cudgelled her brains as to the meaning of the latter happening. Was it something to do with the *war*? Was Vincent—a horrible thought—in the secret service? Had he been spying on the defences of Venice, if Venice had any defences?

Or was it a case of mistaken identity? She rather inclined to a notion of mistaken identity. Had they confused him with some absconding financier? Last (and her heart shrivelled up at the thought) was Vincent guilty of some crime?

If so, what crime? If Vincent had been guilty of something, *what* crime, fo* heaven's sake? For he did not look like a criminal, to say the least. Was he a—murderer? and she almost screamed as she recalled those big staring eyes in that face from which all the blood had fled and left only an artificial-looking coating of tan. She would never see a tanned male face again, without feeling it was somehow phoney.

But there was her mother knocking at the door: asking if she wasn't ever coming down *to eat*—soon there would be no dinner left, as it was long after eight. Whatever was she doing locking herself in—and would she come right now, because *she* was hungry!

As April and her mother crossed the lounge on their way to the table d'hôte she noticed that the reception-clerk and the porter were talking about her in maddening furtive asides, and rudely following her with their inquisitive eyes. When they had sat down, Mrs Mallow remarked, after looking shortsightedly round the dining-room:

"I wonder where Mr Penhale is? Mr Penny-Smythe is all by himself this evening."

"I wonder too," was all April said.

"But didn't you come back together?"

April nodded. "Yes, mother darling. He met a couple of friends."

There was a great exodus from the table d'hôte, led by Monsieur Deutsch, to listen to Hitler.

"Are you going to listen to our Führer, no?" Monsieur Deutsch attached his bold, dark, spectacled eyes almost violently upon the English guests, and especially upon Colonel Neville Tasker whom he regarded as the most obtuse and backward of his class, and a bad influence upon the others.

April and her mother had not started their meal yet. After the second course Mrs Mallow rose and said:

"I'm just going to listen-in for a few minutes. They'll keep our stuff warm. Coming?"

A number of people were gathered in the guest-room or library before the radio. A rather harsh, quiet, voice, picking its words, was coming out of it: a voice speaking in the German language, in a tone of melancholy half-expostulation, half-defiance. And this was the voice that was pronouncing the verdict. Of war for everybody, or peace for everybody.

The faces of the listeners were sallow with excitement— excitement of different kind and degree, from the traditional national animosity which danced upon the face of Monsieur. Deutsch, to the childish appetite for drama of the Italians, or to the ruffled irony of Mrs Mallow. The famous voice droned on. April sat in a bored and melancholy dream, wishing that the horrible voice would stop. Four other English guests listened sternly and blankly to the voice of Fate. But since Fate unfortunately spoke a language which they were unable to understand, they inclined their ears towards the instrument in the hope that they might at least discover if Fate was in a bad temper to-night, or whether the wind was to be tempered to the shorn lamb—in which case a raucous coo or two might be expected out of the diabolical sound-box. As it proceeded, the melancholy monotone seemed to depress them more and more. Destiny was very long-winded indeed, and fearfully lachrymose.

"Tu l'as entendu! Ce qu'il a dit là!" Monsieur Deutsch hissed thickly to his party. "Dieu de Dieu! Quel effronté! Quel mufle!"

"Let's get back to our food!" whispered Mrs Mallow to her daughter. "He'll still be *jawing away* after we've finished our coffee."

Vincent's voice cut like a knife into her ears as April passed with her mother, out into the lounge. She stopped and clutched Mrs Mallow's arm.

"Ah, there is Mr Penhale," exclaimed Mrs Mallow. "He

looks rather annoyed. I have never seen him look annoyed before."

"Why not send a regiment?" Vincent was protesting angrily. "And what's the telephone for?"

He was talking to Martin and the reception-clerk.

The reception-clerk was deferential as usual, but he was gazing at Vincent with an only half-veiled smile of sceptical reserve.

"They thought they would *come for you*, sir, I suppose," he answered. "Evidently they doubted if you would go, unless they came to fetch you."

"But *what for*?—Ah, hello, Madame Mallow," Vincent exclaimed. "Been listening to the old Führer?"

"Yes. What have *you* been up to?"

"Nothing much. I've been identifying a pickpocket." There was a very hard look on his face April thought, and his smile as he glanced at her was a little perfunctory. "Sorry, April, to have vanished. I had to go to the commissary of police to identify a pickpocket."

"A what?" she said, in extreme confusion. It was as if he had been absent for several years. She felt a strangeness and unfamiliarity that greatly embarrassed her. But it did not embarrass him. He did not seem to wish to draw nearer to her for the moment. He was, as her mother had said, very angry and aggressive. Quite a different person.

"Pickpocket!" he repeated distinctly, removing a piece of cigarette paper from his lip, and looking up at her out of his downturned face, as he did it—ironically, she thought, but was not sure.

"Oh," she said.

"A pickpocket? Gracious me!" observed Mrs Mallow.

"Wer-when . . . we . . . were *coming here*," Martin explained. "Per-per-per-Penhale c-caught . . . a pickpocket!"

His stammer was far worse when conversing with women.

"How did Mr Penhale come to do that?" Mrs Mallow asked.

"The fellow was in our c-carriage." Martin gulped.

Vincent came roughly to his assistance.

"I gave a hand that was all. Yes, I turned cop. But I had my reasons. I thought he had picked *my* pocket as a matter of fact."

"You tackled him in great s-s-style, Vincent!" Martin gave a portly imitation of tackling low, in a crowded railway carriage.

April hastily stepped back, and Martin dissolved into buxom donnish mirth.

"I meant to get my pocket-book back." Vincent patted his jacket.

"And did you?" April asked.

"No. I had it all the time."

"Wh-wh-why have they been so longwinded . . . about it?"

"They beat him up pretty badly." Vincent answered. "You saw that detective jump on his face? He's been in hospital ever since."

"What brutes the police can be!" said Mrs Mallow.

"How disgusting!" April put a hand up to her face to show where she felt for him.

"Pretty foul." Vincent made a grimace. "The French police are no joke. But the Italian police hold the record for rough play. Often they kill their man before they ever get him into the box. That's quite common."

"Horrible!" April shivered.

"Ugh!" said Mrs Mallow.

"When I saw them set about him I was half a mind to go and take him back. I had handed him over. I felt it was up to me to see they didn't kick him to death."

"It was t-t-tt-too late . . . the tt-ttrain was starting."

The reception-clerk, dangerously dapper, who had been listening with a smile of bored blandness, his eyes fixed upon Vincent's face with a very curious expression, April thought, now showed all his white teeth at once. He spoke English surprisingly well for an Italian.

"They have to be a little rough with these rats, you know," intervened. "They must be!"

"Why?" asked Vincent, fixing his eye aggressively upon the slightly smiling receptionist.

"The rats *bite*!" the Italian nodded his head violently, smiling with even more forcible urbanity. "Yes! I have seen a pickpocket bite a policeman . . . he bit his finger off. Slipped out of his jacket, and ditabunk!"

"Did they c-catch him?" Martin asked.

The hotel official shook his head dourly—he had stopped smiling. He was not interested in the criminal classes, but he knew that all Anglo-Saxons were, and Martin's question was a natural one. He thought, after a moment, he had better add an encomium or two to show that he was on the side of the angels.

"He had a fine pair of heels. Oh, yes! He showed good footwork! He was a smart thief."

They all moved towards the restaurant, the reception-clerk holding open the door for them with offensive cere-moniousness, bowing with sardonic abasement. As they went in Vincent turned to April.

"Sorry to have walked out on you so unceremoniously, my dear," he said, lowering his voice. "They seemed to half believe, the idiots, that *I* was in league with the pick-pocket in some way!"

April felt at once doubly relieved. Almost, it was like a new lease of life. For this entirely accounted for the odd behaviour of the two detectives, as she now knew them to be. *And* Vincent's feelings for her had suffered no change, he had made that plain. He had only been terribly upset, poor darling—as who wouldn't be?—by this extremely unpleasant experience.

CHAPTER VIII

THE VULGAR STREAK

A FTER dinner Vincent and Martin were seated in the latter's bedroom, between which, and his friend's, was the large bathroom they had in common. Penhale was discussing the Venetian police.

"They have no system," he said. "How they ever manage to catch anybody I don't know."

"But how did they come, Vincent, to make such an absurd mistake?" Martin seemed to resent his taking it so philosophically. Vincent hesitated.

"Cutpurses work in gangs. Like the one I caught. It must be that. They couldn't believe he was operating solo." He pondered. Then he looked up with a grin. "Why they didn't pick on *you* I can't understand. That would have been more logical. You said nothing. And God knows you look suspiciously inoffensive."

"Ner-ner-no; we were together," Martin pointed out.

"True!" Vincent agreed. "Anyhow, the stupid blighters grilled me for the best part of an hour. Even now I don't believe they are entirely satisfied."

"I've never head such nonsense!" Martin was genuinely outraged by all this. "It is in-in-infamous!"

Vincent smiled deprecatingly. "An upper-class attitude!" he said. "Still it is I agree a bit over the odds. Marched off under arrest, like a felon, from one's hotel."

"It is indeed. Why don't you go and see the British Consul, Vincent? I think you ought to."

Vincent shook his head.

"Not at present. Should they come and question you . . ."

"Question *me* . . .?" Martin was startled at this possibility. "What on earth for!"

"It is unlikely. I only mean in case. You would inform them of course of my great respectability—my aristocratic connexions; my solid financial standing."

Martin stared at him.

Vincent got up and stretched—way back, as if about to hurl a stone at God in his heaven.

"I must bathe!" he exclaimed, describing a convulsive arc, from back to front, with his body.

"I thought you were going .out with Miss Mer-mer-mallow."

"Can't be helped. Must bathe! I've been wanting to have a bath ever since I got back from the Lido. It's most necessary."

"What have you bub-bub-been up to—wer-wer-with that girl!"

"What?"

"Sh-sh-she was upset . . . just now."

"Was she? Well, that wasn't *me*. Ask the police why they go about in armed pairs, frightening visitors. I didn't frighten her. She's not frightened of *me*!"

"Ner-ner-no?"

Vincent shook his head absentmindedly, as he took off his shoes. "We get on fine!"

"Have you see-see-seduced . . . ?"

"Have a heart!" Vincent laughed. "What do you take me for? A non-stop Casanova?"

"S-ss-sorry. These things take time . . . I suppose."

"They do. You hunt birds differently to what you do the wild boar, that is obvious. *The moth's kiss first.*"

"I c-c-can see that. But is she . . . a good subject? Is she . . . amenable?"

Vincent sat with his forearms along his thighs, with a slight deliberate frown, as if this clubmanesque catechism had suddenly grown distasteful. Then he laughed, as he stood up again, stroking down the muscles over his belt.

"Is she amenable? Yes, she will be ripe for the kill in a day or so."

"I sh-sh-should not have supposed she was as easy as all that."

"You don't know them!" Vincent laughed boastfully over his shoulder, as he swaggered into the bathroom.

"Pro-pro-professional!" Martin stammered gleefully after him. And then he sat looking at his nails, wondering whether he ought not to have another wash, and whether he was getting a dirty old batchelor, smelling of pipe-smoke, and becoming unnecessarily repulsive.

How the lovely April had shrunk away from him, as he was showing how Vincent tackled the pickpocket, going for the fellow's legs! However, her legs were safe as houses as far as *he* was concerned! Vincent was welcome to his fat Miss Mallow! She was far too big for his modest needs, if he wanted one! Not *too* damned real, and not life-size thank you!—Also the Mallow was of the most preposterous middle-classness. How he *could* . . . ! The sort of thing that would be *heavenly* in the eyes of a railway porter. But that no gentleman . . . !

Martin frowned. He could not help himself. He *had* to read into everything about Penhale now the "humble origin." He fought against it: but Vincent's "confession" had coloured all his thought about his friend.

Things that before he would never have noticed, he could not help remarking at present—gestures, ways of expressing himself—and attributing them to his working-class upbringing. Martin realized that many of these attributions were far-fetched and unjust. But in spite of his efforts to check himself, he felt increasingly conscious of a *coarse* streak in Vincent, that no gentleman would display.

The fellow was a bit of an exhibitionist. That had, on any view, to be admitted. He was exulting over the poor girl, and her feminine weakness under unscrupulous, professional attack. She seemed rather a nice girl than otherwise. Probably never been kissed by a man before—or not in the way *he* would kiss her. Martin had known lots of girls like that himself—sisters of friends and so on. But Vincent treated April Mallow like just another scalp. It was rather beastly the way he had swaggered into the bathroom, just now. Showing off his brawn and making even his calves look *sexy* somehow. Ugh!

There were things you couldn't learn, however good an actor you might be, that was the fact of the matter. Vincent might have acquired the voice and manners (more or less) of a gentleman. But he had not acquired the *feelings* of one! Never would. He was a good fellow in lots of ways and wonderfully gifted. But a *gentleman* he would never be. He had never realized this before, but now he saw it clearly.

Martin, pulling dejectedly on his pipe, sat listening to his too red-blooded room-mate, dashing the water about within. Penhale was all *body* at the moment. A rather beastly experience Martin had not bargained for when he decided on this vacation with him. It was quite unnecessary for Penhale to drag him into all this. And to feel him inside there *gloating* over a lady he'd got into his clutches—a girl of the class he appeared to hate from the bottom of his soul—as he sluiced his body as if it were a tame animal he kept to go hunting with; that he was grooming after a brisk chase. No, *that* was not a phase of the class-struggle he very much enjoyed having opened up for him, nor one for which he desired a ringside seat.

But was it just primitiveness—for he desired to be just? The primitiveness of the artist-nature? No. There was a vulgar exhibitionism that belonged to the children of poor people—who made "raspberries" and vulgar noises as they passed ladies in the street. It was most unfortunate that Vincent had had such a thin time of it as a youngster: but that sort of birth and upbringing *did* taint you for good. It had tainted him.

Where had he met, he wondered, with this uncouth streak before. Of inflamed and unlovely cavemen cow-worship. Oh, where was that? He had seen in a temple somewhere . . .

He dimly recalled a scene . . .? Ah, yes, he had it. It was American! How stupid of him not to have known it must be. That had occurred in New York. The Eastside "strip-tease" theatres was where he had seen this bodily exhibited, to most blatant advantage. What a sodden spectacle of unshamed dog-lust, or bitch-lust, that was! Teeth-set, the American male big business world publicly slumped in orchestra-stalls, a morass of bloodshot eyes staring up at a strutting unclothed female-of-the-species, with her little strip of tease-stuff bobbing.

But Martin experienced a repentant twinge of personal loyalty at this. To think that his inquisitive imagination had led him to the parking of his greatest friend among those lubricious ruffians: those Americans, a laughing-stock for civilized men! Yet, look how Vincent delighted in the "New Yorker," a paper which for his own part seemed as dull as ditchwater. Martin shrugged his shoulder, and gave it up for the time being. Vincent Penhale was probably an enigma: for his case was more complicated obviously than just inborn and inbred vulgarity. He sighed, and picked up a copy of Mussolini's paper, the *Populo*, to see if he could deduce the real intentions of the Axis, from a careful examination of its pages. Martin Penny-Smythe's mind was much more exer-cised by the threat of war than was that of his friend.

Five minutes passed and the door sprang open to reveal Vincent in full evening dress, entering with a rather sardonic smile on his face, as he encountered the disaffected stare of Martin, eyeing this dazzling "member of the working class."

"What, *tails*? Why and wer-wer-wherefore?" Martin demanded.

It came out when a man put on evening dress! thought Martin. It did come out then. That was the acid test. Only a gentleman could wear evening dress and not look a little vulgar or pretentious.

"We're going to the Colonna. Gay togs *de rigueur* my dear man. Hate the things—but the human snob is adamant. Won't let you in if you haven't got 'em on."

He gave a coarse plebeian laugh.

"You better take your sh-sh-shoes away," Martin pushed Vincent's discarded footwear with his toe. "Or, I know I shall be putting them on by mistake."

"And you wouldn't like to be in my shoes, what! . . . I'll bet you *would* like to be a little later this evening when the radiant April is nestling in my arms. Wouldn't you? Come on . . . admit you're jealous, you old humbug!"

Tapping him affectionately on the shoulder this resplendent representative of the submerged-tenth danced out of the door, the last notes of his theatrical laughter dying away in the corridor outside.

Martin picked up the *Populo* again, flushing and frowning. He was extremely displeased with Vincent, but even more so with himself. He sat looking at the paper, without attempting to read it—or trying to extract from it signs pointing to Peace. He was attempting to discover something of quite a different nature: namely, whether Vincent's horrid hint had any substance in it?

Did he, Martin Penny-Smythe, wish that he were in Vincent's shoes, as that by no means modest or unassuming young gentleman had affirmed? Did he or did he not desire sexual contact with Miss April Mallow? He was bound as a good catholic to confess that he would not have been averse just for once, to being in Vincent's place and pressing her body against his. But he was so shamed by this discovery that he hid his face in his hands. He'd never be able to look the girl in the face again. And he didn't really want her in the least! This seemed to involve him in Vincent's goings-on besides. He was under a spell. Vincent had somehow made him an accomplice: had *wished* on him this unsuspected desire.

He took up his Peterson pipe, with its great bulging bowl as if it were permanently enceinte: he puff-puff-puffed at it, the match at its mouth blazing forth or dying down, as he drew on it or ceased to draw. And then great clouds of acrid smoke billowed out into the room. It needed fumigating.

CHAPTER IX

THE BREAKFASTING BRITISH

THE Breakfasting British, upon the morning of Tuesday, September 27, in their Venetian hotel, were glum and excited. The Berlin Broadcast, reaffirming the German ultimatum to the Czechs, had been digested and slept on and wakened up to, and it now overshadowed their bacon and eggs. It made the hot coffee and greasy milk taste better or worse according to their ages, intelligences, pocket-books— to their degrees of suggestibility, hatred, or toleration of Hitler, love of God, stake-in-the-country, hope in an after-life, identification of Christianity with Communism, first-hand experience of war, anxiety for the dog-they'd-left-behind-them, knowledge of Italian, fear of mustard gas. One woman mopped her eyes all the time. She had just received a letter informing her that her only son had joined the Fire Brigade.

Monsieur Deutsch bellowed from the top of the large table, where he sat with his party, as it was too large for a small one.

"Il a peur! *Il a peur!*"

He then would translate for the benefit of the surrounding islanders, whom he treated as a class of dense and noticeably deaf children. Their defective hearing could be directly traced to their intellectual infirmities, his manner left no doubt as to that.

"He funks it! . . . The Maginot Line! . . . Russia is only waiting!" Such phrases resounded in his whiskered mouth.

His voice easily reached a table in the far corner of the room where it pressed a button. An old lady stirred, quietly

65

snorted, then remarked to a startled-looking schoolboy in front of her, as if speaking to herself—

"All bullies are cowards!"

The expression of alarm increased upon the face of the schoolboy, he looked at his grandmother as if ready to get under the table if it happened again. ·

Lt.-Col. Sir Neville Tasker had yesterday's *Times* propped up against the coffee-pot. *The Times* arrived upon the day of publication by air mail, but he refrained from perusing it until the next morning at breakfast. His wife and daughter politely and cordially lent ear to their booming ally *d'outre Manche* thundering for Stafftalks at the next table.

"Yes, when *are* we going to have Stafftalks I wonder?" Lady Tasker enquired testily of the gallant colonel.

"Stafftalks—stafftalks!" he growled angrily, as a much-harassed man. "What about them? What about them?"

"Does it say anything in *The Times*, Neville, about Staff-talks? Surely it's about time . . ."

"Stafftalks! Why Stafftalks? Had 'em long ago!"

"I wasn't talking about the *last* war . . ." Lady Tasker said, with insidious patience. "I was referring . . ."

"I know quite well to what you are referring. We had 'em long ago. We're having 'em all the time!"

Three Americans stooped over their plates, eating and talking with nervous expedition and examining timetables between gulps of grape-juice. And in and out of all these restless people, bowing stiffly as they arrived and as they left, were three bull-like Teutons, two men and a woman. Their attitude was that if there was a bad smell in the room it had nothing to do with *them*.

Mrs Mallow and her daughter sat at a window-table, blinded by the white tablecloth, with the sun glittering upon the hotel cutlery; Vincent and Martin sat at another. Vincent had had the blind lowered half-way.

" I'm wondering," Mrs Mallow was saying to her daughter, "whether we oughtn't to make a move. It looks to me as if war might break out at any minute."

"Monsieur Deutsch says Hitler will climb down," April suggested. "I think he will," she added with superb confidence, gazing out of the window at the flowery windows of the hotel opposite.

"What do *you* know about Hitler?" her mother asked with a benevolent sneer.

"Well, mother darling, what do *you* know about him if it comes to that? It's only what you read in the papers. I read the papers too. You forget I have eyes in my head, and have learnt to read and write."

"Oh, well, since you've become an authority on foreign politics now, perhaps you can tell me what will happen if Germany *doesn't* climb down?"

"Monsieur Deutsch . . ."

"Yes, yes, we know. He knows no more than we do."

"His brother is an ambassador."

"So he says!"

"But mother dear . . ."

"More likely a *sous-prefet* of a colonial canton . . ."

"I don't think Monsieur Deutsch . . ."

"Never mind about him (he's only an Alsacian anyway). We shall be at war from one minute to the next perhaps: probably with Italy into the bargain."

"Not with Italy surely, mother. Let's draw the line somewhere. I don't like the Italians but . . ."

"What did old Mussolini say last week?"

"I never take any notice of what *he* says. I'm sure he doesn't mean what he says. Herr Hitler I agree *does*. But you mustn't listen to Musso, as Low calls him, mother. That would be absurd."

"Herr Hitler! My dear April you are getting very polite."

"I give the devil his due."

"You call him Mister, is that it. Why don't you say, April, you don't want to leave Venice just at present!"

"Shall I? I don't want to leave Venice just at present!" she fixed her eye firmly upon her mother's eye.

"Now we know where we stand."

"It is of course for you to decide, mother. You are the Führer."

"Your excursions into politics my dear . . ."

"Oh, well I *must* take after you mother darling sooner or later, you know. The evil day can't be put off for ever!"

Mrs Mallow cackled bleakly. She screwed up her small wooden yellow face with a certain relish of all this. She stared into her handsome daughter's face in silence, while you could count ten. Then she opened her mouth, held it agape, then snapped it down, in imitation of a dog snapping at flies, in a toothless worldly cachinnation. She threw up her hands, in sign that she threw up the sponge, in comic abdication.

But Mary Mallow was not unsympathetic. A certain criminal gleam in the clever hazel eye of the young man about whom they had been indirectly talking, appealed to her. So they would stop in Venice and give the Wilhelmstrasse another chance to climb down—and Mr Penhale further opportunities to deploy his siege trains about the person of the lovely April. Mary Mallow wished she were younger. She would not have minded those rides in gondolas, and she would have had more to say for herself meanwhile than her poor dear goose of a daughter. How *dull* these young people were to-day! So homely, serious and intensely respectable! (And as to wit!—They had never heard of it). So Mary Mallow arrogantly mused comparing her own dwarfish person with the tall lovely swaying presence of her poor dear "goose" of a daughter.

Penhale appeared before their table, smiling, as if they had been accomplices, at Mrs Mallow, accomplices in something charming and disreputable. The two *fortes têtes* of this outfit, he and she.

"So you think it looks none too good, Mrs Mallow? You think we are going to have war?"

"That was certainly my opinion. But April says I am mistaken. She deprecates all panic."

"Yes, don't let's panic!" Vincent laughed. "May I sit

down? This will be the last holiday we shall get for some time if it's war."

"I know!" Mrs Mallow sighed. "The last I shall ever get!"

"I still think Chamberlain will go on appeasing for a long while yet." Vincent sat down. "I suppose you've heard that the Polytechnic have sent out an S.O.S. to all their parties, recalling them at once?"

"No, have they? I had not heard that."

Vincent nodded. "So it appears. The news has just come through. Panicking at headquarters. Cook's haven't."

"Cooks haven't?" April said. "Good for Thomas Cook!"

"No. Cook's have kept their heads. And we're Cookites, aren't we? But all these people are going."

"At the hotel?" Mrs Mallow quailed very slightly.

"So the manager told me," Vincent answered. "All except the Colonel are off to-day. He is a diehard, like us."

"Three cheers for the military!" April exclaimed, beaming in the direction of Sir Neville Tasker. "I must congratulate him after breakfast."

"Germany has recalled all ships, by wireless," Mrs Mallow observed broodingly. "The Germans don't want to lose the *Europa*. They evidently think they might."

"A precaution." Vincent shrugged his shoulders.

Monsieur Deutsch, at the head of his tribe, made for the door, leaving a great gap in the breakfasters. The Americans rose by common accord, infected by the mass movement, and began precipitately their own evacuation. A page passed the Mallows' table with a cablegram upon a salver. He stopped before Sir Neville Tasker.

"I have some letters to write," Vincent Penhale said, suddenly getting up, as if he had forgotten something.

"Oh, so have *I*!" Mrs Mallow sighed—hadn't *everybody* who was anybody, letters to write, at such a moment as this —yet some people were such great ladies that they refused to be at the beck and call of such obligations.

"I must send a cable—to my man. He'll be in a great stew." Vincent said.

"I have a cable to send as well," Mrs Mallow said—almost offendedly.

"Who to?" April asked with, for her, a dry smile.

"Oh, Roger, amongst other people," her mother replied airily." He will be beside himself, poor dear. And Margery, of course."

"Quite unnecessary." April showed that she was going to have no unnecessary cablegrams. No excitements please. Business and pleasure as usual!

"I have a proposal to make," Vincent began with a cheerful manner.

"Oh?" Mrs Mallow lent her ear, not averse to seconding any proposal, calculated to dispel the gloom, that this resourceful young man might advance.

"Shall we all have dinner at Privitali's! What do you say?"

"What a brilliant idea!" April, was in fact, the radiant seconder, her mother a bad third, with, "Yes, it *is*, an idea! Let's!"

"It's the best joint I know of here."

"I have never been to Previtali's." Mrs Mallow informed them, as if it were a fact that was worth recording, which most people would be surprised to learn.

"It's the best place for food," Vincent told her, "and I feel rather like good food. I don't know about you!"

He eyed Mrs Mallow speculatively, as if to query the capacity of the old carcass, but Mrs Mallow flung his eye off in spirited fashion.

"I feel," she said, ". . . if you want to know how I feel . . . like—getting—drunk!"

"I do too!" the exultant contralto of April Mallow broke out at once. And so the proposal for that party was carried by common assent.

After breakfast Vincent accompanied Martin to the offices of the Wagons-lits. It was Martin's purpose to get English news. The news was black. But as the day wore on the atmosphere became at every moment more opaque with *war*. Like the red exhalation that settles upon a spot where some woman's body has been found dismembered, or some child's body raped and choked—and, like football crowds, butchers by proxy in their thousands have met to inhale the oppressive air—the famous "war-psychosis" settled upon everybody and everything.

War had seeped into every object one touched. The great professionals of war in the Teuton lands were releasing the gases that spread outwards over the European capitals and smiling countrysides. The hotel napkins were tainted. The infected linen left a taste upon the mouth. The very clothes men wore seemed to secrete its stench. The only person who seemed completely immune from these influences was Vincent Penhale.

Martin became very jumpy and morose. He observed his companion's phlegmatic demeanour with mixed feelings of disapproval and admiration. The admiration represented his old attitude towards Vincent, a great deal of which was still intact. The disapproval represented the new attitude—which grew in strength daily, under the surface.

Vincent's complacency he was inclined to ascribe to his radicalism, which he had never quite believed in before. Now he took it more seriously (seeing what its roots probably were) and liked it very much less.

Vincent was positively *smug*. But he still maintained that war would be postponed—to give Hitler time, as he put it, to be so *perfectly* equipped as to make it quite certain he could liquidate Democracy everywhere. Which was what, (so he insisted), Mr Chamberlain and his friends desired.

Martin, who had never been much of a Chamberlain fan, began to see the latter's good points, as he put it.

"Ch-cher-Chamberlain her-her-has his points!" he would stammer.

"Oh, yes?" Vincent laughed derisively. "He stands for the City. That is a great institution. The City *has* its points."

"It her-her-has its points, Vincent, inasmuch as it enables

us to vacation in Venice, more expensively than any it-it-it-Italian could afford to vacation in England."

"You are appealing to me as a rentier?"

"Perhaps."

"And you think my money's safe with Chamberlain, whereas it would not be safe with . . .?"

"No. All I mean is that Chamberlain is a decent old Englishman. . . ."

Vincent for a moment lost his poise.

"Is it decent, Martin," he asked hotly, "to stand by—in a top hat and frock coat—and allow people to starve?"

Martin Penny-Smythe sighed and was silent.

"*We* haven't much to wer-wer-worry about anyway," he presently observed as if as a comment upon Vincent's sang-froid.

"How do you make that out?"

"Well, you and I are . . . over age."

Vincent looked at him, in surprise, then laughed.

"They'll get you old man, never fear!" he said. "A fine stout lad like you will never be allowed to stop out of uniform."

"What would you do, Vincent?" Martin enquired, a little ruffled.

"I? I should join the Brigade of Guards of course. As becomes my station and family traditions."

Martin eyed him bleakly. But he kept his mouth firmly closed. He was going to have no more of that "humble birth" stuff, thank you!

CHAPTER X

HALVORSEN

APRIL saw Halvorsen for the first time under circumstances that startled her considerably. This happened in the following way. The hotel was rather under than overstaffed, and sometimes it was quicker to walk up to one's room than to wait upon the procrastinations of the elevator. That evening about six-thirty upon entering the hotel, she decided to walk up. Having ascended to the entresol, as she was passing round in front of the elevator-gates, she heard a door open. She knew that Vincent's room was somewhere just round the corner. Thinking it might be Vincent she stopped, pretending to peer up the shaft, as if hoping that the truant car might descend.

Vincent did not materialize, but she heard voices. She heard Vincent's voice, in a tone of bleak command, saying—

"To-night. It must be *to-night*. You must not stop another hour in Venice. You understand, Bill?"

Something guttural and blurred was said in answer—she supposed that was 'Bill' responding. Suddenly Vincent's voice was sharper and louder.

"I see that, Bill. I know that. But you must not stop here. An hour is too long. You must sign no hotel-register in this city. They're very hot . . . It would be madness to stick around, as things are."

Another indistinct rejoinder—a rumble of manifest disagreement.

"My God—what of it?" came from the invisible Vincent, impatiently.

Then the low answering rumble rose in pitch and took on definition.

73

"You don't want me here, Vin," it said—oh, in such a vile north-country accent—such as blighted the scenery in the villages near Harrogate. "That's all boloney about the police."

"Nothing of the kind."

"All right. I'll make myself a scarcity, in Venice. I shall get no bloody sleep. But as you would say, what of it?"

April was just preparing to make *herself* scarce, for she heard a movement in her direction, when a large form burst around the corner. A big and unfriendly man stood before her, and perhaps only because he had blue, glaring, eyes, looked as if he could eat her.

"A snooper! Come and have a look at what I've found, Vin!"

April shuddered at the impact of this voice. Who on *earth* was this horror of a man? A big red-blooded, blue-eyed brute who called Vincent, "Vin," who had dropped out of the skies. A dreadful common accent, a *common-and-proud-of-it* sort. The worst sort of all.

But Vincent appeared behind, smiling with extreme bland-ness, and upon the arrival of his easy, a little bantering, good-natured presence all her dismay departed.

"Hello, April!" he sang out, as he came forward. "This silly fellow has got into these fascist lands, somehow or other, without a *visa*. I'm *shooing* him out. Did you hear our altercation? Come down and have a drink, Bill. You really will *have* to do a bunk to-night old man!"

Bill transferred his blazing blue gaze to the smooth and smiling surface of Vincent's face, and April with a grateful "thank you!" in her eyes for that St George, Vincent Pen-hale, beat a hasty retreat to the floor above.

A half-hour later she and Mrs Mallow stepped out of the elevator, and before joining Vincent and Martin, with whom the unspeakable 'Bill' was seated, went to the desk to mail some letters.

"He's there," she whispered to her mother.

"SO I see," said that lady, with a grimace.

In battering muscular tones, Bill laid down the law.

"That would be o-kay, Vin, if they could stop Hutchinson shooting off his great fat mouth. But they know they can't. How are they to stop that old bastard . . ."

"Hush!" Vincent was stopping him evidently from 'shooting off' *his* 'great fat mouth.' April shuddered, as she stuck on the stamps. The fellow had a voice like a can-opener. It was an instrument of the will. He forcibly burst things open with it when they stood in his way. It could still be heard gouging away, Vincent laughing his crowing applause of whatever it was this charming friend of his was saying. Where on earth had Vincent picked this person up? Or had *he* been picked up? It was just like Vincent to allow himself to be drawn into an acquaintanceship with anybody, irrespective of class. He was a queer boy about such things. Much too easygoing. But then the conversation she had overheard as she was going up to her room came back to her. This was no chance acquaintance, it was obvious. What then could it signify? Who and what was "Bill?"

Mrs and Miss Mallow approached the table where the men were sitting and drinking with signs of hesitation. To Messrs Penhale and Penny-Smythe their approach was not visible: but the strange man who had his overcoat on faced them: he stared at them as if they had no right to be there.

"Ah, hello!" Vincent sprang up, as April touched him on the arm. She thought he had been drinking. "This is a friend of mine, Bill Halvorsen. Meet Mrs Mallow, Bill. Bill has to catch the plane for Paris."

Mr Halvorsen was not introduced to April. They had, after all, met before.

They all sat down, now a party of five, and Mr Halvorsen stared at Vincent—he did not look at her, April, or at her mother. Possibly he was a woman-hater, she reflected. He looked a man-hater too, if it came to that!

"Have you examined the tombs of the Venetian patriarchs?" Vincent asked Mrs Mallow, with a condescending boredom, as if he had switched off a very thrilling record

to take place in a dull tea-party chat. "Been to San Zani-
polo?"

"Yes, we have," April replied.

"That is capital! They were a tough crowd! Sea-empires
always breed a tough gang at the top."

Halvorsen laughed coarsely to himself.

"Aren't we a sea-empire?" April asked diffidently. "I
thought we were."

"Like Venice and Carthage," Vincent said. "That's us—
Mrs Mallow feeling tired?"

"Sea sick!" Mrs Mallow told him with facetious Kensingtonian succinctness. "Gondolas don't suit me."

"Nor me," said Martin.

"Speed boats make them roll about," Mrs Mallow rolled
slightly in her chair and cast up her old bloodshot eyes.

"They ought to ber-ber-bar motor boats," Martin was
politely of opinion.

"And we went down a lot of smelly canals," Mrs Mallow
dilated her nostrils. "If Herr Hitler hadn't put me on my
mettle I'd pack up and go."

Martin giggled.

"I like having Venice all to myself," he told her. "It's
far ner-ner-nicer without the ter-ter-tourists."

"Aren't you a tourist, Mr Smith?" Halvorsen asked, with
a sullen yawn.

"I s-s-suppose so!" Martin caressed his paunch.

"But an *exceptional* tourist, huh!" Halvorsen blasted him
with a bilious blue eye.

"A-rar-aren't we all rather *exceptional* people—in our
own es-es-estimation?" Martin was blandly Bellocian.

"Ah! I was going to say!" interpolated Mrs Mallow
approvingly. "Is this gentleman not a tourist too?" (In-
dicating Halvorsen with a wave of a gloved hand). "Or else
somebody concerned with the tourist-traffic? Must be one or
t'other. Otherwise why *Venice*? To be in Venice speaks for
itself."

Vincent laughed.

"Touché!" He turned to Halvorsen, who was glaring fixedly at Mrs Mallow. "Bill is here on business."

"Indeed!" Mrs Mallow examined Bill as if that were the first business man who had come her way. "How very interesting."

"Yes. He scorns delights and lives laborious days. He's not like us. Not above profiting by other people's propensity to globe-trot though."

But Halvorsen scorned also to play ball, in such a conversation, and he stared fixedly now at Mrs Mallow as if he had detected the outline of a natural enemy, beneath that self-possessed old lady's cultured Anglo-Indian tan.

Mrs Mallow stared back benignly, without batting an eyelid. She enjoyed Mr Halvorsen.

"Well, Mr-er-Halvorsen," she said at last. "Mr Penny-Smythe seems to have reduced you to silence, You *hommes d'affaires* are not so easily silenced as a rule."

Martin again giggled. Bill Halvorsen promptly transferred his gaze from Mrs Mallow to Martin. Martin puffed contentedly at his Peterson. The waiter had just brought more drinks.

"Well—happy days!" said Vincent.

"Ter-ter-tootleoo!" Martin muttered.

April raised her glass, and on its way to her smiling lips she gave it a little surreptitious jerk in the direction of Vincent who winked back. In the act of doing so, she caught Halvorsen's eye. A hot neck-flush afflicted her, as she observed the meaningful bantering smile with which this horrid individual took up his glass and emptied it with disdainful finality.

Halvorsen stood up.

"You still have ten minutes, Bill," Vincent told him. "Sit down."

"I guess I'll go now." Bill took up a suitcase, bowed slightly to the company in general, as if he had already forgotten about them, and walked towards the door. Vincent went with him.

"What an extraordinarily unpleasant man!" said Mrs Mallow.

"Is-is-isn't he!" Martin polished the bowl of his Peterson with his sleeve.

"Preternaturally odious!" April breathed. "I wonder where Mr Penhale could have found him? He looks like a dock labourer in his Sunday best."

"He comes from Her-her-hull."

"Not *hell*?" enquired Mrs Mallow. "That's where he should *go to* at all events."

"His father," Martin said, "was a Norse seaman, who settled there. Fer-fer-forty years ago."

"How do you know?" asked April.

"He ter-told me."

"Oh."

April was intensely relieved that this unspeakable Viking had departed: but a meditative frown persisted upon her face, for she could not see why Vincent should tolerate this beastly man or allow him to call him "Vin"; nor was she entirely satisfied by Vincent's explanation of that peculiar altercation outside Vincent's room a half-hour before. Martin Penny-Smythe was the only friend of Vincent's she had so far encountered, and he was of a different class to Mr Halvorsen. Except that he was not a very interesting little man, and well, getting on, Penny-Smythe was the sort of friend she would have *expected* Vincent to have. At least Mr Penny-Smythe was a gentleman, there was no doubt about that— even if his pipe was one of the most repulsive adjuncts of masculinity in her experience, and a monstrous barrier to normal intercourse.

As if in answer to her thoughts, Martin coughed, looked up from his oilskin tobacco-pouch, into which strands of tobacco rather disgustingly depended, dangling from the black mouth of his Peterson.

"Halvorsen saved his life, Vincent said," Martin announced sedately, and returned to the preparation of his pipe for further operations—the object of which seemed to be to fill Venice with dense clouds of smoke, so that he might have it *entirely* to himself.

When they were outside the hotel, Halvorsen turned the full blaze of his eyes upon Penhale.

"What the hell do you think you're doing!" he asked him roughly. "What's the meaning of all that inside there?" He jerked his shoulder back towards the hotel. "Are you right? Ought you to see a specialist?"

Vincent crowed, a little lugubriously, as they walked along towards the landing stage. A number of people were discernible in the twilight a short way ahead, at the landing stage.

"We're different, you and I, Bill. Have somewhat different tastes."

"The tastes you got at Haileybury are different to what I got at the Board School!"

"Don't be a fool, Bill!"

"But hell, man, what is all that inside there? What *is* it? Is it because of *them* I had to be sent off at an hour's notice?"

"Don't be so absurd! I have to pass the time away somehow. Do you object to my playing round with a girl? You're such a damned old puritan, Bill. Why don't you look out for a nice girl yourself?"

Halvorsen heaved his tawny shoulders, and pushed his hat back impatiently till it hung on his neck.

"And that stammering jackass. *He* a pal of yours, Vin? What an outfit!"

"It's just perversity. Put it down to that. I like people to stammer."

"O-kay. But this gets me worried all the same."

"It needn't."

"No? Are you toying with the thought, Vin, of making a little downy nest for yourself, lined with lousy dividends, among the 'Upper Clarsses' what? Think of retiring? Got your eye on a little shooting-box, Vin—shall I have to get past a butler when I come to see you, one day soon? '*Mr*

*Al-vor-sen, sir? Yes, sir. May I know your business, sir?
Does Sir Vincent expect you, sir?'*—All I ask is for some
warning Vin. I might die of shock. You know my ticker's
none too strong."

"Don't be a silly ass, Bill!" Vincent said.

"I don't want to look too big a fool!"

"I see your meaning. But you've got this all wrong. Anyhow . . ." He pointed to the launch. They had now reached
the waterfront. The last of a group of passengers was crossing the gangplank.

"Well, Vin, so long! See you in a week or so. Yes?"

"Yes. So long old man," said Vincent heartily, patting
him on the back. "I shall hear from you before I leave?"

"Ay, ay, Sir Vincent!" Halvorsen rushed into the
crowded launch.

CHAPTER XI

DINNER AT PREVITALI'S

VINCENT re-entered the hotel, after seeing Halvorsen off, sat down and pulled up his chair till it touched that of Mrs Mallow.

"Seen off your boy-friend?" asked Mrs Mallow.

Vincent nodded.

"Thank goodness *he* is eliminated!" Mrs Mallow sighed.

"Don't you like him?" asked Vincent, smiling. "He's no lady's man is Bill. I like him though. He once saved my life."

"Did he get a medal for it?" enquired Mrs Mallow.

Vincent hesitated, then shook his head. "No. No one knew but us. Another round of drinks before we go?"

The hotel had emptied completely in the course of the day, and the place felt so empty that these four English people had developed a Robinson Crusoe air. They were the object of much lazy speculation, on the part of the Italian hotel staff, who covertly watched them to see if any *restlessness* could be detected in these extraordinary Britons, or to surprise the first symptoms of a belated panic. At any moment, it was felt, they might start up, thunder for their accounts, rush up to pack, and stampede for the railway station.

The secret of their resistance to crisis-stimulus was canvassed in the reception desk, in the restaurant, and even in the sweltering tumult of the kitchen. Mainly, it was ascribed to bravado. Of this rather showy spirit Vincent Penhale was regarded as probably the chief exponent.

Since the visit of the police Vincent Penhale was watched very narrowly from behind the reception counter, and his true vocation was debated hotly. There was something phoney about him, but they could not decide exactly what it was. Halvorsen had started all their tongues wagging again. But they were afraid of Vincent, whom they looked upon as a very tough customer indeed. His stern eye daunted them. Why he should wish to stop on in Venice they could not divine: but it was *he*, they felt, held the little party together.

Registering all comings and goings as they did, it had not escaped their notice that Mr Penhale and Miss Mallow had become potential love-birds. Winks were exchanged when the party of four, so matily gathered within view of the reception bureau, informed the management that they would be absent for the evening meal. Only the Colonel and his two womenfolk would be there that night for dinner: even the three Germans had joined in the exodus, bowing stiffly and sticking their arms out fraternally at that part of the *Axis* in the reception desk.

The male reception-clerk came over when the fresh round of drinks made their appearance. He bowed, he deferentially kept his person in the background, yet he made his smile seen. He caught everybody's eye in turn, except Vincent's. If Vincent was firm with him, he also was firm with Vincent.

"So the ladies and gentlemen," he took what he considered an opportunity of observing, "are not so timid as the rest! No *wind up* . . . ! not like the remainder of our clients?'

Vincent did not trouble to conceal that he was in no mood to play to-night, not with Italian hotel-servants, of whom he showed he was not overfond.

"No," quavered Mrs Mallow, with her half-smile for servants. "No, we none of us have the *wind up* as far as I know."

"The British Prime Minister is speaking, to-night, at nine," the receptionist informed them. "You listen to him, no?"

"On the radio?"

"Yes, Radio Roma. It will be relayed."

"We shall not be able to, I am afraid," Mrs Mallow answered.

"They say he is to *lift the veil*," smirked the clerk.

"Ah. *Lift the veil*?"

She let it be seen that she had no great belief in *veil*-lifting. She had never known any Prime Minister to lift a veil yet. She questioned if that was what he was going to do. (She belonged to the *sealed-lip* school herself). She turned her back upon this over-coloquial foreigner. "There is nothing I deprecate so much as colloquialism in a Wop!" she told them later, when they had left the hotel.

Smiling with great effrontery at Mrs Mallow's back and bowing again, the hotel clerk withdrew. The Anglo-Saxons still had the jack! Less of it every day. But for the hotel trade they still added up to more than a Teuton, with his peculiar, parsimoniously-allotted marks.

They started off to walk to Previtali's, which now could not be reached by gondola. There had been a shower of rain but now all the bright stars used by Italians for the *Adorations of the Magi* came bursting out overhead, in great steely clusters, though Mrs Mallow pushed up the collar of her fur coat, and Vincent passed his hand inside April's arm; and, as if to protect her against the chill of the air, drew her against him as they walked.

"Mr Penny-Smythe, let me take your arm?" said Mrs Mallow to Martin, who found himself advancing, with his forearm cuddled by a little befurred old lady, having been compelled hurriedly to remove his Peterson pipe and adopt the reverential pace of an undertaker's mute. What they were all coming to as a result of this abominable Crisis and the still more abominable courtship of his companion he did not know. For there was he on ahead, the old ruffian—Vincent and April had seemed to leap away, in an ecstasy of juvenile athleticism, and indifference to the locomotive problems of age (to whose snailish chariot *he* poor chap had been resolutely hooked), playing the Faust for all he was worth. To what end—except to be thoroughly tiresome.

"Those two seem to *hit it off*!" Mrs Mallow panted in his ear, nodding her head in the direction of the love-birds.

"They do in-dud-dud-*deed*!"

"I've always liked . . . er . . . *Penhale*. He is a very intelligent young man. One does not often meet them."

"Ss-sometimes . . . he's intut-tut-tut-telligent!" Martin stuttered morosely, casting a critical glance ahead at the back of the gentleman in question.

"Yes! I can imagine he might be rather dense about some things. I can see that."

"V-v-very dense." Martin scowled.

"All intelligent people are. We all have our blind spots. My husband was a very intelligent man in most ways. But he was a perfect *fool* about *women*!"

Martin emitted a strangled stammer. He had *tried* to utter an old-fashioned compliment, which the occasion appeared to demand. But it stuck in his throat: his tongue rebelled, cleaving stubbornly against the roof of his mouth.

"A perfect idiot!" Mrs Mallow pursued, almost in a shriek. "He thought that all women were in love with him—except me. He *knew* that I wasn't!"

A sound that was not mirth, and was scarcely intended to be, was emitted by Martin.

"April is like *neither* of us. Neither like Theodore nor myself. She is a curious girl. She is cold . . . she quite frightens me sometimes. The man who likes her must be jolly fond of icicles!"

"In-in-deed!"

"But she will *melt* one of these days. Then there'll be a bit of a mess. I frankly dread that moment."

The old lady tittered naughtily at his side, and he felt that an almost obscene warmth was communicated to him by the medium of the expensive fur—dampened by the rain, a slight shower escaped from it.

"April is getting on. I always tell her," Mrs Mallow confided. "Next month she'll be *thirty*. You wouldn't think it would you? I should give her twenty-five if I didn't know. Not a day more."

The other two—the young ones—had stopped to look in a

shop window, and Martin, determined to overtake them, quickened his pace as far as possible. This was preposterous! He positively dragged Mrs Mallow along.

Blessed if they weren't choosing their trousseau! The shop, Martin discovered as they approached, was one where Venice lace was displayed. By God—*undies*! He crossed himself inwardly. This was getting past a joke. As they came up he coughed in a warning manner. But this merely drove them off. They started forwar d again without turning round, with peals of laughter coming from April.

At the restaurant, the selection of their table had been dictated by some obsession with the romantic. It was withdrawn from the rest of the mere eating and drinking majority. It had a window opening upon a starlit canal, of very old and shadowy palaces, with a great drooping church, weighed down with a plastron of tormented sculpture, dripping in its bath of moonlight.

As Martin heavily took his place, he looked at his friend. The look spoke volumes.

Like Mrs Mallow, Martin was 'attracted by intelligent people.' Really he *had* a great affection for Vincent—in spite of confessions; in spite of his now detecting vulgar streaks of which formerly he had been quite unaware.

But *this* was not Vincent Penhale at all. This man he had before him was an impostor. A vulgar impostor. He resented his impersonation of his friend Vincent Penhale. And he would jolly well like to tell him so!

This was a nightmare version of Vincent. Moreover, the confession staged in the gondola he could not quite believe in either. That was rather nightmarish too.

In spite of everything, Martin clung to his picture of the gentleman. The picture of his friend as he had always thought of him from the start. He *would* not have this bounder thrust upon him—as in a spirit of mischief Vincent seemed determined to see that he should.

What of course made that horrid "confession" seem

particularly unreal (and perhaps, after all, it was a hoax?), was the patent affluence of this "working-class boy." Members of the working class do not as a rule inherit fortunes from aunts. As a matter of fact, if at all, *never* from aunts! They didn't have aunts—people like that. Vincent certainly had indicated that his legacy derived from an aunt. But, who ever heard of touchy old ladies with big bank balances, hovering deliciously in the background of a son of toil? They were a strictly upper class phenomenon.

No. One day perhaps Vincent would come into his room and tell him it was all a hoax, and show him a photograph maybe of a House-group at Haileybury. The house-master in the middle with his mortarboard on his knees, and with a cross marking the position of the little Penhale. He would be very angry with him if this happened. He'd tell him what a stupid crack he thought it, and point out there was a limit to practical joking between such friends as they were.

He had been a fool at the time not to ask Vincent how it came about that this abject working-class family of his had coughed up an aunt overflowing with dough. She must have been very fond of him to leave him so much money. Had he lived with her as a boy? Why had he never talked about his sister Victoria? And so on. But he had felt a bit shy about asking such questions.

So he stared at Vincent, as the latter moved about and talked; for it was one of those dreams where you cannot speak for yourself. Being outside the scene—quite as if it had been of his own making—Martin was by turns attentive and inattentive. But, above all, the unreality was so greatly increased by the extreme vivacity of Mrs Mallow. *That* it was that bereft him of speech and depressed his spirits to an absolutely sub-normal plane.

Vincent had been speaking in an undertone to the *maître d'hôtel*, and shortly an enormous ice-bucket made its appearance. It contained what could only be a magnum of champagne if not a jereboam.

"My dear!" protested Mrs Mallow to the bustling Vincent. "You don't expect us to drink all that! This is not the Lord Mayor's banquet."

"We are to enter a still-born war," he reminded her.

The mummy of a moonlit Canaletto through the glass of the window; this desiccated voice of the old woman, like the voice of a gnat, humorously rationalizing everything with her veneer of a fetid gaiety: and on top of all that, Vincent's elaborate pantomime, gave Martin the sensation of being seated upon a stage in a theatre, rehearsing with the actor-manager some stock farce.

"Pray silence for this solemn toast!" boomed Vincent. "Ladies and gentlemen. To the poor little war that missed the bus."

"If it *has*!" said April, raising her glass. "Aren't you drinking, Mr Penny-Smythe?"

Martin, who was sitting between Mrs and Miss Mallow, touched both their glasses in turn.

"The poor little war *has* missed the bus," Vincent informed them. "The manager has just told me so."

"How do you mean—he t-t-told you?" stuttered Martin.

"Mr Chamberlain's speech, to which the manager has just been listening, makes it clear that the threat of war has passed."

"Thank god for that!" Mrs Mallow exclaimed.

"Yes. I second that!" said Martin, drinking.

April stared in front of her for a moment.

"So it's all over!" she said as if to herself.

"Yes," smiled Vincent. "All over. For the present."

"Well, I suppose we ought to be very thankful," she said, dazed and uncertain.

"What for? For the Crisis, do you mean?" Vincent bent his head towards hers. "I'm rather grateful for *that*, darling!"

And he squeezed her hand under the table. He looked over at her mother and Martin, who were conversing earnestly. The great news had affected them both in rather the same way. Both had been very exhilarated by it.

"I can see you two are plotting!" Vincent broke in, with a

wag of his finger. He filled Martin's glass, with a bubbling overflow, then Mrs Mallow's. "A Stuart Putsch—am I right?"

"No. An Anti-red Front!" squeaked Mrs Mallow.

"I thought it might be some sort of witch-hunt."

Vincent's hearty "you two" was a displeasing reminder to Martin. It damped for the moment his exuberance. He had been thawed into *bonhomie* with his aged neighbour, whom he now eyed with a scowling interrogation.

"Yes, my dear. 'We two!'" she said and gave a shriek, that was a sort of fragile war-whoop. He drew several inches away from her. This woman was perhaps a witch. The "witch-hunt" should perhaps start with her. Martin would not have been at all surprised to observe a mouse jump out of her talking-trap.

Shellfish of odd colours and shapes appeared and were eaten. Previtalis for good food! Martin noted the presence of the good food and subsequently it's disappearance, that was all.

"Herr Chamberlain believes you can defend a world-empire with umbrellas," Vincent was proclaiming. "He believes in the goodness of man. He believes in the sanctity of work—at quite low wages. What is more, he believes in the sanctity of No Work. Blessed are the out-of-work, for they shall inherit the Dole, unto the third and fourth generation. Who will drink to our wonderful P.M.?"

Vincent's hands remained in his pockets. But Martin took up his glass and announced—

"I will! I will drink to Mr Chamberlain!"

He drank.

April, whose cheeks were flushed, exclaimed prettily, "Pray Silence!" and half rose, gracefully waving an empty glass.

"I have a toast, ladies and gentlemen!" she mildly piped. "I should like to drink to *us*. Just us!"

"May we live long to enjoy our ushishness!" Vincent added, lifting his glass to his lips.

"Bravo!" quavered Mrs Mallow, nodding her head at Martin. She stamped her miniature feet, feebly cymballed with her ringed hands, and hooted in Martin's ear "hooray." The latter shied away.

Martin was surprised to find a large bird upon his plate. Several large birds appeared and were eaten. But Martin had grown definitely mellow. He wished to propose somebody's health, but he could not remember their name. What *was* their dratted name? He had had it on the tip of his tongue. Theo—something. Was it Theodore? Then Mrs Mallow claimed attention for a really important toast. Raising her glass she announced it in a firm schoolmasterly voice, incorrigibly slangy, with a stern twinkling eye;

"Jolly good luck to Earl Baldwin, wherever he may be!"

"More power to his Garter!" Vincent added.

"You *are* interested in politics!" April whispered to him.

"Not really," Vincent said.

Martin and Mrs Mallow came out of a huddle about Monsieur Deutsch, for whom both had conceived a great secret antipathy. Mrs Mallow came out of it snapping for air with her slightly moustachioed lips. The champagne was gradually wearing down her veteran corpuscles. A cup of coffee now stood before each of the four diners, the meal had reached that point. The ruins of a *Soufflé (en surprise)* of proportions analogous to the magnum had just been wheeled away. A large flask of *Fine* made its début upon the table; one of *Chartreuse*, too, and one of *Kümmel*.

The waiters, out of their sallow masks, were eyeing the English party like a ring of slovenly birds of prey, with an impolite semi-oriental fixity, of bold black eyes. They were far enough gone, they judged, these preposterous Englishes, for it to be no longer necessary to dissemble. They gathered in a scowling ring.

Martin brooded over his goblet of brandy. Vincent was a damned smart fellow! No question about that. He had known all along there would be no war. How did he come to be so infernally smart? He was too clever by a long shot to be a gentleman! Too *knowing*. Must be his low birth that had sharpened his wits.

He was disturbed in his meditations by a movement at his side. He looked up frowning: there was Mrs Mallow unsteadily making her way among the nearby tables, guided by a waiter.

"I think I'd better go after mother," said April. "She doesn't look awfully well."

He got up and allowed April to pass. When he was seated again, Vincent slipped into the place April had vacated.

"What are you brooding about Mart? Your lost youth?"

"N-no-no," answered Martin. "About *something* I had lost. But it was not youth."

"What was it Martin?"

"About a friend I had lost," Martin answered. "That was what I was grieving about just then."

"His name?" Vincent enquired softly. "Do I know him?"

Martin nodded.

"Ah!" Vincent laughed. "A certain rather tiresome fellow born in the lower walks of life. Am I right? You old goose. You haven't lost him at all. He is at your side all the time!"

He filled Martin's goblet. He reached for his own and filled that.

"Martin, let *us* have a little toast, all to ourselves."

"I'm not Miss Mallow, Vincent! I'm not a wer-wer-woman."

"Now don't get cross. I shall drink to our stopping friends in spite of all my faults!"

The two ladies had returned, and Vincent and he rose, to allow them to regain their seats. Mrs Mallow was a greenish white when she returned. Martin said nothing, he was feeling rather stand-offish. He fixed a frowning eye upon his glass. Mrs Mallow was getting into her fur coat. A waiter assisted her. Soon they had all plunged out into the extremely chilly Venetian night. And then once more the obscene warmth of the befurred arm, and the small gloved hand which was like a snuggling head to it, was communicated to Martin's arm.

"I don't know I'm *sure!*" the small and cultivated Kensingtonian accents at his side joined in his meditation. Then later, "If I don't *soon* reach that hotel!" And again. "Mr Pennyishmy! Did you hear that man . . . No of *course* you didn't. You . . . weren't there. Were you? Or *were you!*"

"I wer-wer-was not. As y-you know . . . qu-qu-quite well."

"You are premtry . . . Pennishmy! Aren't you! or *aren't you?*"

He snorted and tried to shake off the little befurred old lady. But she only shrieked and faintly hooted in his ear.

That morning at six a.m.—it was September 28—the door of April Mallow's bedroom opened and Mr Vincent Penhale stepped out into the passage. His dressing-gown, of an aggressive red, was held like a toga. He closed the door, nodded to a man who was removing shoes from before the door of Mrs Mallow's room, and made his way to the head of the stairs which led to the entresol, where his room and Martin's were situated. When he reached his room he took a sheet of note-paper out of the drawer of the desk, and scribbled the following message:

"Don't want to be disturbed till noon. Been busy all night instructing Miss Mallow in the arts of love. She's an A.1. pupil. I feel all in. Respect my slumbers when you rise at the unearthly hour of eight.

Vincent."

Passing quietly into the bathroom, he went down on one knee and slipped the sheet of notepaper, face upwards, beneath Martin Penny-Smythe's door.

Chapter XII

THE INVALID

VINCENT PENHALE was stretched out, spectacularly re-laxed, upon the terrace of a water-front café, with the air of a convalescent. He sucked glumly at a straw, his tall drink standing upon his chest, both hands cupped around it. Four days had passed since the night of the dinner-party.

"I'm all in," he complained, "this honeymoon's getting me down."

Martin sternly refrained from comment, but smoke stole out of the sides of his mouth as he very slowly removed his Peterson.

"I shall have to make my escape," Vincent said, as the other remained silent. "I am not a robot."

Martin put his pipe back into his mouth again, and his teeth closed tightly upon it's stem. This exhibitionism was more than he could stomach! He was in the same case as Vincent—*he* would have to escape too—and that jolly quickly—if Vincent persisted in his present impersonation of a rank outsider.

"Now we know there's going to be no war," Vincent spoke again, "should we go back by way of Vienna? What do you think? It's a grim place these days they say. But I have never seen it."

"I don't think you'd like it."

"No?"

"Not now. I know I shouldn't."

Martin was so unspeakably repelled by *the invalid* and his objectionable languor, that he refused to turn his face in that direction. At least this actor should be without an audience —his ears he could not stop up, but he could avert his eyes.

This time he had struck. He declined to have anything more to do with Penhale's vainglorious theatricals.

He sent his gaze, in a stony meditation, out over the Grand Canal, doing his best to recall what all this stale beauty had looked like when first he saw it as an undergraduate. *Stones of Venice*! Ah, that was his companion then. Ruskin instead of Penhale.

Out of the tail of his eye he remarked two painfully familiar female figures, emerging from the great square at their backs, drifting out, woman-fashion, upon the Piazzetta. It was Mrs and Miss Mallow.

Almost at once they were spotted, and the two ladies, still pretending to drift, altered their course, and came slowly towards the cafe, Mrs Mallow hoarsely calling as they approached—

"Ah, there you are!"

"Yes, here we are," Vincent drawled through his nose, without removing the giant tumbler from his chest, or the straw from his mouth: going limper rather than the reverse.

Martin lumbered to his feet.

"No, we won't disturb you . . . do please sit down, Mr Penny-Smythe," said Mrs Mallow.

"Ner-no disturbance. Really," Martin murmured—but he could not bring himself to look at Mrs Mallow otherwise than askance. Indeed April was the only other member of the party his eyes ever rested on now with comfort. The more Vincent came back with accounts of her hot-bloodedness, the chaster the poor girl seemed to look—almost as if butter wouldn't melt in her mouth. She looked perfectly madonna-like this morning, in her aloofness from fleshly things.

She was, however, as she stood there with her mother, making a great effort not to appear crestfallen. At any moment she might burst into tears, he felt. That probably was what Penhale wanted.

Sliding her hand inside her mother's arm, she attempted to draw her away, biting her lip and keeping her face averted from the odious convalescent.

"April, darling," drawled Vincent, very offensively through his nose, "take your mother home, there's a good old girl. She looks tired."

"Not half as tired as *you!*" Mrs Mallow protested.

"Yes, I expect I do look a bit fagged out, Mrs Mallow. I feel it."

"We've all been under a bit of a strain, I suppose. It's the strain of these last few hectic days."

"I expect it is."

"Thank god it's all over, anyway." Mrs Mallow sighed dramatically.

"Amen," said Vincent.

"Another week of that . . . " Mrs Mallow fanned herself.

"Heaven preserve us from *that!*" Vincent quailed, in mock alarm. "April, my sweet, *do* take your mother away. She ought to have a little rest before dinner. You've already dragged her about too much."

"No, it wasn't April. *I* wanted to go and look for you. It was I who dragged her, poor girl."

"Come along, mother!" April, on the verge of tears, implored Mrs Mallow.

"Well. A reviderlo!" Mrs Mallow cast Martin a gaily reproachful look.

"A rer-re-riv . . . viderlo!" he answered, sitting down.

The two women moved away.

"Hunting us!" Vincent grumbled, the straw still in his mouth. "We shall never shake those women off, as long as we're in Venice."

"You mean you won't," Martin put in a sharp protest at the 'we.'

"The old one's as bad as the young one," Vincent said.

Martin however was boiling over with suppressed reproof.

"Why are you so beastly to that girl, Vincent!" he asked him.

"I? Beastly?" Vincent looked up in affected amazement.

"You know you are bub-bub-being . . . brutal."

Vincent laughed.

"I like that," he said, bitterly. "She doesn't *pay* me does she. I'm a voluntary worker. She has no right to come routing me out like that. I must have an evening off occasionally." Then he looked up and grinned. "So must *you*, old man."

"Me? H-h-how d'you mean, I must?"

"Oh, I don't know. You and Mary M. seem to hit it off pretty well."

"Don't be so absurd, Vincent," Martin gulped. Mrs Mallow is an aged person. She's old enough to be my grandmother."

"April Mallow is not so terribly youthful either."

"There is a difference."

"Not in kind, but in degree."

And there they stopped, for Martin could not trust himself to continue this extremely distasteful conversation. He knew Vincent was talking like that to get his goat: just as the horrid stretched-out limpness was done to annoy, as much as anything.

What on earth was happening to Vincent, he pondered? What did the "confession" mean—whether true or not? What did *this* mean? He seemed to be tormenting that wretched girl now, who, it was plain to see, was madly in love with him. Was it his intention to shake her off now that he had got what he wanted—for neither of them made any disguise of the fact that they were lovers? Or was this part of a plan to attach her still more closely to him? Odious thought!

The text of the "confession" so far as he was able to remember it, seemed to indicate that the latter might be the explanation.

The filthy party at Previtali's, with the lavish alcohol, what had been the meaning of that? In times of crisis and emergency, the female restraints tend to break down. Had Vincent availed himself of the emotional tension of the last ten days (a tension in which he did not himself participate, for he had never believed in the likelihood of war) to put over a matrimonial *coup* since his funds were getting low? And was the party at Previtali's a part of the machinery—the *pièce de résistance*, as it were? If so he had put himself to a lot of unnecessary trouble. The girl was only too eager to become his melting victim. But there you were! Vincent was nothing if not ingeniously dramatic. It was the *vulgar streak* coming out.

Vincent had declared on one occasion that all his money had now been dissipated. Was that true or not? Martin really did not know which was the more unpleasant notion (1) Vincent the fortune-hunter, or (2) Vincent the lady-killer (with the emphasis upon the *lady*).

Before this happy reversal of fortune, which had overtaken Vincent some eighteen months before, Martin, with his small private means, had been obliged always to consider whether his friend could afford or not a quite moderately-priced restaurant, when they went out together. Afterwards, all that had been changed. Now it was rather Vincent who had to give thought to the modest proportions of Martin's purse. But the transformation occurred silently, and almost as if Vincent had been ashamed of his good fortune.

That his friend had the makings of a great actor Martin was positive. His parts had been mainly in Chekov or Shaw plays, in a semi-amateur capacity. He hated to be thought of as an actor, too—as a *pro*. As a dress-designer he was very skilful—although he had no training as an artist—and he had designed the dresses for several revivals of seventeenth-century plays, and for one small highbrow ballet that had been put on in Eastbourne. He had done a great deal of dress-designing. And, rather than describe himself as an actor, he put "artist" on his passport. As an artist, or dilettante of the arts, he had given himself out here in Venice, and frowned whenever Martin inadvertently mentioned the Stage.

That he had great talent for the arts, and a great flair if not understanding in everything to do with artistic expression, was unquestionable. Under happier circumstances he would have risen to great eminence in one or more of the fields where his especial aptitudes had been demonstrated, Martin was quite certain of that. And he admired him very much—though regretting there was nothing more substantial for this hero-worship to feed on than a few brilliant performances of parts in unpopular plays, or a few sketches of costumes, or little Conder-like scenes in projected ballets.

Loud and long had been Vincent's protests against the malign fate that had denied him a glorious career, which his qualities as a personality and his talents seemed to entitle him to. When he had come into money he had without delay rented a studio and launched into an ambitious programme of 'creative' work. He had undertaken some film-projects. (which had come to nothing) and made a few attacks upon the London Stage. For six months it had been a whirl of speculative activity. Held back for so long by lack of money, obliged to 'pot-boil,' *at last,* he was free to do what he wanted. That was the idea.

Martin had been delighted to feel that his friend's troubles were over, and that he now would come into his own—*how* was not very clear, but probably in a combination of ways. Several times he was mentioned in gossip-columns. Vincent's was such an unusual mind, his friend had felt, that it had been a great shame he had been forcibly confined to the production of mere bread-and-butter stuff, by which he was more than once almost sent mad. He had thrown up more than one important stage or shop job, in a moment of acute impatience with the standards demanded.

Vincent's great attraction for Martin Penny-Smythe was therefore—even as the former had asserted during his confession—a matter of personality, even of personal beauty, rather than of mind. This stumpy, scholarly, little man, himself of the 'tweed and waterproof class' had been dazzled by the vitality, the good looks, rather than by artistic attainments of his friend.

But, after a furious spell of work, not unattended by success, Penhale's activity had dried up. This did not prevent him from announcing—and of late this had been of especially frequent occurence—that he had been commissioned to do something—what it was he did not reveal in detail—for which he was receiving a handsome fee, Martin, knowing from his own work as a civil servant, the disastrous state of all the markets involved, was sceptical. But in making these announcements Vincent's object could only be to induce others to believe that a substantial proportion of his income was derived from work of his own hand, rather than from those hated *dividends*, which when he saw other people enjoying them roused him to such ferocious denunciation.

So that, whichever way you looked at it, Vincent's economic position was an enigma. Martin felt, however, if they were to remain friends—in the same way as before, that is—he should have *some* understanding of what was going on, and at least not be hoaxed as he felt more than ever had been happening a week ago on their sketching-trip in the gondola.

"Ver-ver-Vincent!" he stammered suddenly—and the stammer showed that he had gone back to the old footing, and desired to be reinstated as his old Bellocian self. "Are you rich?"

"Eh?" Vincent looked up frowning.

"I hope you don't m-m-mind my asking, old man. Did your aunt leave you . . . much?"

"Depends what you call much . . . But I'm practically broke now." Vincent, after his first astonishment, had gone still now, and started sucking at the straw.

"I'm s-s-sorry to hear that."

Vincent shrugged.

"What's it matter?" he said.

"What will you do now?" Martin was going to have this out. He was not going to be put off. Vincent had imposed for long enough upon his genteel inhibitions.

"Do? What will I do. How do I know?" Vincent stood up and stretched, calling out for the waiter. "Ask me next month. I've got enough money till then. But I feel in no mood, let me tell you, *for confessions*, to-day, old man!"

"I don't wer-wer-want you too . . ."

"I was sorry afterwards I had told you about my working-class origins. You've treated me quite differently since then."

"Oh!"

"You talk to me now sometimes as if I were the under-gardener. Your voice has a bossy note in it. 'Let me see, my good man—did you say you'd put a little money away against a rainy day?' That sort of thing. You've been quite horrid at times!"

"Well . . . !"

"Oh, I'm sure you didn't mean a thing. Just habit. The master-class state of mind."

"Really, Vincent! I'd been thinking that *you* had been behaving a bit oddly."

Vincent laughed, handing a new twenty lira note to the waiter. "Exactly!" he said. "Everything I do seems *odd* now. One of the 'lower orders' dressed up to look like a toff cannot be otherwise than *odd*."

PART II

LONDON

CHAPTER XIII

BROTHER AND SISTER

MADELEINE MORSE rapped upon the taxi window for the man to stop, pointing at a low white house in the centre of an irregular block of buildings standing directly upon the River Thames. Only the white building was used for residential purposes.

White-washed, its shutters, doors, and other woodwork painted a penetrating blue, which picked it out as a smart gentleman's residence among the shabby neighbouring offices and warehouses, it suggested an original taste in the occupier: for who but an original man would choose such a site? Two shrubs standing in white buckets impressed by their beautiful hair-cuts, on either side of the door. A neat yellow gravel-path led from the iron gate to the dazzling white door-step: and when Mrs Morse gave a gentle rat-tat upon the exotic brass knocker, a white-coated domestic opened the door.

"Good morning, Willis," said Mrs Morse. "My brother is expecting me, I think."

Willis had 'old soldier' written all over him. He stood aside, smiling a respectful welcome.

"Mr Penhale is upstairs. I will tell him you are here, m'm."

He pushed open a door on the opposite side of the small octagonal hall, on the walls of which hung six framed drawings of costumes for a performance of *The Winter's Tale* signed V.P.

"Thank you, Willis. How are the rheumatics?"

"Not too bad, thank you m'm," the man gratefully answered. "It's difficult to keep the damp out in this place though."

103

"It must be. My brother never gets any twinges does he? Then he's as strong as a horse."

"He is that, m'm. He's a young gentleman with a constitution of iron, as they say. I wish I had half the health wot he has. Have you been keeping fit madam?"

"Fair to middling." Then the rather statuesque face broke into a swift, intelligent, smile. "Mustn't grumble, Willis, you know. Mustn't grumble!"

"No m'm. That's right m'm."

They had moved into a large room, its roof supported by cedarwood pillars. A grandiose—and quite superfluous easel loomed at the side of a quite superfluous model's throne! Shallow steps led up to the windows, which ran the whole length of the river-front.

Willis withdrew, quietly closing the door behind him. Madeleine Morse ascended the steps and looked out at the dung-brown flood surging almost immediately beneath her eyes. It appeared a most at eye-level—a swirling convexity. Gulls rode up and down upon it like large toy birds for a child's tub.

The door opened at the farther side of this rather bleak apartment and the voice of Vincent Penhale called to her softly.

"Maddie! I came you see!" He advanced rapidly towards her, his face lighted up with an almost school-boyish pleasure.

Madeleine came down the steps without speaking, her large earrings swaying as she moved, in the shadow of her sweeping sable hat, dating from Chelsea's 'gypsy' vogue.

Vincent took her pale statuesque face, with its sad red lips, in his hands, and kissed her cheek. She gave his arm a quick squeeze, and stood back, with the same absence of expression, almost wooden—but withal sensitively-carved. They looked at each other, he smiled, a little nervously for him.

"Well, Maddie darling. What did the mysterious summons mean? I flew—literally, flew—in answer to it. I arrived from Paris only an hour or so ago."

"Vincent," she said, and stopped. The impassive, bloodless face began to writhe a little at the mouth, then suddenly, it broke up and went to pieces. She sat down abruptly upon a large bench, and covering her face with her hands, burst into tears.

"What is it, Maddie?" he asked softly, going up and bending towards her. "You have something to tell me, haven't you? What has happened, dear?"

"It's dad," she said. "It's daddie. He's dead."

For a few moments Vincent's face was strikingly like his sister's. It became wooden: white and stately, but with the lips thin and tight. Then ever so slightly, just as his sister's had, it began to writhe in the neighbourhood of the lips. His nostrils dilated. But it did not break up, as had his sister's. It began to go harder still, instead.

"Poor old dad!" he said at last. "He's gone has he. He must have been glad to get out of it."

Maddie continued to cry. Vincent stood gazing at her, in wooden, impotent, distress. Then he went over to a table by the large red-brick fireplace, where drinks stood upon a tray. He poured himself a Scotch and soda.

. "Have something, Maddie," he suggested. "A whisky? Stiffen you up, sister! You've had a lousy time of it I expect."

His sister got up, wiping her face with her handkerchief.

"I'm sorry to be doing this, Vincent." She took out her compact from her bag and began to repair the effect of the tears.

"Poor old Maddie!" He went up and put his arm round her waist and led her towards the fireplace. "I know how terribly you feel it darling. . . . You didn't tell me, Maddie, when you wrote that anything was wrong."

"I know, Vincent. There *wasn't*. He was only ill three days. I'd just heard the news when I sent you the cable."

"What was it?"

"Pneumonia."

Maddie's face was now as white, solemn, and unsmiling

as before. She was his junior by a full decade: seven-and-twenty. More than Vincent's, Maddie's features were beautifully regular, altogether of the 'classic mould', with eyes and hair dusky like his. But if nature had endowed Vincent with too irritable a sense of humour, it had equipped Maddie with an almost startling absence of it.

Before her marriage with Richard Morse, a young hack cartoonist she had met at her brother's, Maddie had sat for the head, as portrait-model, for a number of years. She had first mounted the model's throne at eighteen. And there she had queened it, till four-and-twenty.

Sitting without more movement than a thing of stone (for she was conscientious) for hours at a stretch—inspiring, as she felt herself to be doing, with her rounded Graeco-Roman beauty, herds of flattering students, yet whom she had to keep at a distance, and whom she actually rather frightened by her noble severity of looks and carriage—this inexpressibly sedentary, this peculiarly lifeless occupation, had stamped her for good. She always gave a little the impression of somebody *posing*, and constrained under penalty of dismissal to keep quite still. Not that it was her nature, anyway, to relax easily into a smile.

In some ways, however, this mask of a girl, with her static face, served as a key to her brother—who was not so unsolemn as all that himself. In spite of the fact that he made such an active and as it were, over-deliberate use of his personality, and went suavely smiling through his mortal part, he was born to the tragic rôles as much as she. They were very near together in some respects, these two. Both took life with such a black seriousness at bottom. Everything that happened to them set up so dark a tension. One covered up with masculine veneer, of fearless laughter. The other faced life unsmiling and unwinking, with great dark rounded eyes that looked like shock-absorbers for something much more lively and sensitive within.

There was another link between these two—of which this guarded aloofness, and even stateliness, was the expression.

The relentless pressure of the English *class* incubus had poisoned the existence of one as much as of the other. A morbid condition obtained in both cases: both had suffered a deep infection.

This had even to be allowed for in accounting for Maddie's impassibility. One reason why she held herself so stately and unsmiling—perhaps a little *queenly*—was because she had had to be always on her best behaviour. Maddie had not sufficiently mastered the arts of careless ease of those who had never had to think about class—about accent and deportment. She so remained aloof in her ivory tower of classic physical perfection, where she could be a girl of few words, and those words picked beforehand, without haste, so that no grammatical slip might escape her.

Maddie was beginning now to outgrow her first discomforts: her marriage had provided her with a status of sorts, and a husband who had 'people' ('professional' instead of 'labouring'), and who at Manchester Grammar School (the 'Westminster' of Manchester) had received a suitable education. His accent was therefore quite good. But she still kept her impassive, rarely smiling, mask. And her beauty, paradoxically, was of such a *noble* order, that she could scarcely help herself. Physically, with her, it was a kind of *noblesse oblige*—which at the same time *did* serve to explain Vincent.

Her love for Vincent, for all her studied coldness, shone warmly out of this blanched immobility, and her lips still trembled slightly as she gazed at him now—full of admiration for this wonderful brother of hers (so much nearer to her than was her husband, Dick)—such a gallant figure; such a perfect gentleman; so loyal a friend.

"Did he die . . . easy?" Vincent asked stirring things about on the table with his finger. "He had everything he wanted? Or he was not *in want*. He was all right was he?"

Maddie wiped her eyes for a moment with her handkerchief.

"You know what mother is, Vincent."

He looked up quickly.

"Oh, what about her? Didn't she get the doctor at once?"
Maddie shook her head.

"Of course she said Dad was putting it on—*sprucing*. You know what she is like. The poor old man was delirious for the best part of a day in the back room. Mother was in one of her tempers. In the end I think she got frightened. I think dad frightened her by the things he said. . . . Then she got a neighbour to 'phone for me. I found him *raving*."

Vincent sat, his face contracted, staring at the floor.

"*Sprucing*. The domestic discipline that is aimed at getting the wage-slave off to work each day, whether he feels up to it or not. When he falls ill he is treated as a *malingerer*, until he grows delirious. . . . Pretty awful isn't it?" he said. "Pretty bloody awful, what!"

"Oh, Vincent, it's terrible. It really is. You should see the place now. It is a perfect pig-sty."

"But why couldn't they *move* from that filthy den? They've had enough money."

"Mother refused. I tried to get her to move. She said she liked the neighbourhood."

Vincent laughed. "She thinks the *Kenilworth Arms* and the *Load of Hay* can't be improved on?"

Maddie hung her head. "She's worse now than ever," she said. "As soon as your cheque arrives on the first of the month Minnie says she starts on a drinking bout. Almost all of it goes. Half the time she's without money. Dick has none, as you know. I can't ask him for more than a few shillings. Lately I've thought I'd go modelling again. But Dick objects."

"But why didn't you *write* to me, Maddie? I could have sent more *easily*. I'm broke right now. But I could easily have done it."

"What's the use, Vincent? Any money you sent would go the same way."

"Into the cash-register of the *Kenilworth Arms* or some other pub?"

"At once. Sometimes Dad went with her. But he got

precious little of the cash, and he often said he wished he hadn't given up his work."

"I wish he hadn't. The poor old devil ought to have been left in harness till the last."

"His asthma got awfully bad, Vincent. I doubt if he could. Then he never used to get proper medicine. You know what the panel-doctors are like. Dr Stockton refused to prescribe what he needed."

"Why?"

"Well, Dick says—I don't know how true it is—that if a panel-doctor prescribes expensive medicine . . . medicine that costs the country . . ."

"Costs *the state.*"

"Yes, costs the state . . . costs the state a lot of money—if he prescribes it for people who . . . who are . . ."

"For poor people, you mean? For the poor. Yes. I see."

"Well, the country . . . or the *state*, doesn't like that, Dick says. A doctor he knows, who is a panel-doctor told him he was hauled up before his board and threatened if his bill for medicines for the month was over the regulation figure, which allows only for the cheapest sort of stuff. So panel-doctors you see, often *can't*, if they want to, prescribe for their patients medicines that they know quite well they need if they are to get well."

Vincent sprang up.

"The bastards! The bastards!" he exclaimed, his face almost as pale as his sister's with anger. "The inhuman brutes!" He paced up and down in front of her, as if seeking some path to action—some path out of the despondent maze; but turned back every few feet, met by insuperable barriers.

"Maddie, excuse me. I'm sorry. But this is really too much!—Imagine a doctor—imagine a man with all the advantages, the training, of a medical man—lending himself to that shabby, *criminal*, system: hiring himself out as an *alibi*: being paid his fee to see that the poor are left where they drop. To refuse to succour them: to help these jolly masters of ours to push them off the earth! To take money for *that!*"

"It is terrible. It is! But what can you do?"

"Do? I should like to go now to that filthy little doctor and wring his vile little money-grubbing neck! That's what I am half a mind to do before he can preside at the torture and slow death of any more of what he calls his *patients*. Ah, *patient* indeed. All of us are that! As mild and submissive as sheep."

He turned upon Maddie, who jumped slightly.

"Why didn't you go and see him, Maddie, and tell him what you thought of him? He wouldn't have *dared* to do that if he knew he was being *watched*. They can only do these things, believe me, because the poor have no means of defending themselves. It's only because no one is there to *see* them in action—or in no action—that they can carry on. You should have threatened him with a writ. He would soon have made out the necessary prescription!"

"But that's just what I did, Vincent. I did go and see him, I mean. I said I was dad's daughter . . ."

"Ah, you shouldn't have said *that* . . . you should never have allowed him to see that *you* were one of the poor yourself! That is fatal."

This philosophy, typical of Vincent, appeared to confuse her only.

"I suppose I shouldn't," she answered half-heartedly.

"What did he say? How did he receive you?"

"He was . . . he was very insolent, Vincent. He was rude to me." Again the heroic, beautiful, mask showed signs of breaking up. A slight flush began to creep up to the eyes—a flush of shame at the memory of the insolence of the panel-doctor, when that official had realized that she was the daughter of his two elderly working-class patients, who inhabited a slum-flat of two small rooms and a kitchenette. He told me that if I could treat my father better than he could I'd better do so, and save him the trouble. *He* didn't mind, if I preferred it that way. He said that with such a bad asthma and at his time of life he was lucky to be alive."

Vincent, who had sat down again, leaped to his feet.

"I *will* visit that foul little pill-wallah. I *will* not let him do that to . . . to *me!* To *you* . . . He *shall* not get away with it!"

"He's not *little*, Vincent. He's a big fat red-faced fellow. And he can be . . . very, very rude."

"I can be rude as well."

"He made me feel very small beer I'm afraid . . . and oh, so awfully *helpless*. I said I'd pay for the medicine. But I think he didn't believe I had the money. In the end of course I bought it myself, out of some money Dick gave me—though he couldn't afford it, poor boy."

Vincent in savage contemplation gazed at his sister and she gazed back, resigned and stately, at him. But their eyes both held a consciousness of the same injustice . . . for which there was *no help*—unless one could obtain it by fraud or force. Both had tasted for too long the hopelessness of rebellion.

"Honestly, Maddie, it almost compels me to agree with Halvorsen. That's saying a lot. There's nothing I should like to do so little as to agree with Halvorsen."

Maddie shook her head. She meant that she wouldn't care much to be in agreement with Mr Halvorsen either.

"So what must we do now, Maddie?"

"Well, there's the stone . . ."

"Oh, yes. The *funeral* you mean . . . nothing has been done about that yet?"

"Not yet.'"

"Well, let us go to . . . mother's. Let's go there now." He rang the bell.

"A taxi, Willis," he said, as soon as his white-coated 'man' appeared. "Look slippy!"

"Have you enjoyed yourself, Vincent?" Maddie asked. "You've been away a long time. Let's see, it's about two months since you left Venice . . ."

"Have I enjoyed myself? Is that the question? Yes, I suppose I have. I have just got married."

"Married?" Maddie was so astonished that she lost her impassibility, and borrowed one of Vincent's frowns.

"Yes. Last week in Paris. You didn't see about it in the *Daily Mail?* Quite an occasion. The bride, Miss April Mallow, wore a gown of white satin La Vallière, with a veil of Venice lace. A great show. Bride given away by her uncle, Sir Lionel Mallow. Reception afterwards at the Crillon. . . . Oh, yes. It was very posh."

The statuesque serenity of the face before him began to show signs of emotional collapse. It's surface commenced to writhe. But Maddie lowered her face and said in a husky voice:

"I think you might have told me, Vincent. I know I'm nothing. . . . I'm only your poor little ex-model of a sister . . ."

"Whom I certainly would cut if I encountered her as I was coming out of the church, my bride upon my arm! . . . It's true. I should!"

"How *hard* you are Vincent!" A single stately tear descended the pallor of her cheek. She spoke without reproach.

"Ah, that I *have* to be. Who is better able than you Maddie to understand all about that? . . . But now it is all over—thank God—you must meet April. I may send for her to-morrow. She's quite a decent girl you'll find."

"But very high and mighty."

Vincent laughed.

"Not half as high and mighty as you, darling Maddie."

Willis opened the door.

"The taxi is there, sir," he said, his face as much a mask— and for the same reason—as that of Mrs Morse.

CHAPTER XIV

THE FUNERAL

ALL, the neighbours protruded from the windows of the slum-alley—there was Mrs Atkinson, who had called Minnie "a mare," upon hearing herself referred to as "no lady"; Mrs Powder whose dog 'Zip', bit the Penhale dog once a month, and had killed Mrs Cotton's whose eye had been blacked for interfering; and Mrs Simpson whose ex-policeman hubby had prostate trouble, and Mrs Chenil, who had won twenty-seven pounds in the pools. A black suited Vincent made all catch their breaths, then click their tongues, as preceded at arm's length by an enormous wreath, he alighted—and no word but that could convey the graceful translation of his richly-trousered legs from the seat of the hired car to the muddy cobbles. He ascended the steps to the flat-door followed by the chauffeur with the wreath.

As Vincent Penhale entered the small room there was a hostile hush. There had been a hush before he arrived. His father lay in state beneath the mantelpiece. But the hush imposed by Mr Penhale lying in his varnished box was as nothing to the *dead* silence that supervened upon the entrance of his son.

Nine women and one man were inside. The man was Vincent's elder brother Harry. His two sisters, Minnie and Maddie, his two sisters-in-law, Flo and Bessie, and five lady-neighbours were the nine women.

Maddie, his confederate, the only friendly face in this company, greeted him, placing a hand upon the swagger wreath.

"What a beautiful wreath, Vincent," she said. "It is lovely. Will you go in and see mother?"

113

"How is she?"

"Not well enough to get up. Her cough's pretty bad." She lowered her voice. "I think she's angry with father for dying. It's mostly temper, Vincent! Still . . ."

"Where shall I put this—here? Thank you Minnie. Poor old Minnie, you must be all in. Did you get any sleep last night? . . . no, I don't expect so. Ah, hello, Harry? Keeping pretty fit? 'Lo Flo!" (to Harry's wife): "'lo Bessie —how's the kids? Fine. Ernie left Christ's Hospital? Ah, Mrs Armitage, pleased to see you again. In the pink? That's capital, sure—I'm bearing up. Mustn't grumble. What do you say? No, mustn't grumble. Well I'm damned! (excuse me!) if it isn't Mrs Cooper!"

"'Ow are *yew* Vincent? We hardly dare 'ope—did we 'Arry?—wot *yew'd* be able to come Vincent. 'Arry and me thought the weather would prevent you. Still, I'm sure we're glad to see you, Vincent, aren't we, Flo?"

"I can stand up to rain as well as most people of my years," said Vincent smiling blandly.

"*I'm* sure yew can!"

"Besides it's stopped raining," Vincent looked towards a dirty window-pane, from which it was impossible to gather what was happening outside. "I think it'll keep off don't you?"

"I really couldn't say Vincent. I really couldn't. It *might* do."

Mrs Cooper (who was a great pal of Mrs Penhale) refused to commit herself about the weather—she seemed to suggest by the loftiness of her reserve that it was not exactly a delicate topic.

"Well, Vincent!" said his brother Harry. "I see you're much as you was last time I see you."

"Mustn't grumble, Harry."

"Well . . . Dad's gone, Vincent!"

"Dad's gone, Harry. Poor old dad."

"Mother's poorly too. She's getting old, Vin. . . . We're all getting on."

Harry shot a hard ugly look at Vincent's well-tailored sveltness. Himself he was a bald and dusky wage-slave of forty-five about. He was a mechanic, whose work was in a truck repair shop. A fine straight nose, as good as Vincent's, and fine darting dark eyes incongruously embellished his hard and mournful visage, well-scrubbed with Lifebuoy soap for the occasion.

"How have things been treating you, Harry—pretty lousy?" Vincent genially enquired.

"Oh, not too bad, Vin. Mustn't grumble. Stan's 'ad a bad bout 'er bronchitis, por kid—same as you used to 'ave, Vin, when you was young. You 'eard Ernie'd gone out to work, 'adn't you?"

"Ernie? No, what's he doing, Harry?"

The attraction exercised by such fine clothes, and such fine manners-to-match, had caused Harry's wife, in spite of her rugged 'independence,' to propel her small and sweaty East End person grudgingly towards Vincent.

"Ah, how are you, Vincent?" she said. "Ernie's a paper boy now. He started last spring."

"Delivers papers in the morning does he?"

"And evenings," Flo amended sullenly. As if Vin didn't know what a paper-boy did!

"How much does he get, Flo?" asked Vincent.

"How much does he get? Oh, five bob a week. Some wages, isn't it! I don't think! Still, he has to do something."

"That's right," Vincent agreed heartily. 'We all have to do something. Healthy occupation, carrying the *Times* round at seven in the morning, and laying it reverently upon people's doorsteps."

This flippant interpretation of the duties of a paper-boy sent up Flo's blood-pressure in an instant.

"I don't see there's any call, Vin, to be funny about it," she remarked, her face dark red—quite a different coloured blood to what a blush is made of. "What else can the poor kid do? He's seventeen. He must do *something*."

"Corse 'e 'as to," said Harry. "'E has to bring *somethink* in!"

"It's a shame he should earn so little," Vincent said mildly. "Can't he be apprenticed to some trade?"

"Where's the money coming from?" asked Flo disdainfully. "Next year 'e may get 'alf-crown raise I 'spose. I don't know."

Vincent sang, low and sweet,

> "*It'd be a risky thing*
> *To lose me job*
> *For thirty bob*
> *And NOT be England's King.*"

"This ain't 'ardly the time nor place is it to sing! Its' not exactly respectful to the dead, not to my way 'er thinkin'," commented Flo, and turned her back upon her brother-in-law.

"Terrible is it not, Vincent! Wasn't you shocked when you 'eard? I know I was. I only 'eard yest'day tea-time." Bessie had come up. Only an *in-law* (the widow of a dead brother) Bessie consequently was less moved to anger by the costly Bond Street suit, the fashionable overcoat, the regal wreath, and generally by this super-Penhale who had brought them all round (either upon his back or at the end of his white-cuffed arm), surmounted by his controversial face, so arrogantly alert, briefly to shine upon his proletarian kin. *She* didn't mind all this . . . he was a nice uncle for her kids to have. She could remember the time when he was one of those down-at-heel pros—she *much* preferred him this way! "Yes, I couldn't hardly believe my ears—*yew* know. It was Flo come round and told me yest'day. It wasn't 'arf sudden too was'n tit! Two days . . . hardly that was it and he was gone. Por ole dad!"

She wiped a tear away from her eye, then another tear.

"Man's life is but a day . . ."

"Ah! That's right." He *had* a beautiful voice, Vincent had, she reflected. He could have been a proper slap-up clergyman with that voice of his, or a radio announcer. "It doesn't some'ow seem right does it! And 'im so hale an hearty too like he was!"

Vincent caught sight of his father's face with that military look it had of bronzed distinction, its placid immobility suggestive of a trick—just as his mother appeared to regard it. "Old escapist!" Vincent inwardly addressed the corpse. And a warm and friendly smile played on his face—as he spoke, tonguelessly, in his disembodied mind, to the dead.

A sickening odour of heavy white funeral flowers pervaded the small shabby room. Vincent glanced towards the table, and saw that at least two wreaths as large as his were there, sending out doubtless their quota of perfume. The attractive rather rakish personality of the old man in the death-box had moved two of his former employers to dispatch these massive tokens of appreciation.

"You don't know me, sir. I'm Amy," said a live voice, of great volume. It came from a towering wall of flesh of which he had been conscious—a back that had been turned towards him, blocking his view, but which had now slowly revolved to face him, and in so doing had dislodged Flo.

Flo had not been able to drag herself away from Vincent, but had been standing as if angrily mesmerized by this provocative apparition—pretending to come to them out of another world.

"I knew your por father," Amy rumbled, "when he was quite a young feller."

"So you are the Amy I thought you were!" Vincent exclaimed heartily. "There is only *one* Amy isn't there! Didn't dad once say he wished he'd met you first, before mother had nobbled him?"

"I don't know about that, young man. He never said that to *me!*"

"We never met, did we, Amy?"

The word 'met' amused this giantess. The furrows of her massive face, the colour of cold mutton, were trenches out of which the dirt was seldom picked—if it *could* be extracted at this time of the day, which was questionable. Eyelids of lead always threatened to drop over what was left of two eyes of bilious blue, which had disintegrated into a green, blue, and yellowish mosaic. Her hair was a sickly saffron white, but her eyebrows, which long ago had agreed to coalesee, still disposed of a strong black pigment. She was as large as Falstaff: and this great presence had all been built up with Bitter Beer in unremitting attendance at the Four Ale Bar.

"Yes, I'm Amy!" she purred out, in a great giant pussy-cat purr, which had more of the growl than the purr. "And I knows who yew are better'n you know yourself! 'Ow did you know 'oo *I* was, Vinshunt?"

"I guessed it from your back!"

"From my *back*?" There was a coquettish commotion in the neighbourhood of her shoulders, which she sought to wriggle and failed; but she did succeed in reconstituting what once had been a famous dimple. Now it reappeared as a deep and unclean cavity—like a bullet wound, rather. It formed, and melted away again, half-way up her left cheek.

"Mother always said Dad liked big women. I do too, Amy. I suppose that was how I knew. You must at all times have been *big*, Amy. You started as a pretty big girl."

"You aren't 'arf a caution, Vincent! I'm blowed if I know 'ow your mother ever come to 'ave you, young man—do *you*, Harry?"

"You mustn't mind 'er, Vincent," Bessie told him. "Mrs Tucker's what you might call a *priverleged person*. Don't take no notice of her."

"Amy was before your time, Vincent," Harry said.

"Aren't you coming in to see mother?" Maddie took his arm. "She wants to see you. Come along."

"I was just coming, Mad."

As Maddie and he passed into the room beyond, the others watched them in silence, with expressions of derision, bafflement and dislike. Harry laughed, shaking himself and stamping about a little as if he had been standing in a cramped position and was relaxing. He rubbed his eyes with his hand, as if to wake himself up.

"Wot do you think, Amy, of our young toff?" asked Flo, with a sneering nod towards the door. "'Ow's 'e strike *yew*?"

"I don't really know, Flo, wot to think!" said Amy. "I s'pose it's all right. But it can't be 'elped if it isn't, can it?"

"You're right there," said Harry. "It's not *our* fun'ral!"

"'Arry!" Flo admonished him, as the word funeral fell from his lips.

"Eh?"

"Mind what expressions you're using, 'Arry, please! Remember where you are!"

"Where's the sense," asked a neighbour with militantly folded arms, "in bringin' children up above their station, I should like to know? That young lady . . . young Maddie, I should say—she doesn't never seem *happy* do she, for all her dollin' up and puttin' on the talk?"

"It wasn't 'ere she learnt that, Mrs Fitzsimmons," Flo told her, wagging her head. "Madeleine wasn't *brought up* as you call it to act like that."

"That's right," Harry agreed. "Mad was a quiet sort of kid before she began going about with them artists, Vincent took her to see."

The bedroom was all bed and no room. Vincent and Maddie stood in the narrow trench between the bed and the window. Vincent looked down at his mother.

"How do you feel, Mother?" he asked, with a simple tenderness, taking her hand.

Mrs Penhale choked off a coughing fit and patted her chest elaborately. Her flannel nightdress was frayed and unclean. The crumpled sheets had smears upon them. One stain she tried to hide. He guessed what sort of stain it was. The sweet odour of whisky was clearly discernible in the dark air.

The old woman looked up at her son rather with the expression of a particularly double-faced child, who is conscious of being loved by her parents in spite of everything, but who has so many disdemeanours to conceal that she expects some reprimand at any moment, and is ready to bluff it out. Vincent was pappa and Maddie mamma, and they had come to her bedside to ask her how she was. A great gulf naturally was fixed between the child mind and the adult mind. She could never quite tell what they were thinking—only by guessing at it. But *Vincent* she could always manage.

"I'm a weenie bit better than wot I was, Vincent," she told him hoarsely. "It's the bronchitis."

"I can hear it."

Maddie left the room quietly. In her large shock-absorbing eyes was a curious expression. It seemed indicative of some unkind emotion.

"Vincent!" His mother hissed his name pompously as she always did. Her accent in the presence of this odd son of hers tended to be a caricature of the way of speech of royal princes and princesses, conferring loftily in their palaces, as imagined by their subjects. Generally aitchless, her aitches suddenly abounded (as aitches, she felt, would probably abound in palaces), forcing an uncalled for aspiration upon any word beginning with a vowel—eddy became *heddy*, or interfere, *hinterfere*. But in order to 'put on the talk,' Mrs Penhale adopted a rather disagreeable and displeased expression—a *haughty* expression, as she thought, to go with the elevated accent.

"Yes, Mother," Vincent said, bending over towards her differentially. "Is there anything I can do?"

"Yes, Vincent, there is!" she classily hissed—and a blast of stale whisky struck him in the face. "I can't manage to get out of bed, Vincent." She broke into a spasm of coughing. "I want you, Vincent, to ask Maddie to do somethink . . . for me. See, Vincent?"

"Mother—what?"

"Ask Maddie, Vincent . . . to kiss him for me."

Vincent bowed his head and left the room.

Entering the sitting room, he pushed some of the company

rather unceremoniously aside, and delivered their mother's message to Maddie.

"I can't, Vincent!" Maddie told him, in a terrified whisper. "Must I? I'm sorry, Vin. Ought I to do it?"

"All right dear. I understand."

The hush that his presence always tended apparently to produce fell again upon everybody, except for the growling-purr of Amy. Everybody, covertly or openly, was watching the two of them, and attempting to catch the words of their whispered conversation.

Vincent left Maddie's side and went over to the coffin. At this the hush was so entire that the breathing of some of those present could be heard.

His father lay motionless, his romantic head of a slightly disreputable *grand seigneur* in the great relaxed peace of death. Vincent stood beside him, with his back to the others, aware of the battery of eyes, and took one of the cold hands in his and held it. His attitude was suggestive of that of a physician taking the pulse of a patient.

Gently he replaced the hand and stepped back. As he turned away from the coffin, his own face was white and still, as if as a reflection of his communion with the dead. Harry, who had been watching him, turned his head away. Vincent returned to his mother's room. Maddie and Minnie were there.

"You can't let him go like that, Maddie!" Mrs Penhale was vociferating. "Maddie, it isn't respectable. I mean it isn't respectful, Madeleine. Minnie has only just told me. Of course, Madeleine, I didn't know he 'adn't them. 'Ow could I?"

"It doesn't matter really, Mother," Maddie shook her head distractedly. "Does it, Minnie?"

"I don't know," said Minnie. "I suppose Dad *ought* . . ."

"What is the trouble?" Vincent enquired. "What ought dad? What is it, Minnie?"

He was informed by his younger sister that Mr Penhale was without his false teeth. Minnie had just revealed this fact to Mrs Penhale.

"He looks better without them," Vincent told Minnie. "Those teeth were too big for his mouth. I shouldn't bother about putting them in, Mother."

"They was the best teeth we could get, Vincent. They wasn't too large . . . was they, Minnie? I know your dad, Madeleine, wouldn't like to go, not without them in, Maddie!"

There was a knock at the door.

"The undertakers is here," said Harry, coming inside.

"Are they?" Vincent went out at once.

"'Ere, Harry, your father 'asn't got 'is teeth in," Mrs Penhale protested.

"Wot's that! Dad 'asn't got 'is teeth? Is that right, Madeleine?"

Outside three men in black frock coats were discussing the weather with the assembled women. Amy was towering benignly over one of them, whose eyes twinkled in his regulation grimness of feature: and another laughed "not half!" as Flo asked him something that required that rejoinder.

At the appearance of Vincent, who held his head high, his nostrils dilated, with a frown of bored command on his face, the muted bonhomie died out altogether, as gossip in a work-room is extinguished by the entrance of the boss.

"Are you the undertaker?" he asked the most important looking of the three men.

"That's right, sir," said the man with respectful alacrity. "Mr Vincent Penhale, sir? I thought so, sir. I'm in charge. Is everything ready, sir? We should like to screw down as soon as you are all set."

"Go ahead," said Vincent. "I believe there is nothing else we want. Is there, Harry?"

There had been an exodus from the inner rooms. Harry had been the last to emerge.

"Half a mo. Wot is we to do, Vin, about . . .?" He came nearer and lowered his voice. "Wot about dad's teeth? Eh?"

Vincent shrugged.

"You can put them in, Harry, if you think it's really necessary."

It was a new idea to Harry that it would devolve upon *him* to insert the dentures in his dead father's mouth. Vincent was footing the bill for the funeral, so it seemed *his* show. He became distinctly less interested in the matter at once.

"Well, Vin, it's as you say."

"Not at all, Harry. It's as much to do with you as it is with me. You are senior to me. If you really think . . ."

"No, old man, it's only wot mother thought . . ."

"Well, you'd better do it now, Harry, without more delay, because these gentlemen here want to get to work."

Vincent walked away to the window and looked down into the street. In the windows opposite were more women just the same as those in the room: the so-called working-woman, who in England does so little work. Maddie came up to him.

"I don't know what possessed Minnie," she said, "telling mother about dad's teeth!"

"It will be all right in a minute, Mad," he told her. "Harry and Minnie know where the teeth are. It's up to them.

Minnie came up behind them. None of the Penhale good looks had fallen to Minnie's lot or she had worn them out long before. A settled look of righteous indignation was imprinted upon her sallow face.

"Will it be all right if they screw the lid down now? The men are waiting . . ." In a tone of reproach.

"I'm not holding them up, Minnie. I told 'em to go ahead. You must ask Harry."

"I don't think at a moment like this one, Vin, you ought to adopt that attertude!"

Vincent smiled patiently.

"Minnie, you old goose. I have told Harry that if he wanted to put in dad's teeth he ought not to be too long. That's not *adopting an attitude*, is it? Don't be so stupid, Minnie . . ."

Minnie flushed darkly.

"Stupid? We know, Vin, who's got all the interlecks in this

blinkin' fam'ly. I know I'm nothing. I'm a *charwoman*, that's wot I am and not *ershamed* to say so. I'm not *intellergent* and don't set myself up to be, I don't,'' She bridled at her young sister.

"He didn't mean you are *stupid*, Minnie . . .!'' Her sister interposed. "That's not what Vin said.''

"That's quite sufficient, Maddie! I don't want to be told by *you* . . .!''

"May we begin screwing down, sir!'' the undertaker asked Vincent.

Vincent moved over to the coffin and looked at the face of the dead man for the last time. "No one ever hushed their voices because of you while you lived,'' he thought. "But it is Death, not you, they honour at present. Well, good-bye, Dad. If I stand here any longer I shall arouse their jealousy. So long then, Dad. Now they must screw you down, old fellow.''

He turned, to find Harry observing him sourly.

"Can they screw it down now, Vin?'' he asked in an aggrieved tone.

"Of course,'' said Vincent. "Am I stopping them? I'm sorry.''

There was silence in the room while the sound of screwing continued. Maddie began to cry; then several of the neighbours followed suit. Minnie had just been about to do so when she noticed Madeleine starting. She pulled herself up and went over to the glass to put on her hat and veil instead.

They had a grand send-off, with all the street out watching and nodding, arms bracketted upon aproned stomachs, and as they approached the church the bell was tolling.

How many strokes for a man, how many for a woman, Vincent tried to recall? For a child fewer of course. Did girl children get less than male children? They ought to. As they reached the church the tolling bell, which had been getting louder and louder, seemed to fill the entire universe with its great ominous pulse.

The service was without choir: the vicar was not officiating, it was the curate. A poor man's passing! It had been suggested to Mrs Penhale by the vicar that there should be a service gratis. The only reason even so much was allowed (and Vincent had seen no object in offering to finance a full cast of choristers) was because for so many years, among an ever dwindling congregation, the deceased had always been in his place on Sundays, roaring out *Lead Kindly Light*; and a minimum of twelve bob per annum in threepenny bits had flowed into the Vicar's pocket, to which had to be added periodic subscriptions. It was the Widow's Mite; but it had helped educate the Vicar's young at better schools than the Penhales attended. So the bell tolled and the curate put on his surplice. Such perfunctory homage as was indicated by the passing of the Widow's Mite.

On the way to the cemetery afterwards Vincent and the curate sat in the first of the funeral coaches, namely Vincent's hired car. The spectacled young gentleman of "the cloth" had his overcoat over his cassock, as the rain had begun to come down in earnest.

At first this youthful priest(C. of E. a 'broad churchman,' but willing to play at the real thing and not above a spot of incense, if the customers liked it) could not make head or tail of Vincent, whose offhand command outside the church, "Come, hop in here!" had been obeyed with silent dignity. He had pulled his cassock away as he sat down, as a woman, put on her dignity, removes her skirt from contact with someone whom she regards it as unsuitable to be in skirt-contact with, until she knows more about them.

Vincent appeared oblivious. As if *he* had been the curate and desirous of being polite, occasionally he made some observation, such as, "Dear me, how this neighbourhood changes!" or, (as they passed some particularly hideous slum dwellings) "when are they going to learn, I wonder, to design a standard house for the Worker, that is both sanitary and beautiful?" With such lofty commonplaces the curate was fed from time to time. When Vincent enquired about his work as a clergyman his remarks almost were prefaced with a 'my good man.'

Harry, Minnie and Flo sat in an owlish row facing Vincent and the curate, who had insisted on occupying the fold-up seats. This trio of mourners blinked malevolently at Vincent, and listened-in, in scandalized amazement, when he patronized the young cleric. When the latter, evidently impressed, began to address Vincent as if he were an equal, the trio of mourners exchanged glances. Minnie started to cry. But the curate took no notice of her at all. He was engaged in a discreetly animated conversation with Vincent upon the Victorian Gothic in church architecture. Vincent, with careless condescension, was conferring enlightenment upon his backward class-mate.

In the other coach, where Maddie had elected to sit, the world wore a different aspect altogether. Amy sat in the centre, beads of sweat standing upon her face that was the colour of cold mutton. Up under the mourning-veils went cheap handkerchiefs, to mop up either perspiration or tears, Maddie and Bessie were upon either side of Amy, and Mrs Cooper and another crony of Mrs Penhale were packed in too.

From the eastern limits of the Harrow Road it was a long way to Hanwell Cemetery, the principal burial ground for West London, and the hearse, for most of the route, set a smart pace. The rain came down: Maddie found herself watching it splash upon the bald skull of a road-mender, who stood cap in hand, surreptitiously attempting to count the number of wreaths, as the hearse hurried past him.

The old saluted with greater unction than the young, she noticed. It was not her dad they were saluting—the same reflection came to her as it had to Vincent. Fundamentally they were baring their pates to their own prospective corpses —but as this cruel thought struck her the white mask writhed, and a dark lace handkerchief Vincent had sent her from Venice stole up under the veil, to dissipate a tear.

A dying horse, lying in a pool of blood at the side of the

road, was watched by a group of men. They looked to Maddie as if they had attacked it and were watching it die. There was no truck standing near it. Of course *they* were not responsible for the conditions of the horse! The sight had shocked her into a distortion—into *blaming* somebody. The pathos of the great bloodstained horse—struggling to live, its giant muscles striking out for it, in feeble stampings of the air—had torn away the screens, behind which human death is enacted off-stage, its reality sublimated.

She had an inartistic glimpse of a delirious old man, whose equally aged wife had refused him when he had asked to be taken into bed beside her to be warm when first the great chill descended on him. She saw the old man thereupon, like a dying animal, his teeth chattering, crawl out into a closet-like chamber beside the kitchenette and sink panting upon a rickety camp-bed, to face death alone.

Then it was, no doubt, that the delirium came down. The cold of the limbs and back was forgotten in the drunkenness of fever. He imagined himself warm again, perhaps, under an august sun, back in his hey-day among the young men he grew up with on the land.

The tears fell faster under the veil, as the dying horse stained her mind with its blood like a terrible sunset, where a moment before she had been unconscious of anything except the rain, and the general greyness and senselessness of life, and the smell of Amy. Are horses visited by delirium? She hoped they might be—and just end in a fevered dream, no worse than an ordinary nightmare, such as everybody had.

Upon arrival at the cemetery, the lodge attendant indicated the spot where the grave had been dug for the remains of Mr James Penhale: the cortège moved a certain distance, but for the rest of the way the coffin was carried by the four undertakers; the party, led by the clergyman, straggling grimly after it, the rain drenching the veils of the chief female mourners.

When they reached the grave, it turned out to be a deep pit, waterlogged at the bottom. Cheap graves are not sheltered from the rain with boards and tarpaulins, or any fancy things of that sort, Vincent reflected, as he stepped up to the edge of it and gazed down. Down *at death*. And since half the year it is wet in London, often it would be true to say of the poor, Vincent went on to consider, as he stepped back, that when they die, in their deal boxes they are *launched* into their resting place! The coffin is apt to float, if it is far enough down, in a sort of baptismal font of sepulture—as his poor dad's would almost do, he was afraid.

In silence the four undertakers lowered the heavy box into the opening, paying out the broad tapes that they had passed beneath it. At last with a hollow splash it reached the bottom. Vincent said nothing, but his eyes were fixed upon the clergyman, who was preparing to liquidate as rapidly as possible, with a few beautiful words, this squalid event.

The mourners stood on one side of the grave, the clergyman opposite them, and beside him two of the mutes, looking genuinely down-in-the-mouth as the rain streamed off their black backs. Maddie had placed herself beside Vincent. Her great beauty was remarked by the young spectacled cleric, who made a mental note to visit these parishioners, who seemed to blossom out in such unexpected directions —into beauteous damsels and male offspring fitted out in Savile Row and the Burlington Arcade.

Dead and cold though he was, Maddie felt she *could* not leave her daddie at the bottom of this awful hole in the earth, filling up with water. Why did all this have to be done—was there no other way? Could not she and Vincent perhaps have the coffin removed? To leave her jolly, laughing, father, who had been so fond of her, down there in the cold and mud was a terrible ending. She felt for Vincent's hand and gripped it despairingly. Vincent gripped back with his hand, without looking at her, and so they stood, until that part of the burial service was reached where the spectacled young clergyman had to bend down and scoop up some dust in his hand for the climax of the ceremony.

"Dust to the Dust!" he declaimed, and taking up a lump

of mud—there was nothing else in sight—let it fall in the pit and it could be heard to smack the wood of the coffin. Maddie could bear it no longer: she flung herself upon Vincent's shoulder in a spasm of weeping.

Minnie had her own private grief. Secretly, as it were—since everything with her was undertaken with a fearful privacy—she had wiped her eyes. Furtively she had blown her nose, as the burial service proceeded. But through the stingy, secret, tears she espied her baby sister's antics. And the service ended with a dry-eyed Minnie, and a general feeling that Vincent and Maddie were as usual standing out and apart from the body of the family, in splendid isolation, and, as usual, making an unnecessary exhibition of themselves.

CHAPTER XV

VINCENT IN THE FAMILY-CIRCLE

HARRY, Vincent, Minnie, Maddie, Flo and Bessie had sat down to a sandwich dinner at the table upon which the wreaths had been stacked earlier in the day. The six black-clad figures with their pasty masks (except for Vincent's) were like a wax-work reconstruction of a mid-Victorian print, purporting to show the slum-poor at their Sunday meal. Even the room itself resembled an exhibit. It was where two old persons had lived and dreamed their drunken dream of old age. It was too small for the six persons now sitting there, stiffly adjusting themselves to the demands of table-manners—all except Vincent, who gave a spirited performance of the Mayfair way of negotiating a ham sandwich or devouring an uncooked tomato.

It was three o'clock by the rose-gold clock with the dirty face and amputated minute-hand. The rain rapped the two small windows painted thick with factory dirt. The funeral repast of sandwiches had been prepared by the Penhale sisters. A big sinister tea-pot, grotesquely surmounted by a blousy cosie, propped upon its spout, was refilled from a saucepan kept on the boil in the kitchenette.

But two bottles, of Port and of Whisky respectively, were also present upon the table, and Vincent, declining the black tea, had poured himself a Scotch.

"I only drink China tea," he announced provocatively, his eye upon Flo. "Can't drink that stuff. Sorry!"

"'Ark at Sir Vincent!" Flo barked derisively, rising promptly to the bait.

"The gentleman I works for," Minnie observed disagreeably, "and 'e's a *real* gentleman, 'e is, born and bred, not the jumped-up tuppenny-'alfpenny sort—doesn't never drink anythink, 'e says, except black tea like wot me and you 'as."

"Ah, I've 'eard gentlemen—*and* ladies—say wot they'd sooner 'ave a good cup o' tea wot 'as stood ten minutes or so"; Flo robustly bore out her sister-in-law.

Vincent raised his glass, grimly and gayly, winking at Maddie—whose eyes still held a lurid reflection of the pathos of dying horses.

"Well, here's to my continuing to prove myself no gentleman, but a china tea-drinking upstart of the working class!

"Our Sir Vincent don't 'arf fancy 'is luck! Think's 'e's at the blinkin' Guildhall, along er the Lord Mayor and Lady Mayoress!" Flo told Minnie.

"I have none of those proletarian tastes of the toffs who hire you, Minnie, for a bob an hour. Ladies and gentlemen— I drink to the working class!"

"*Wot* class was that you said, Sir Vincent, you belonged to!" Flo asked him bleakly. "Was it *workin'*?"

But Harry laughed with easy-going restraint, for his brother's firm stand against tea had emboldened him also to break through to the whisky bottle (sent round that morning by Vincent's wine-merchant) and he had just helped himself to a good solid whack.

"Work!" Minnie told her brother. "A fat lot you know about work!"

Harry drank—presumably to the working-class. His eye had been a lot softer for some time now, ever since he had learnt that not only his father's Gold Hunter watch-and-chain, but also the mother-of-pearl cuff-links of the deceased, as well as his gold tie-pin were his undisputed property.

Mrs Penhale's insistence that Vincent should have the tie-pin was disregarded by the latter who protested that he regarded tie-pins as ostentatious.

Vincent's restrained affability, as well as his indifference to tie-pins, was creating a good impression. He had been making some headway even with the implacable Flo.

Things were more harmonious than might have been expected. Conversation became general, with Vincent's cultivated voice dominating the family board, however. When its accents of embarrassing refinement broke out among them (all the others had to do was to close their eyes—to believe they heard the boss speaking), they tended to still their own voices to listen.

"What has happened to that nice gentle old ex-scene-shifter—who used to talk about Henry Irving in 'The Bells', remember? Who had a sick old wife," enquired Vincent. "Wilks was it now?"

"Wilkie you mean, Vin," Minnie told him. "That was Mr Wilkie."

"Was it Wilkie? He had a little beard."

"Wot 'ad a Irish setter?"

"That's the lad."

"'E's dead, Vin, 'e is, last Febry," Minnie looked grave. "You 'eard, didn't you, Vin, 'ow 'is wife took her life?"

Vincent shook his head politely.

"Poisoned 'erself, por old lady."

"So she did, Minnie," said Bessie.

"Swallered a bottle er Lysol."

"I did feel sorry fer him, poor old body," Bessie commiserated.

"How beastly." Vincent grimaced.

"She did do it *to* 'erself any'ow which is something!" Flo was heard to mutter darkly, as she sawed at a cold sausage with a chain-store knife, to which the sausage was doing a lot of harm.

Vincent, his head on one side, asked her with frowning innocence, "Was Mr Wilkie murdered, Flo?"

Flo returned his gaze suspiciously, but answered notwithstanding:

"Murdered! I shouldn't wonder if that wasn't the word."

"You said it, boy!" said Harry.

"Murdered is wot 'e was, por old feller, if you ask me," Minnie nodded. "If it isn't murder it's the next thing to it."

"How did that come to pass? You do see life in Linlithgow Terrace!" Vincent laughed.

"Not 'arf they don't!" Harry agreed.

"Same as Dad 'e 'ad bronchal asthma," Flo stated, in her crisp dogmatic coster tones. "Two months after 'is wife died por old chap 'e 'ad a bad attack. They sent 'im to the High Road Infirmary."

Vincent slapped the table. Everyone looked up in uneasy astonishment.

"You need go no further! I know the rest!" he cried dramatically. "I know *how* he was murdered now."

"How was he murdered, Vin?" asked Bessie. "I never knew anything about *that*."

"What an institution!" Vincent growled.

"Ah, they *are* pretty 'ot at High Road," Harry agreed. "Vin means, Bessie, once they got the por old chap in at High Road . . . Well you, up at High Road . . ."

"That's right. No one round 'ere won't go there not if they can 'elp it," Minnie said. "Old Mrs Heasley was supposed to go there last week. But she won't let them move 'er. She kicked the ambulance man wot come to take 'er."

"Small blame to her," said Maddie. "I know I wouldn't go."

"How long did they take to kill him off?" Vincent inquired. "Did they make a quick job of it?"

"Not above a week was it, Minnie, 'e was in there, before 'e died?" Flo, sipping her black tea, hiccupped, and said "pardon!"

"It was more than a week, Flo," Minnie replied, apologetically—for upon a point of this sort Flo was not accustomed to tolerate contradiction. "'E asked Mother to go and see 'im and 'e'd bin there some days then I know."

"Did Mother go?" Vincent asked.

Minnie shook her head, and looked towards the bedroom door.

"Mother don't like goin' there, Vincent. She says it gives 'er the willies."

"Kind of afraid they might keep her, what!" Vincent laughed.

"They do be'ave awful though from what I've 'eard, with some wot they get in there. Por old Mr Wilkie they knocked about something crool, por old chap. Mrs Dates 'oo went to see 'im said 'e 'ad a black eye as big as a plate. Mr Wilkie told 'er the nurse done it. E' wanted to get outer bed . . . well you know what I mean. . . ."

"I know what you mean," nodded Vincent. "So it was a *bed-pan* crime was it? All the quarrels of the poor with hospital staffs centre round the *bed-pan*. The theory is apparently that the poor do not need to urinate so often as other people—as nice people. And as to evacuating their bowels, they should be jolly glad to be allowed to do *that* at all. Once a day is the most that that trim gentlewoman, the nurse, can be expected to co-operate in *that* orgy of nastiness— which if encouraged, out of sheer beastliness the poor would go on indulging in!"

"Draw it mild, old man," expostulated Harry. "There *is* ladies present, old man."

"A fat lot of notice 'e'd take of *that*!" said Flo.

"'E got outer bed, Mr Wilkie said," Minnie pursued her story, "'an the nurser knocked him down and blacked 'is eye. *She* said 'e 'it 'is eye fallin'. But 'e said she done it. Por old chap. 'E wasn't 'arf a dear old man too!"

"Ah. A proper old sport!" Flo heavily assented.

"His wife was bedrid for two years," Minnie told them. "'E nursed 'er like a baby, 'e did. When she swallowed the Lysol 'e was 'eartbroke."

Vincent watched them curiously.

"Can nothing be done about that slaughter-house for the aged poor at High Road?" he asked. "It was once a workhouse, wasn't it, before it became a so-called 'Infirmary'?"

"That's right," said Minnie. "It was a Workhouse once, Vincent."

"Who would be one of the poor! What an inferno it is "

"There 'as to be poor people, Vincent! We can't all be toffs, not like yew," Flo told him.

"But doesn't it make you *angry* to know there is a place in your district, where a staff of trained nurses and doctors are paid by the state to brutalize and kill aged people, who have no one to care for them, or protect them against these ruffians, and who their panel doctor pronounces as too ill to remain by themselves? Would it not be better to supply these poor creatures with a cup of poison so that they could make away with themselves—rather than to knock them about: black their eyes, sock them with the fists of callous bitches who receive a good wage from the tax-payer?" (Harry coughed, to remind Vincent again that ladies were present and to moderate his language). "If Dad had been so situated that he had had to go to High Road Infirmary, I would rather have seen him put away with a big shot of morphia, wouldn't you, Harry, rather than have his last days darkened by this fearful ill-treatment and neglect —the aim of which is to stamp out the spark of life as quickly as possible short of murder. That of course was why that poor woman Mrs Wilkie swallowed Lysol. Better *that* than the High Road Infirmary. I'd give that nurse who is so handy with her fists a life-sentence if I were a judge and she came up before me!"

They were all silent, cowed by this classy humanitarian invective but even more so by the Public Schoolboyish delivery—by the command of master-class accent displayed. The picture of Vincent in the ermine of the Judge, however, in the awful seat of Justice, brought a nasty light in Minnie's bloodshot eyes, which Maddie remarked and wearily turned her head away. It would be so much better if Vincent wouldn't talk!

Though temporarily abashed, the women communicated by means of glances. After a few exchanges of this kind, especially passing between Harry's belligerent wife and Minnie—semaphoring by means of glance and counter-glance—Flo spoke up.

"Well, Vincent, if you was a *magistrate* you'd do this and you'd that. You've told us wot *yew'd* do. Those old people in High Road has 'ad their day. It's the *young* wot ought to have a break and 'asn't. That's wot I'd say if you ask *me*."

Vincent sighed at this stocky little East End sister-in-law.

"I'd say that too, Flo," he said. "But what goes for the old goes for the young. If they are callous with the old wrecked bodies, they are callous too about the welfare of those setting out in life. Well, like your kids, Flo, who are put to no trade, but scrape a few shillings together when they leave school doing something that demands no more intelligence or special knowledge than a duck."

"Never mind about Ernie, Vincent. We can take care of 'im, thank you, without any help from you."

"It was you, Flo, mentioned *the young*. When *I* was young I found that no one was able to help me much—any more than you are able to help Ernie. I was in just the same fix as Ernie is, poor kid. So I helped myself. See? That, in your eyes, is my great sin. I dragged myself out of this inferno." He looked around him. "For this is an *inferno*."

"Infer'nl—'ere steady on with that foul language, Vin! Easy! Draw it mild, old man. There's ladies present," Harry mildly protested yet again—feeling that that kind of unbridled language *had* to be checked, but that on the whole a brother who supplied one with Haig *ad lib*, should not be too much discouraged.

"If the young," Vincent continued to assert, "have the gumption, they effect their escape. Take Victoria."

"Ah! Take Victoria," Flo mocked.

"Victoria set everybody in this family an example. She did a bunk, didn't she, into Western Canada—where she has a beautiful home, plays bridge every night, has a Japanese gardener, and a Negro house-man."

"*And* she lets us all know it! 'Ouseman! She calls it *butler*, that old nigger wot she 'as. We never 'ear the last of 'im nor of her Jap gard-in-er. I thought you'd bring *Victoria* up,

Vin!" Flo laughed bitterly. "Thought we'd 'ear somethink about *Vicky* before we'd done."

"But was that intelligent of her—to get out of this? Do be sensible. America has a classless society. In principle . . ."

"In principle's right!" Harry interrupted him noisily, the old shop-steward coming out strong. "There isn't no classless society, Vin, not in America no more'n wot there is here, and don't you believe it, boy, when they tell you so. They kid you there is. That's all baloney. Use your intelligence, Vin."

"Very well. But even a *principle's* something, Harry! It is only natural, hang it all, for a person bowed down under class-taboos here . . ."

"I isn't bowed down," protested Flo. "Is I?"

"No, but you speak a slave-jargon and can't help yourself—would it not be highly sensible to escape to a place where one is free from the stigma—at least from the *stigma*— of class? Here the poor are treated as creatures of *another clay*. That is the point, Harry. Since there are no niggers here, they had to create niggers. The poor are the niggers in this country."

"So they is over there," Harry replied.

"Would Victoria—I just put it to you—ever have had even a black butler in this country; let alone a Japanese tree-surgeon to stop the teeth of her decrepit sycamores?"

"You 'as one, Vincent—accordin' to wot Maddie says: you 'as a butler. He's white too," Flo retorted, with a kindled eye that showed she felt his armour had been pierced.

"You mean Willis? Ha ha ha!" Vincent rocked in easy Mayfair mirth. "I'll tell Willis he's a *butler* the next time I see him! But whatever you say, she was a live wire, was our sister Victoria!"

At the first reference to Victoria, Minnie's face began to work angrily. She squirmed in her chair, as if attacked by an insidious parasite she was attempting to dispose of by heavy hip and shoulder exercises. Upon hearing Victoria—the outstanding success of the family—described as 'a live wire,' she, however, broke into bitter words.

"Same as you, Vincent, Vicky thought 'erself too good for us. She was ashamed of belonging here. Last time she come to the ole country she threw a lamp at Mother and 'it 'er on the chin . . ."

"No, Minnie!—with all due respect! She threw that lamp at *you*."

"At *me*?"

"I'm afraid so, Minnie. I agree Victoria is only half-civilized and she reverts to violent modes of self-expression at times, when revisiting the scenes of her savage youth. But you hate Victoria because she's *got out of the mess*, just as you hate me . . ."

"I don't 'ate anybody. But if you think this is a *mess*, Vincent, as you call it . . ." Flo was breaking in hotly.

"Isn't it a mess?" Vincent stopped her, gazing round him at the slum-room and its occupants. "Look at us. Look at the place our mother occupies!"

"People 'oo looks down on others wot they belong to," Minnie returned to the charge, "I do 'ate and detest I owns I do. I call it contemptuous."

"Contemptible. Got the word wrong," Vincent corrected her. "Go ahead."

"Contemptuous, I call it!" Minnie stuck to her guns.

"Call it that if you like." Vincent shrugged.

"'Ow is Vicky better'n wot we are I should like to know? She always give 'erself airs, Vicky did, same as wot you did, Vincent. I belong to the working-class an' I'm not ashamed to say so. Some people would turn their backs on their own mother as if she 'adn't 'ad them but was some old lady wot they didn't 'ardly know. Ah, I'm speakin' about Victoria. You know 'oo I'm talking about!"

"I know Minnie who you're alking about. I'm every bit as bad as Victoria."

"It's you saying it isn't it, Vin!"

"Every time I open my mouth you think I'm high-hatting you, I understand that, Minnie. It's because of my Oxford Accent."

"Oxford Accent! You haven't never bin to Oxford, let alone studied there. You a Oxford Man! You make me laugh."

She threw up her head, her mouth distorted with disobliging mirth.

"As you say," said Vincent. "I've taught myself to speak like this without even going near Oxford. Cheaper, wasn't it?"

Harry had been watching his brother, more amused than angry.

"You must have wanted something to do, Vincent," he laughed, "to teach yourself the talk. You wasn't *born* to talk like wot you do."

"Ah, *born*." Vincent seized upon the word with satisfaction. "There you've put your finger on it, Harry."

"'Ave I?"

"You are a fatalist, Harry. People ought, according to you, to stop upon the spot where they happen to be born. That's where we differ. I'm all for changing things, and *myself* to start off with."

"You've done that sure enough," Flo said.

"I was born to be a bus-conductor like Albert wasn't I, Harry? Pre-destined to snip the tickets. Or to be a mechanic like you. And to marry a charwoman like Minnie here. Well, I just thought I wouldn't stay put."

"A little bit less of your charwoman if you don't mind!" Minnie interposed, ruffing bellicosely.

"Spades not to be called spades? O-kay. Everything—to proceed—is done in this country to secure that everybody stops just where they happen to be born. It is the law of the social *status quo*. And we—the British working class—are the worst snobs of the lot. Worse than our middle class which is saying a good deal. For we accept our status as sub-human inferiors: we do everything we can to help our masters to keep us down. And if one of our number makes a move to get out of line, we do our damnedest to stop him. We pursue him with our indignation and hatred. As to a girl of our class that shows signs of restlessness and a desire to move *up*, rather than horizontally, our women do their best to drag her back. But how, Harry, can we ever break the class-system—this awful spell of superstition about 'gentlemen' and common people—if we go on like that? Once you called yourself a socialist. You once wanted to break this unjust system, this snob-system, as much as anybody. Don't you still?"

The silence that followed this rhetorical attack of Vincent's was of longer duration than the first silence, a short while before—which had been broken by Flo's muscular, argumentative, tones.

Harry sat looking sullenly down at the table-cloth, observed expectantly by his wife. Maddie—looking very upset—had, followed by Bessie, left the table and gone into her mother's room. At last Harry looked up and said,

"I still think same as I always have. *I* haven't changed, Vin."

"I'm glad to hear that, Harry."

"But I don't want no *butlers*, see, and no *gardiners* . . ."

"Quite—nor to play golf nor bridge. But can you say conscientiously that you are satisfied with your standard of life? Was your garden big enough for your kids to play in? Had they *anywhere* to play—except the gutters of Kensal Rise? So what? If you decreed a change of society, in which you would get your deserts, you would move onto the middle-class plane, would you not, where you had decent conditions for your growing kids, a few luxuries for yourself, whisky like this and cigars on Sunday, as good clothes as a teller at a bank; and Ernie would have learnt to speak proper English . . ."

"Proper English!" Flo broke out. "You don't half fancy your grammar don't you, and the swanky talk you put on! See here, Sir Vincent, our way of talkin' may not be *grammatical*, we know that."

"I know what you're going to say, Flo."

"Oh, *do* you!"

"Let me say it for you—only I will put it in better English than you would . . ."

"You 'ave got a proper sauce 'aven't you? To hear you talk anyone'd think we come from the slums . . .!"

"Well, don't we? Where else do we come from?" Vincent laughed. "You, Minnie, myself, and poor old Harry here? For instance I was born within smelling distance of the New Cut."

"Oh, cut it out, Vin," said Harry, drinking as if afraid he might have to leave his glass at any moment, before he had finished his drink. "We've 'eard enough about us not speakin' right, an' . . ."

"*Our not speaking correctly*, you mean," Vincent smilingly amended. "Must pick the jolly old g's up, Harry. Just as important as the aitches. That's the way our rulers *wanted* us to speak, I know. That's no reason to oblige them and go on speaking Kitchen English, or Pub English . . ."

Harry got red in the face at this and looked angrily over at the beautifully tailored, lounging and smiling figure in front of him, whom he found it difficult to think of as a brother.

"Kitchen English! Thank you!" Flo gazed at him stupefied. "You'll be told off one of these fine days, Sir Vincent, right and proper! You isn't a kid any longer you know, not by a long shot. It's time you was your age."

"Why don't you and Flo," Vincent asked his brother, in a confidential undertone, as if it were not for Flo's ear, "allow me to give you a lesson or two in the proper way to speak? You'd never regret it. Why be so sentimental and touchy about it?"

"About what? Are you quite all there?" Harry asked him roughly.

"No, 'e isn't!" Minnie said, getting up and going towards the bedroom. "Don't take any notice of 'im, 'Arry. 'E never was like other people. 'E's wrong in 'is upper story."

"Fill up again, Harry." Vincent pushed over the bottle of whisky. "We don't meet often, Harry. Why not be matey when chance throws us together?"

"I don't mind if I do," Harry answered, pouring himself hurriedly another whisky. "Prime stuff this, Vin. Thanks, old man."

"Have a shot, Flo?" Vincent indicated the bottle.

Flo shook her head. "No, thank you all the same. My bowels is acid." She tapped her mouth, and produced a miniature belch. "Pardon," she said.

"Of course," Vincent answered, casting a forgiving eye in the direction of Flo's offending mouth. "Look, Harry. *I* had to learn how to speak . . ."

"Is you still talkin', Vincent, about grammar?" Flo asked incredulously.

"Harry understands!" Vincent looked flatteringly towards his brother. "He is a mechanic. He knows if you don't submit to instruction you'd never learn anything about the functioning of an engine. Isn't that true, Harry?"

"Sure thing, Vin. You 'as to be taught, else you don't know, do yer?" He drank heartily.

"Certainly not. If we were ashamed to ask we should never understand anything. Ignorance is not a thing to be ashamed of. What one ought to be ashamed of is *inability to learn*. Or laziness of course."

"You 'aven't got through such a mighty sight of *work* in your time, Vin, old man, that you can afford to talk."

"*Manual* work you mean, I suppose?"

"Yes, 'Arry means man-u-al work," Flo broke in fiercely. with a mincing imitation of Vincent's way of speaking. "We can't all be fancy *thinkers* like wot some of us thinks they is. . . ."

"No need to put in the *wot* there," Vincent politely pointed out. "Just leave out the *wot* and see how much better it sounds."

Flo got up.

"Oh, you're *crackers*. You're nuts. That Sir Vincent stuff of yours will get you down! Come along, 'Arry. Let's go in and see Mother. It's time we was gettin' along."

"We *were*—not *was*." Vincent reminded her. "I can see,

Flo, you're past help. But *don't* for that reason, when my young sister Maddie wants to try and get rid of that slovenly way of speaking her native tongue, always gird at her and try and laugh her out of it."

"'Oo girds at 'er! We 'aven't, as we 'Arry? I've never laughed at young Maddie, I'm sure."

"Maddie is *not* a snob," Vincent said. "She just doesn't accept the handicaps fate has imposed on her as you do. You shouldn't persecute her. You're very hostile both to her and to me, without any reason. But I won't stand by and see her sneezed at because she picks up her G's and puts her aitches in the right place."

"Oh, 'ark at Sir Vincent again. *'E won't stand it* 'e won't. 'Lor lummy milord, I'm sure I ap-polergize," his sister-in-law mimicked.

"Me and Flo," said Harry heavily, "ain't interfered with Maddie and we isn't here not to be insulted. We come 'ere, Vincent, to bury poor old Dad, that's wot we come 'ere for . . ."

Vincent had risen too. His head held high, chin out, in characteristic challenge, he went up to Harry, and placed his hand upon his shoulder.

"Harry, you're right. We mustn't have words just after putting poor old Dad to rest, must we? I haven't wished to be offensive, Harry. But Maddie, poor kid, has been given a pretty thin time by her family. I don't want her interfered with any more, that's all."

"Who's interfering with 'er?" Flo demanded. "It doesn't matter to any of us what she does with her life. That's *'er* business."

Harry and Flo moved towards the bedroom. Vincent stood beside the table watching them.

"Remember, Flo," he said. "It isn't snobbish to talk the way I do. It's assisting to perpetuate all the snobbery in England to go on talking the way *you* do."

"Oh, rats! Shut up, do!" Flo exclaimed.

Harry made a gimlet-like movement with his forefinger at

the side of his temple, as he was passing into the door of the bedroom, to illustrate the strictly cerebral seat of his poor brother's trouble.

"Where's Vinz-sunt?" he could hear his mother demanding. "Tell 'im to come 'ere, Flo!"

He could hear by her voice that his mother was drunk. He did not want to see her in that condition any longer than was necessary, so he went to the window and stood watching the rain. Alcohol, he told himself, as he had many times before, was *de rigueur* for an old working-class woman, in this damp and lowering island slumland. He hoped his mother was properly drunk. He preferred not to see her—but that was another matter.

As she was taxied home by Vincent, Maddie scolded him.

"Minnie is furious," she said. "As to Flo! Why can't you let sleeping dogs lie, Vincent? It doesn't do any good."

"Why don't I let sleeping underdogs lie? Because to start with they don't sleep. They keep up a quiet snarling and eye one as if they would tear one's throat out for two pins. After a few hours I lose patience."

"You might have been patient *to-day*, Vincent."

"I know it. I suppose I have got a streak of *them* in me."

"Oh no, Vincent."

"Yes, I'm rather stupid really. Do you ever feel like Minnie? I often feel like Harry . . . something hard, and stupid."

"Vincent!"

"I'm afraid, Mad, I'm . . . wanting in something . . . essential. I can't quite define it. As I was looking out of the window just now I *almost* saw myself. Almost. Then it all became muddled and blurred again—just as I thought I was going to know what I *really* was like . . . Mad my dear: I wish I knew what I was really like!"

Chapter XVI

BUCKING ON YOUR HAMS

Vincent Penhale and his sister Maddie sat in the 'throne-room', as Halvorsen called it, in Vincent's Thames-side residence. Both their faces wore an intent look. The family-likeness was very much to the fore. They gave the impression of two people engaged in a séance; a séance in which one was subjecting the other to his will, as if in the case of an entranced medium and a hypnotist. Vincent, of course, was the hypnotist.

Pale and monumental, Maddie sat staring in front of her and waiting. In view of her past profession, her attitude might have most aptly suggested that she was posing—say for a period-portrait of a defunct Infanta: of which august original she had the pasty cheeks, the vacant, haughty eye. She gazed ahead, in expressionless calm, except for the faintest pained contraction of the brows.

But Maddie was neither being subject to hypnotic-suggestion, nor was she posing for an Infanta. Vincent sat squarely in front of her. Beside him, propped upon a chair, was a drawing-board. To this was pinned a large sheet of white paper. Upon it, in bold black lettering, were the words

BUCK-ING-HORSE

Vincent's index finger, pistol fashion, pointed at the bold blackly-lettered words.

"It is quite easy," he observed, "once you've got Bucking Horse. But you *must* master the words Bucking Horse first."

"Yes, Vincent. Of course."

"Think of *Buck*. A 'young buck,' see? Then think of *King*. Like King Henry the Eighth. Then think of *Horse*. The

145

notorious quadruped. Think of them separately. That is the important thing. Have you thought of them in isolation, Maddie."

"Yes, Vincent."

"Well now. Let's start shall we? First say, *Buck*."

Maddie gathered herself together, wetted her lips, and said slowly and carefully,

"Buck."

"Next say *King*."

"King," she said.

"Now *Horse*."

"Horse," came from her lightly parted lips.

"Very well. Now say, after me, Buck-king-horse. Now! Buck. King. Horse."

"Buck. King. Horse."

"Capital. Now we will say Bucking Horse altogether; as if they were two words instead of three. Say after me Buck-ing Horse."

"Buck-ing horse," mournfully intoned the defunct Infanta.

"Wonderful!" exclaimed Vincent, enthusiastically. "And now we can go on to Buckingham Palace, can't we? It is *not* Buck'nm as I heard you saying yesterday. You see, the difference between *Bucking Horse* and *Buckingham Palace*—the thing that makes Buckingham Palace more difficult for slum children like us—is the *ham* in Buckingham."

"I know, Vincent. It *is* the 'ham' I see that."

"It is indeed. That's where we fall down. If it were *Bucking Palace* that would be a relatively simple matter. Then you would be called upon to rap out the g, good and strong. But it is not. It is Buck-king-*ham* Palace. So let us concentrate on the *ham*."

"Right-ho, Vincent. I think I can do it, though."

Vincent sprang up and began dancing about, slapping his hips.

"Think of your *hams*, old girl. Think of your *hams*, whenever you have occasion to mention the palace. Come, stand up: bring kinetics into play. There's no memory system so good as one rooted in movement. Come and *buck about on your hams* with me—see, like this."

Laughing, Maddie rose to her feet.

"Slap your hams, Maddie, slap your hams!"

Maddie smiling doubtfully, placed a flat and tapping hand upon her hip.

"You must get much more kick in it than that. Watch me. Buck about on your hams!" and he suited the action to the words. "Say ham, Maddie, over and over again. Strike your hams, the way I'm doing, and utter the word *ham*, as if you meant it and *ham* represented *a great deal* to you. Like this!"

Vincent engaged in a sort of Kaffir dance, noisily slapping his hips, and vociferating over and over again "Ham—ham—ham! Ham-ham-ham!"

His sister followed suit—striking her hips, hopping up and down, and uttering in a non-stop monotone the vocable *ham*. Both of them *bucking on their hams*, sprang up and down. And the 'throne-room' echoed to the mystic word *ham*.

"What ever are you two up to!" asked the astonished voice of April.

They both stopped as if shot at the sound of the astonished voice, and Vincent stared at April without speaking for a moment. His wife had come into the room while they were absorbed in 'bucking on their hams' and now stood by the door staring at them.

"Are you practising a dance, Vincent?" she asked, coming forward. She embraced Maddie who remained flushed and confused, and the sisterly accolade consummated her embarrassment.

"It's a game we used to play as children," Vincent answered. "An old nurse used to teach us to say *ham*. Ha, ha, ha! It must have seemed damn funny to you, darling."

He went up and kissed her.

"It was, I confess, an unexpected sight. But please go on. Can't I play too?"

"No, darling—it amused Maddie and me but it wouldn't amuse you. . . . Why are you here? *You* are a bit of a surprise too! You said you'd be arriving by the six-thirty."

"I know, but the timetable has been altered."

"Ah. Because of the Christmas holidays. Probably that. We are invited to have dinner with Mary Mallow to-night." He turned to Maddie. "I promised to bring my little sister along."

"What a bore, Vincent," said April, grimacing. "You *are* coming, aren't you, Maddie? *Do* come. Mother is dying to meet you."

"I should love to. I want to meet her too!" Maddie replied.

"She's an aggravating old woman; but she does herself quite well. Doesn't she, Vincent? At least we shall get a good dinner."

"I'm sure we shall," Maddie said. "Vincent has told me it will be a *banquet*."

April caught sight of the drawing-board with the words BUCKING HORSE.

"Oh, look! *Bucking Horse*. I do wish, Vincent, you'd teach me how to play your game. I think you're being very exclusive and cagey."

Vincent laughed and shook his head, then he passed his arm round her waist.

"I'll teach you Bucking Horse to-night, darling!" he said. "Wait till we're in bed."

Both April and Maddie had blushes now around their embarrassed smile. Maddie a new blush for Vincent's coarseness. But all reference to *Bucking on one's hams*, and the scene of which April had been the unwelcome and unexpected witness, was effectively banished by these tactics.

Maddie looked as smart as a debutante on her way to the photographers in a new semi-evening frock which had come that morning from Harrods (sent her by Vincent). She had reseated herself, with her manners of a defunct Infanta, staring into space, and April thought how young and beautiful she looked. If the rest of the Penhale family were as handsome as Vincent and his sister she reflected they must be a wonderful sight when they were together. But as his parents were both dead, and the rest of the family scattered, she was unlikely to make the acquaintance just yet she knew of any except Maddie.

As to her, she was a strange girl. Indeed, a very strange girl. She was *so* reserved, and *so* shy, that half the time she scarcely seemed to be there at all. April confessed to herself that she found her rather frightening. But she had been rather frightened by Vincent himself to start with.

If she had not known that Vincent's father had been a lawyer, she would have guessed these two to be the children of say a musician (like Sir Thomas Beecham perhaps, or Sir Henry Wood—the knightly kind of music-maker of course), or even of Sir William Forbes-Robertson—a great Hamlet-actor: a to-be-or-not-to-be knight. Something artistic, anyway, and quite out of the ordinary—though the fact that (in a quite non-professional way) Vincent had acted, would have suggested the stage.

"You won't have any tea, April? No, it is a bit late." Vincent put two more logs on the fire and attacked them with a medieval bellows.

"Oh, did you see the house-agent?" April asked. "I meant to ask."

"Messrs Guthridge and Crossland? No, I have spent the entire afternoon with Mr . . . where is the fellow's card? . . . ah, yes, *Mr Herb*. He is the hire-purchase gentleman. With him I had a very instructive conversation."

"Oh, really. What did he have to say for himself?"

Vincent mixed himself a drink.

"A snort? Not yet? Maddie?" He seated himself by the side of the roaring wood, upon an immense hassock.

"Mr Herb is a cynic," he said. "I knew when he entered

this room he took it for granted I was a crook. He was only uncertain what *sort* of crook I was."

"Oh, Vincent!" April exclaimed. "Are you sure we oughtn't to go to Harrods after all?"

"Darling, neither your purse nor my purse can stand up to Harrods. No, the ancient and honourable establishment which Mr Herb represents can supply us with all the luxury that is good for us."

"It is a pity they employ such a horrid man as Mr . . . is, it?" April made a face at this indiscriminating Mr Herb.

"Herb is all right. We got on famously. I told him I had been flat-hunting and asked him why all these new blocks of apartments they are running up have such preposterous rentals. Beginning at £225 a year in unfashionable Bayswater. Two rooms the size of a closet and a bath big enough for a pygmy!"

"They are awful, aren't they?" Maddie agreed. "Every day the rents seem to mount."

"Well, I put it to Mr Herb, that there cannot possibly be enough people in London with incomes adequate for such rentals. But he replied that there were not.—How so, said I? —Well, said he, It's simple, sir. Only half ever pay.—What is that! said I. What are you saying, Mr Herb?—It's a fact sir, said he. These luxury flats are built by the Banks and Insurance Companies, who nowadays hardly know what to do with their surpluses. (Ostensibly they are built by some man of straw. But the Bank sticks him up to act for it). Now—says Mr Herb—the Bank stipulates that the rental of the flats should be such that if only *half* of them were occupied they would get the return they regard as justifying the outlay. *And* (again says Mr Herb) this is on account of the recognized fact that fifty per cent of London tenants of luxury flats never pay their rents."

"But what an extraordinary thing, Vincent. Mr Herb was pulling your leg I am afraid," said April.

"I was incredulous at first. But he convinced me. Mr Herb says he knows it is true for the excellent reason that his firm supply the furniture for the apartment—on the hire-purchase system—and in 50 per cent of the cases the hire-purchase is never paid. They take the furniture back and it goes out to another customer—who presumably pays twice as much as he should, to compensate the firm for their losses elsewhere."

"I still don't understand," said April. "If you take a flat, how can you get out of paying for it, if you are that sort of person?"

"'That sort of person' is good!" Vincent said.

"Well, *we* don't intend to cheat our landlord do we, Vincent!"

"I certainly should, my darling, if I got a chance—and if I thought he had a lot of dough and I hadn't any! But we don't *need* to, darling, do we? We are the suckers who pay twice over—for ourselves and for somebody else."

"Vincent!" Maddie cried, as if he had struck her in the face. April started at her sudden cry. (What a queer highly strung girl she was!) "Don't please say such things."

"Let me proceed with the story of the excellent Mr Herb. He told me how it was done. He says he is asked to go to a large apartment and there is a very well-dressed woman, smoking a cigarette at the end of a long holder (he was very insistent upon that detail). She goes from room to room with him and orders tons of beautiful furniture. Grand pianos, £200 radios, superb rugs, a welter of Chippendale, Queen Anne and Louis Seize: if it's a roof-garden flat overlooking Hyde Park, or Regents Park, thousands of bushes and dwarf trees—in short a 'home' worthy of an archduchess. It is duly delivered and fixed up. Then a large car arrives with a quantity of luggage. The car (hire-purchased) eventually takes all the luggage *away* again. Supposedly the aristocratic tenants have gone away for a short holiday: the splendid commissionaire touches his hat with his white-gloved hand, and off they drive. And no one ever sees them again. The landlord usually waits about ten days: then, with a sigh, the hire-purchase company come and collect all their goods—

the grand pianos, tallboys, and refrigerating plants are re-moved. The untraceable tenants are written off as a bad debt—by the landlord, the furniture firm, the tradesmen. By everybody. A new set of probably crooked tenants move in."

"Impossible!" said April. "I don't believe a word of it. Mr Herb is romancing."

"I was not satisfied. I said to Mr Herb: You have ac-counted for rent, and furniture; and shown me how to live in style on zero, or next to zero. But how about *servants*? Do they do up the place themselves? Some of these large apartments would keep them pretty busy if so, and it would look somewhat odd.—Oh, said Mr Herb, *that* is simple. And he proceeded to tell me about one set of people he knew (clients of course) who occupied a maisonette in Holland Park. They had two maids and a cook, all from the Dis-tressed Areas. Welsh girls. *Cheap!* They got them from one of the agencies that handle that kind of cattle. They paid them the first month's wages—a pound or two. Then at the end of the next month they asked the girls if they would mind wait-ing for a little while for their wages. Sure, said the trio of Welsh sluts; we'll wait.—At the end of a year they hadn't received a penny piece more. They were fed. Mountainous bills at the tradesmen's caused food to be plentiful. They had privileges of course: could bring men in, who left a few shil-lings I expect on the poor girls' mantelpieces. Anyhow, that was how Mr Herb got round the servant problem."

"How horrible!" said Maddie. "I do hate hearing about all this."

"I don't think I should like Mr Herb," said April.

"You never know who you'd like darling till you've tried. Mr Herb didn't impress me to start with. But I soon learnt to appreciate his sterling worth. His is a dark view of life perhaps. But it is nearer the truth than that of most people. He has no illusions, has Mr Herb. And he enjoys the sound of his own voice."

"So it seems," said April. "He discussed none of the things he came to talk about, I suppose?"

"Do you know, I was so fascinated by his picture of the unreality of the stately London scene—with its gilded portals, dazzling footmen, and be-medalled doorkeepers—that I clean forgot the practical purpose of his visit, altogether. I believe he forgot it too. After all, he doesn't mind much whether we order a thousand pounds worth of goods or not since as likely as not we should never pay for them.—So he went on telling me all about this fantastic House of Cards that is *London*! I felt as I listened to him that if you blew on it good and hard it would fall to the ground. Half the people who *do* pay never have any food—they haven't any money left for that after they've met these inflated rentals, the most ruinous income-tax in the world, and all the rest of it. They get thinner and thinner. The only fat ones are those who slip between the gaps in the net.—If you see a fat man in London to-day, you may be sure he's a rogue!"

"You are absurd, Vincent!" said Maddie, with a shadow of a smile, blowing two plumes of smoke out of her wonderfully straight Greek nose.

"No, Mad, it's not *me* who's absurd. It is the crazy system that produces such a world of façades."

"So you took no steps, Vincent, about the Chelsea flat?" April enquired.

"None whatever. It is Mr Herb's fault and then Maddie's who wanted to play *Bucking on her hams* with me."

Maddie blushed and was speechless. Infected by her embarrassment, April blushed too.

"I think I'll let you interview Mr Herb to-morrow, April. Also Guthridge and Crossland. You are not only richer than I am, you *look* richer darling. It's no use my trying to take them in. I'll leave it to you my sweet."

CHAPTER XVII

MADDIE'S CLUBMAN BEAU

CROSSING from Burlington Gardens to the west side of Bond Street, Vincent Penhale and Martin Penny-Smythe made their way up in the Brook Street direction, Vincent once sweeping off his hat to someone in a slowly moving Rolls, in a manner worthy of more spacious days, and of a harder, higher, hat than the one he wore.

"Lady Meltingbrook," he informed Martin with quiet unction when his hat was back on his head again: "Great pal of my mother-in-law." The perfect snob-mask of owlish solemnity did credit even to Clubland.

The aloof 'my mother-in-law' for Mary Mallow, however, annoyed as well as amused Martin. Just as if Martin had not been present in Venice when Vincent first encountered the Mallows—and afterwards been in Paris with them on the way home. Just as if he had not been privy to Vincent's beastly courting of his prosperous bride. Just as if he didn't know that it was all because Vincent had got Miss Mallow in the family way, and so compelled her, as it were, to compel *him* to marry her! At least he had manœuvred things in such a way as always to appear the *hunted*.

"I'm sure the place was somewhere hereabouts," Vincent muttered, looking to right and left, as they moved down a side street, studded irregularly with small shops. "Damn!" all of a sudden he exclaimed and bolted into a chemist's, with such a rat-like velocity that Martin caught his breath, as if an express train had burst past his ear.

Martin halted uncertainly, removed his pipe from his mouth. There was a time when he would not have dreamed of smoking a pipe in Bond Street, when he was very young, or walked up it with a brown paper parcel under his arm. He had just done both. But the days of the Meltingbrooks and the Ribblesdales were past and over. Bond Street had become an ordinary thoroughfare, where no especial precautions had to be observed—lest one met Lord Meltingbrook emerging from the barber's just south of Burlington Gardens, or Lord Ribblesdale jauntily issuing from the doors of the Royal Watercolour Society and starting to amble down to Whites in St James's Street.

A big man, with a baldish staring face, and protruding eyes, had got out of a taxi-cab a few yards ahead of where Martin and Vincent had been, when the latter bolted. He threw a baleful glance or two at the chemist's, while he sorted out a handful of change. Then, to Martin's intense surprise, Madeleine Penhale came out of the taxi-cab and stood beside the tall, fat clubman, and said something that made the latter's fat shake sardonically, without looking up at her. They were on talk-without-looking-terms, these two!

It was now obvious to Martin that his friend had been seeking to avoid this encounter; though why he should wish not to see Maddie, of whom he was so passionately fond, he could not imagine. But the towering bull-dog stranger, with the protruding eyes, advanced, and in his turn entered the small chemist's shop, leaving Madeleine Penhale to drift towards a furniture store at which she had negligently pointed and he had nodded *okay*.

Apparently she had not noticed Martin; who, replacing his pipe in his mouth, passed quietly into the shop as well.

Inside, antiseptically bright and neat, with a woman's weighing-machine in one corner, it was as pokey as the most romantic American tourist could desire. The last comer remained just inside the doorway; he discovered the vanished Vincent and the stranger, both tall, occupying most of the available space. These two stood back to back. One was studying a row of bottles of laxatives and skin-creams; the other balanced in the palm of his hand an indigo tube of Parke-Davis's Shaving Cream. For a few moments silence reigned—a kind of artificial silence, as if the next moment everybody would begin shouting.

"How much is this?" demanded at last, fierce and matter-of-fact, of the deferential shop assistant, the man who had issued from the taxi-cab. A stare of fish-like effrontery accompanied the words, and the assistant quailed politely and cast his eyes down as he answered him.

"Ah, hello, Penhale!" boomed out immediately afterwards, panting as he spoke a little thickly through his copper-red moustache, Maddie's boy-friend. "I thought I recognized you."

"Oh, hallo, Dougal! What are you doing here?"

Vincent Penhale wheeled round, unsmiling, to confront his pursuer. He did not disguise the fact that he had been merely awaiting the unwelcome summons.

"Nothing much. I've just got back from Berlin."

"Berlin! What took you to that unwholesome spot."

"Curiosity," said the other. "And you?"

"Oh, I and my friend here . . . this is Mr Penny-Smythe—Mr Dougal Tandish . . . we have been to the Queen of the Adriatic."

"To Venice? What for?"

"Just to look at pictures."

"Were you doing any sketching yourself?"

Vincent shook his head.

There was a pause; it had the aspect of an armistice. Penhale handed a bottle of laxative to the assistant. Penny-Smythe frowned upon the floor, drawing upon his heroic pipe: and Dougal followed Penhale's movements with his eyes, which were dancing with belligerent lights, pointed with ironic fire. Then he gave his muffled bark again.

"Well, things are pretty grim, aren't they, Penhale!"

"Indeed they are."

"What's going to happen now?"

"I beg your pardon?"

"Munich postpones things for how long do you suppose?"

The embattled Clubman, Mr Tandish, stood with his elbow out, holding his cigarette in his mouth and drawing on it in little puffs, his hand drooping down on to it, like a hinged mechanical hand to administer the cigarette from above.

"What's your view, Dougal?" Vincent asked.

"I haven't got any views any more. I shall emigrate I think! We shall all get poorer and poorer."

"It is a question of money with you."

"Money enters into everything doesn't it? If we'd called their bluff in September the whole thing would have been over by now."

"How do you make that out?" Vincent asked with studied politeness. "You haven't made much preparation for war, have you? According to what, as a mere man-in-the-street I hear, we are strangely unprepared to engage in warfare with a major power. Why didn't you put industry upon a war-time basis long ago, Dougal, or is that an impertinent question?"

"Why didn't *I*? My dear chap, I wish I *had* had something to do with it."

"Haven't you? I've always regarded you as one of the dominating figures in our national life."

"Have you, Vincent?" Dougal inhaled deeply and fiercely, looking through slitted eyes past Penhale's head.

Dougal arched himself forward, and stamped out his cigarette butt on the floor.

"We're much better prepared than is generally supposed. If it rested with me I would call their bluff to-morrow," Dougal said fiercely, drooping his slack cheeks and rather bloodshot eyes, mastiff-fashion. "The City will go on dickering with them till we sink into the position of a second-rate power."

"We shall," replied Vincent. "You are right. But where are the arms with which to call their bluff?"

"We've got enough."

"I'm very glad to hear it. But I was talking to a man last

week who is a squadron-leader in a Defence of London unit. He told me that if war had been declared at the time of Munich he shuddered to think what would have happened. London could have been flattened out."

Dougal shrugged his fat shoulders.

"It's a pretty awful mess!" he said.

"That's what it seems to me."

Vincent Penhale affected to get in motion, but his area of manœuvre was too restricted to do much more than to take one pace forward and then one back. Dougal fixed his gaze upon Penny-Smythe, his face floodlit with a sardonic light, one eyebrow held up by an obliging muscle. Penny-Smythe avoided the bilious and berserk eye.

"Unusual part of the town to encounter you," Dougal said.

Vincent flushed, but his voice was civil as he answered.

"Is it? Yes, I suppose it is the preserve of the affluent."

Dougal had planted himself in the doorway. Now he blocked it squarely, with his fat shoulders. He quizzed the other and shuffled nervously with his feet.

"Someone told me Penhale, that you had become a rentier."

Penhale shook his head.

"That was unkind gossip," he answered.

"I hope it's true though."

"A very small legacy," Penhale picked up a bottle from the counter, looked at it, and carefully replaced it. "I'm spending it. I have been looking at Europe. I thought for twelve months' I would belong to the leisured class."

"I see. You still paint of course?"

Vincent Penhale shrugged his shoulders and nodded.

"What happened to that portrait you did of me, Penhale?"

"I painted it out."

"That's a pity!" Dougal, with his head back, looked down at him along his nose, from which smoke was escaping.

"Why?"

"Oh, I don't know. It seems a waste of energy. I'd have given you a tenner for it."

Vincent gazed back without a change of expression.

"Well, it has been destroyed. Dougal. I think we must go now," he said. "We have some shopping to do."

Dougal sprang, with a flapping of wide trouser-legs, away from the door.

"I'm sorry. Have I been standing in your way?" As he did so, with a shaky hand he withdrew from his breast-pocket a note-case, and opened it. Fumbling for some seconds, he produced a five-pound-note, and held it up.

"Can you change this for me?" he asked with solemn airiness, with lifted eyebrows and half-closed eyes. He straddled, vaguely belligerent, in front of Penhale. There was a light of dim banter in his eyes.

"I must look like a crook, I think. The Bond Street shop-keeper looks with suspicion upon a fiver, I find. One said he had no change the other day. That was a tenner it's true."

Penhale took the five-pound note, leant against the jamb of the door, and held it in his hand, looking down at it, as if it belonged to some obscure exotic currency. Then he held it up to the light. He returned it to Dougal Tandish.

"It looks to me as if it might be a phoney," he remarked.

"Oh, why? I'm sorry you cast doubt upon my notes."

"I'm no authority," Vincent said. "I know a man who could tell you in a minute. But he's in jail."

Dougal Tandish was moving out of the shop. Vincent and Martin went out after him.

"Oh, Penhale. I've got your sister with me. . . . There she is. Maddie!" he called out. "I've just run into your brother."

Vincent went extremely white. As Maddie came over towards them her face was quite colourless too. The brother and sister stared at each other as if they were strangers whose appearance filled them mutually with distress. Maddie's lips were slightly parted, Vincent's were closed tight.

Without addressing a word to his sister Vincent moyed off

up the street, with the silent Martin at his side. They had not gone above a dozen yards when Vincent left him and rapidly retraced his steps. Going up to Dougal, who was standing on the edge of the sidewalk with Maddie, and placing his face within a foot of the latter's, he said in a guttural voice, of which a great deal of genteel gilt had been removed,

"Dougal, if I ever meet you with my sister again I will break every bone in your body!"

"What the devil's the matter with you . . .!" Dougal barked.

"Try it and see!" Vincent retorted fiercely, turning on his heel.

"But, wasn't it you introduced me to Maddie?. . . You're not Maddie's husband, are you?" Dougal straddled and blustered indignantly.

As he heard this last remark, and the crack about not being Maddie's husband, Vincent turned quickly round. For a moment he looked so murderous that Dougal Tandish expected an immediate assault upon his person and stepped away from Maddie's side to receive it. But Vincent turned about instead and rejoined Martin, who had removed his pipe and taken a step towards the quarrelling men.

Immobile, Maddie stood looking after Vincent, the white mask writhing, tears beginning to start out of her eyes.

"Vincent!" she called, and it was the voice of their mother being lofty and tony. But Vincent was out of ear-shot, striding along, Martin keeping up with him with difficulty.

"Down here," Vincent said, and turned into a side street. "Sorry, old man, to have made a scene."

As he wheeled in response to Vincent's command Martin cast a glance behind him down the street they were leaving, and saw Dougal stooping over Maddie, who apparently had dissolved in tears.

Vincent shook himself, like a dog, when it comes out of water, after a compulsory immersion. For the first time in his experience Martin saw his friend's face angry.

"I will not have that individual fooling round with Maddie. There are limits." Vincent said.

"Who *was* that man, Vincent?"

"That was Dougal," Vincent replied, as if imparting a piece of momentous information. "Dougal."

"Yes, but Doo-doo-Dougal . . . is he not a little odd?"

"I find him, on the contrary, typical."

"Typical . . . to-too typical."

"He stands for his class. What more can a fool do? He looks every inch the topdog does he not?"

"He does certainly ler-look that."

"He is a rich top-dog out of the second-best top-drawer of our snobbish plutocracy. He has not a drop of blood in his veins that is not grocer-blood, or Birmingham slum-blood. But, as you see, he feels himself the cat's whiskers. He's yellow except when he's whisky inside him: yet in his own view he could stand as the model for the bully-beef fed to the Bulldog breed, and would make a fine poster for it. Like some of the most typical Britons he is Irish—though British public-schooled and London-clubbed." He took a breath, and added: "I am afraid he gets my goat."

"I can see, Vincent, he der-der-does that!"

But although his words were violent—much to Martin's astonishment, who had never seen his friend like this before, his voice was now devoid of emotion. His mind seemed occupied with something else.

"Wer-wer-what does he do?" Martin breathlessly enquired.

"Nothing."

Martin Penny-Smythe croaked.

"Dougal is an artist. He is an artist in words. He is an explorer. He has explored Finland and Egypt, and I believe pushed as far as Iceland. His style is very beautiful. He has a touch like my charlady's. Hers would be like his if she wrote up her travels in Southend and Margate. So we are both artists, he and I.

"He is v-v-very warlike isn't he?"

"He is a gallant gentleman. Do you know what Dougal really is—if you are curious about him?"

"W-what?"

"In Dougal you see our English fascist."

"A fascist . . .! G-g-got it. Your-your-you're right!"

"As near as we can get to the beastly thing."

"Yes, he's our sort of fascist!"

But Vincent Penhale was not averse to giving more information. He had not done with Dougal yet.

"Pukka fascist lands, too, exercise an irresistible fascination for Dougal. You heard he had just been to Berlin? Doubtless he is petted by the Nazi boy. He has been twice to Franco Spain."

"T-t-twice?"

"At least! He hobnobs with the *Falange* and the *Sturmabteilung.* They make a great fuss of him everywhere I imagine. His status of rich bulldog impresses, it is a pleasant *passe-partout.* The poor muts believe him to be John Bull in person, because he is fat, stupid, and has sagging jaws and more spittle than if he drank less whisky."

"He *should* go down well in G-g-germany."

"He is our local brand of Junker."

"He-he-he's . . . the grocer . . . turned Junker." Martin was enjoying this. His friend laughed, coming out of his abstraction to applaud the image.

"You have it, Mart. I can see Dougal in a white apron, with great distinctness, can't you? Selling rotten Russian eggs as English best new-laid. How truculent he would grow if you caught him out—in the act of handing you short change, affecting to have mistaken your half-crown for a two-bob piece. How I can watch him at it, in my mind's eye! And *what* a pillar of the Chapel he would be, roaring thanks out to his ugly god, for abetting him in his plunder!"

"I can s-s-see that too!" Martin had no difficulty in imagining the heretic at his crooked devotions.

But, as they marched along, Vincent continued his unmerry chatter of gossipy invective, uttered in a low, almost confidential tone.

"Preposterous old baby!—born with a silver spoon in his mouth which his father obviously came by dishonestly! What is one to do with such a man? His romantic claptrap will sink him, there is always that. All that rotten stock have *Finis* branded on their backs. Branded on their strutting rumps. *Someone*—cleverer than the likes of us—will gut them till their pocket-books are as flat as they now are fat. I give them a decade to do it in. There will be no Dougals infesting this earth by 1950. Neither British Dougals nor German Dougals, nor any other Dougals."

Martin was puffed. He took out his handkerchief and began patting his neck and forehead.

"Wer-wer-where are we going, Vincent?" he panted.

"I thought we'd go to your club and have a drink," said Vincent pulling up. "Sorry, old man. I have been tearing along. The fact is I haven't quite recovered from Mr Tandish yet. I'm afraid he made me mad."

He made no reference to his sister.

Chapter XVIII

A ROTTEN ACCENT

VINCENT was pacing irritably up and down in front of the fireplace, while the whistle of a tug outside the window made speech for the moment impossible. Maddie sat tearfully watching him. It had all the appearance of the quarrel of a married couple—only the wife a phenomenally docile one, and the husband oddly authoritarian for 1939.

When the uproar from the river had abated, Vincent stopped in front of her. He spoke with a deliberate harshness, and Maddie stiffened tremulously against the attack.

"I have no right to interfere," he said, "in your love-life . . . That is Dick's business, if it interests him."

"Don't be absurd, Vincent!"

"Very well. But I am able to say this. If you continue to see that bad smell I shall see *you* no more. To me you also will stink."

She shrank back as the word *stink* hit her.

"Vincent ple-*please*: why do you threaten me like that! *Of course* I won't see him if you tell me not to."

"I can't *tell* you to do anything."

"It is terribly unkind of you to go on in this way, Vincent! You, Vincent, are responsible for Mr Tandish aren't you? It was at your place I met the wretched man . . ."

"True. But I didn't expect you to go and succumb to his attractions."

Maddie wiped her eyes with her handkerchief.

"Vincent, you told me didn't you," she expostulated, "to 'seek every opportunity'—those were your words you know —of conversing with people who were . . . who were . . ."

Vincent laughed crossly.

"Yes, yes—who were liable to speak the King's English rather than Minnie's. I remember."

"Upper class if possible you said, instead of middle-class . . . like Dick, you said."

"I didn't say anything about Dick, Maddie!"

"I think you did, Vincent."

"I oughtn't to have done that. Dick Morse is a gentleman —which is more than one can say for Mr Tandish!"

Maddie sighed heavily.

"Dougal is a very 'nice-spoken gentleman,' Vincent, as Mother would call it," she smiled wanly. "It's like going to have a lesson more than anything else, when I have a date with Dougal Tandish."

"A lesson in what?"

"Oh, it's as if I were going about with somebody who was teaching me Portuguese or Dutch."

Vincent laughed crossly again—finding himself hoist with his own petard.

"That is an ingenious way of putting it, Mad. You're not a woman for nothing are you!"

"But it *is* just like that, Vincent. Really it is. It's hard work what's more. Often it gives me a headache. I get terrible headaches sometimes. I took three aspirins after our *Bucking Horse* lesson—I didn't tell you . . ."

Vincent bit his nails and stared away out of the window. Was he *nuts*, as Flo said he was? he asked himself quickly, and then turned to his sister again, very firm and full of authority, but less severe this time.

"I shouldn't give yourself a headache any more—not with Mr Tandish. I exempt you from these painful exercises. He has got a very bad accent anyway. Very middle-class."

"Has he, Vincent? Is it *middle-class*? I thought it was like . . ."

"No. It's rotten."

"Well, I certainly won't see him any more if his accent's rotten. I only saw him at all because I thought his accent was so good."

Vincent laughed shortly—a thoroughly checkmated sort of laugh.

"Has he taken you about much? Dancing and so on?" he asked gruffly.

"No, Vincent."

"Does he kiss you a lot?"

Maddie threw up her head, and looked at Vincent as a statue in a park might do if you asked it if it rained sometimes, or if the wind blew on it ever.

"He has done so," she answered. "You told me once when I asked you, that although a gentleman was always supposed to act like a gentleman, the proof that he *was* one was often that he didn't."

Vincent burst into so hearty a laugh this time, that Maddie felt comforted and gave a timid smile.

"Well I will see that friend Dougal hasn't another opportunity of demonstrating with my sister what a gentleman he is! I'll cut his hands off if I catch him within six feet of you!"

Maddie's smile suffered a violent death.

"I'll beat his mouth into a pulp!" her brother said this quite quietly, looking at her sideways. He held his hand out in front of him and opened it and shut it. *Shut*, it menaced the mouth that kissed—not Cæsar's wife, but Vincent's sister.

"Don't go on like this, Vincent . . . I have told you I shall not see Mr Tandish again, haven't I? So please let us talk about something else."

"What's the matter with Dick?" Vincent asked her, suddenly and angrily. "Doesn't he love you?"

"I think Dick does, Vincent," she looked doubtfully at him. "Yes, Vincent, of course Dick does."

"Why have you got no children? Are you really as cold as you look? You ought to have children. You have been married for nearly three years."

The perfection of beauty, hearing itself denounced as *barren*, broke up its features into a hideous mask of grief.

Wailing, she fell sideways upon the couch, where she lay and gave herself over to weeping.

Vincent immediately left the room. Except for the reading-lamp by the side of the fireplace, the 'throne-room' was now quite dark.

When Vincent returned, in about five minutes' time, Maddie was sitting up. She did not look at him. He sat down beside her on the couch, and gave her arm a friendly squeeze.

"Terribly sorry, Mad . . . I have behaved very badly. I know it. Deep apologies."

She shook her head—it made her *more* unhappy to hear him apologize. Why do that when, as always, he was right?

"I'll explain," he said. "You don't understand, but that nasty snob treats you as an uneducated girl, who is fair game for gentlemen disinclined to marry and too particular to go to a tart-shop. But, Mad, my darling, you are *my* sister. You are more than a sister to me—I love you very much. You are a part of me. If he insults you, he insults me. And he knows that perfectly well. He insults you by treating you as if you were just any girl to have a good time with (your social standing gives him the privilege of the master over the slave) and meanwhile quite likely upset your married life with Dick. But I don't like this man. He knows that. I don't say he takes you about in order to annoy me merely. That would be leaving out of account that lovely face of yours and your unspoilt trusting heart. But I *do* come into it. See? And I am not going to come into it with *him*—not at your expense; not in that way. I feel his damp whisky-shaken hand roaming round on you is like a cockroach in my bath-tub. He is nosey with it too; nosey about things that are no business of his. He is a dangerous old devil. . . . You know, Mad, that I would not lightly talk to you like I was doing just now. Not without very strong motives. Something very important." He stood up. Maddie's face had become grand and expressionless again.

"I'm sorry, Vincent, if I made a fuss, but I've had a . . . an . . . upsetting day."

"It's I only who have to apologize, Mad," he said.

"Minnie rang me up this morning," she announced. "That's how the day began."

"Oh." He frowned at the mere thought of the 'charlady.' "What did Minnie want? Money?"

Maddie shook her head.

"Mother was brought home practically unconscious by the police last night."

"Ah."

"At her age! It's terrible. She couldn't walk. She'd been out with Mrs Cooper, it seems . . . She can't drink so much as she once was able to."

Vincent stared at her in silence.

"The police knocked Minnie up at three in the morning." Maddie's mask began to wriggle at the lips. "It's so . . . *humiliating*, Vincent!" She made an effort to hold her face still at the mouth. "It's *awful* . . . Vincent!"

She placed her face in her hands, as if to hold the stern mask together.

"It's not *pretty*, Mad, I admit," he said after a moment. "Of course it isn't. But nothing is pretty is it, about life as it has been lived by us? If an old female slave gets drunk! . . ."

"But it is our *mother*, Vincent!" his sister wailingly protested.

And again, just as when the brother and sister had been discovered 'Bucking on their hams,' April had entered the room, and was saying pleasantly—

"What an illumination! . . . Am I interrupting a private conversation? . . . I'm sorry!"

"Not a bit!" breezed Vincent. "When Maddie and I get together we always look more hopelessly dramatic than we really are. Poor old Mad's overwrought. All the Penhales are temperamental. Mother was *full* of temperament, wasn't she, Mad?"

Maddie rose, wiping her eyes.

"I'm sorry, April, I am such a fool. I get . . . easily up-set."

"I'm sure you don't," April said, going up to her and putting her arm round her shoulders. "Is there anything *I* can do, Maddie darling?"

"No, April, thank you." She gave April a gauche, shy, hug. "I shall be all right in a minute. Really I shall."

Vincent came on the other side of her and put *his* arm round her too. She gasped as the two of them squeezed her, and laughed shakily.

"My little sister wants a good night's rest," he said. "You must lie up for a couple of days. A staid old married couple like April and I now—you should observe *us* and imitate."

"Mr Halvorsen, sir," Willis announced.

"Hallo, Bill!" Vincent exclaimed, breaking away from his sister.

"'Lo, Vin!" sang back Halvorsen, and he brought his blazing blue eyes and salmon-pink face into the area of light by the fireplace.

"How do you do, Mr Halvorsen," said April. "Do let's have a little light on the subject, Vincent."

"'Lo, Maddie. Quite a family gathering!" Halvorsen was in a jolly mood. "I saw your friend this afternoon, Mad. What's his name . . . Standish!"

"Mr Tandish, do you mean? He is not my friend, Bill," Maddie said. "Only an acquaintance."

"Is that so? I'm glad to hear that."

"Why?" asked Vincent, coming back from the light switches by the door.

"Why? Oh, dunno, Vin. He's a kind of a nosey Parker, isn't he?"

Vincent nodded sombrely.

"He is."

"I met milord in the Underground. He asked me where I lived. I asked him if I might hope he'd pay me a call—said I was sure I'd be awfully honoured. He said he might drop up one day and see what sort of kennel . . . or was it bugwalk? . . . I occupied."

"What did you say?" Vincent asked.

"I said—*Cave Canem*. That's good straight latin that is. He laughed and said he'd risk it. 'But seriously, Halvorsen' —you know, very toffish—'we're really equals, don't you know! I'd welcome the *appertunity* of a talk one of these days with you Hal-*vor*-sen!'—'Why, thank you kindly, sir,' said I, 'but I'm a busy man. I have no time for small talk! . . . I couldn't shake the bastard off—oh, forgive me, ladies, won't you! I'm always disgracing Vincent, Mrs Penhale! I am that, madam!'"

"Bill's tongue is rough!" Vincent told his wife heartily. "But he's never had our opportunities. A Council School is all old Bill's folk could run to. So—*que voulez vous?*—Is my accent good April? We had a rotten French master at Hailey-bury. And I was always bottom of the class!"

"Who is this objectionable Mr Standish?" April asked.

"Not Standish," Vincent said. "The fellow's name is Dougal Tandish. Most offensive citizen."

"He sounds very bad," April agreed limply.

"I must go, Vincent," said Maddie, who showed even less relish for the society of that flower of the Board Schools, Halvorsen, than did April.

"Vincent," said April, "you'd better ring. Willis wants to get the table ready I expect. . . . Come along with me, Maddie darling."

April and Maddie left the room. Vincent rang the bell.

"So you're stopping here for the present, Vin?" Halvorsen remarked, pouring himself a Scotch and soda.

"For the present, Bill. When April has her child we shall want more room. Just now—well, money's scarce."

Halvorsen approached him, holding his glass.

"I thought money was plentiful now. Why don't you re-consider your decision, Vin, if that's the case?"

Vincent shook his head.

"April has to be considered, Bill. Then . . . I shall have a kid. See? No, Bill, I must be serious now."

Willis came in to lay the table for dinner—for this was a 'studio,' a study, a dining-room, and drawing-room all in one.

CHAPTER XIX

"I SUPPOSE I SHALL HAVE TO
SHELL-OUT"

THE January sun cast its bleak light over Palace Gardens Terrace, and provoked Mrs Mallow's parrot into incontinent epigram.

"Pretty Polly!" it observed smugly and sedately. Then with its strong nasal accent: "*Cet animal est méchant. Quand on l'attaque il se défend!*"

It spoke in the bay-window at the west end of the drawing-room. Near the window facing east, from which could be seen the Victorian turrets and battlements of 'Millionaire Row', sat Mary Mallow and her daughter, April. Both looked rather harassed and grave.

"Well, there's nothing for it!" said Mrs Mallow, shrugging and grimacing. "I suppose I shall have to *shell-out*. Shan't I?"

"I don't know, Mother," April looked distressed.

"You know I shall. So does he!"

April moved deprecatingly, to deny responsibility on the part of Vincent.

"You see, Mother, all this property in Canada is realizing nothing, for the moment. There is one very large house, Vincent says, which *may* be let as a school. His lawyer is negotiating. It is a Victorian eyesore—oh, like one of those houses over there," (pointing at the skyline of Millionaires' Row). "In these days nobody wants that sort of house, that is the trouble. The new rich class in America have built themselves 'modern homes.' But as a *school* it may serve some purpose."

"Has he *nothing left*?"

172

"Practically nothing," said April reluctantly. "He has been living on an overdraft. He has always hoped against hope, poor boy, that the property would find a purchaser. Get let! He has a lot of it, it seems. But it is all *dated*."

"All right. As I said, needs must! I will see Mr Hackett about it, to-morrow. I don't know what he'll say!"

"Thank you, Mother."

"Who are his lawyers? . . . Never mind. Mr Hackett will attend to all that."

"It won't be for *very long*, Mother," said April anxiously. "Vincent is seeing his agent to-morrow."

"You mean he's going to act again?" her mother cackled glumly. "That's not going to make much difference is it? The highbrow play generally runs for a week or two and then comes off."

"He thinks perhaps one of the good repertory companies . . ."

Mrs Mallow shook her head.

"Shakespeare? Pretty precarious. People hate Shakespeare! They want American gangster stuff."

April hesitated.

"He thought he might get an engagement in America as a matter of fact," she said. "Not in gangster plays, of course. Several people, friends of his, have made a good deal over there."

"Why doesn't he *write* a play. There is money in that now!" Mrs Mallow nodded her head knowingly.

"Yes, that *is* an idea, Mother!" April lit up her face.

"I should think he could write a *jolly good* play." Mrs Mallow warmed to the subject. "He's a very clever young man—and he knows all about the theatre, which is more than most playwrights do."

"He has acted quite a lot. Mostly Chekov and Shaw."

"You must make him do that at once."

"I'll take it up with him this very night, Mother. We're going to the theatre to-night . . . if he doesn't say at the last moment he doesn't feel like it, and hates the theatre! He's been very nervous lately. He often changes his mind . . . he will say,—Let's do this or that. Then when the time comes he cries off. It worries me rather. I don't think he's well."

Mrs Mallow listened with growing interest.

"Yes," she said, "I've thought he was behaving rather oddly once or twice. I like Vincent! But I can't quite make him out. *Nor* his sister for that matter. There is a queer girl if you like!"

"She is queer. I like her, but she rather frightens me."

"If one didn't know it wasn't so . . . I mean if she wasn't Vincent's sister, I should have suspected that Madeleine was a quite uneducated girl."

"Madeleine? That's never occurred to me, Mother." April looked pained.

"Well, it has to me. I know it isn't so. But she often uses very funny expressions. Did you hear her say that night she came here to dinner—'Oh, Vin, don't turn me up,' when he pushed her over on the sofa. 'Oh, you *muss-sern't*!' she said. Instead of 'mustn't'—Just the way cook would say it! I don't suppose you heard her."

April shook her head. "No, I did not. She's an awfully shy girl. Often she doesn't open her mouth for hours."

"I expect she had a cockney nanny, poor child," Mrs Mallow decided magnanimously. "Children pick up the most extraordinary things. Young Meltingbrook used to say, 'didn't ought,' for a long time, until Lavinia cured him of it. He still says it sometimes. They pick up things from grooms or anybody."

"I expect it is something of that sort. Vincent and Maddie are very close to each other. I found them some time ago, playing a horse game of some kind, they used to play as children. *Bucking Horse* they called it. They were hopping about and shouting *Ham-ham-ham*. Over and over again."

"How remarkable!" Mrs Mallow gave her solemn blank monkey-stare. "Father had an orderly in India who taught him *horse-language*. He used to neigh at a horse, and make it do whatever he wanted."

"Really, Mother? I can see Grandfather talking to all the *horses* at a Meet instead of talking to the people. I can see that! He always said he much preferred horses to men."

"He did!" Mrs Mallow confirmed, with extreme relish. "He *hated* people. He was just like me!"

"Vincent says he hates people," said April.

"All intelligent people do."

April paused and turned something over in her mind.

"Vincent says he likes poor people better than rich," she said doubtfully but deliberately. "He says he hates *snobs*. That makes me a little uncomfortable, because I'm not sure I'm not a snob . . . in some ways."

Mrs Mallow laughed hollowly.

"Vincent is a bit of a Red," she told her daughter indulgently. "But that doesn't mean very much."

"I am sure it doesn't," April hastened to declare.

"All young people are like that, to-day. It's part of the reaction against Victorian pomposity and smugness. It's a pose. It's a *young* pose. Vincent is still a young man, but he's not averse to adopting the *young* point of view. He is after all old enough to want to do *that!*"

"I don't think it's that, Mother, I don't believe it's a pose." April frowned. "That wretched man Halvorsen has a very bad influence on him."

"Oh, *him!*"

"I just can't understand Halvorsen. I can't see the point of that horrid man."

"He says the man saved his life," Mrs Mallow reminded her.

"I know." April shook her head, with a puzzled wag, reminiscent of her mother.

"What play are you going to to-night," Mary Mallow asked.

"*The Happy Minx*. I think it is."

"Oh, yes. From the notices it doesn't seem much of a play."

"Well we probably shan't go," April sighed, "so it won't matter."

The telephone rang. Mrs Mallow sprang up and moved with venerable expedition, in a little trot, over to the telephone.

"Yes . . . ah, Vincent—good morning. We've just been talking about you—talk of the devil . . . with April . . . yes, she's here. . . . You want to cut out the theatre engagement for to-night? . . . Yes, well April *said* you would do that . . . eh? No, she *foretold* that—she says you are as variable as the shade—she never knows from one minute to the next . . . my dear man I'm sure you don't. . . . Put it all onto God. . . . Ah, that's where the devil comes in! . . . You once acted the? . . . Dostoievski—of course I remember. I helped Mrs Garnett. . . . He does—and women also? . . . no I mean women do . . . yes, w-o-m-e-n—the poor *shes* . . . cheap? . . . the weather's o-kay at this end . . . yes, well, look here, Vincent, if that's so, you take my advice, an old woman's advice, and go and see Mr *Perl* . . . oh, well he calls himself a psychiatrist, but he is a very intelligent fellow . . . no, silly, not to be *psychoanalysed*, just to have someone *outside yourself* tell you what you look like from the outside . . . that may be so though it has not been my experience that actors are very *objective* about themselves. . . . No, I know you're not. Now listen to me—and this is *a command* . . . and I feel like him sometimes! But listen, young man— take down this address. Have you got a pencil . . . right. Fifty B., Wimpole Street. Name—Humbert Perl. He's a refugee . . . yes, but it's time we had a bit of new blood here. I make a great point of this. Telephone him at once and say you wish to consult him—say I'm your mother-in-law, say you want a *Heart-to-heart* . . . Yes. And tell him the truth, unless you've forgotten how to tell it. . . . No, I should refuse to listen, if he wanted to tell me. You don't sound *at all* yourself. The visit to Mr Perl will make a new man of you.

He will turn you inside out. Now here is April who wants to speak to you. Hold on—here she is."

After April had exchanged a few words with Vincent, purred her *good-bye* to him, and returned to her seat, her mother spoke.

"April," she said, "see that Vincent pays a visit to that man you heard me telling him about. *I* thought I was going to die! It was Mr Perl who proved to me that I wasn't. I quite forget his reasoning. But he is my Halvorsen. He saved my life."

CHAPTER XX

A HEART-TO-HEART WITH MR PERL

M R HUMBERT PERL spoke English very well, with a
powerful, chugging German accent. He was fat and
tall, with a beaked face like an inquisitive bird. When Vincent was speaking he looked at him meditatively out of one
eye. Occasionally he jotted something down upon a sheet
of paper.

Vincent Penhale and he were closeted together in a large
room, whose walls were lined with books, paper-backed and
polyglot. It was very dark: an opaque green fog, and a green
shaded reading-lamp, imparted a sickly cast to the faces of
the two confreres.

"Well, what shall we do, Vincent?" Mr Perl was in the
habit of affirming that after a half-hour of *heart-to-heart*
he and his clients knew one another better than most so-
called friends of ten years standing. At a certain point in the
interview with a new client (usually just after the latter had
confessed to having raped his sister, or to having designs
upon the savings-bank balance of his old cook), Mr Perl
would begin calling him by his first name. If the client was a
woman it was the same procedure, except that then with the
use of the first name went a tender guttural syllabication.

"Now that you have told me your story, Vincent," he said,
"shall we try to generalize about it, no?"

"Why not? That would be fun," said Vincent.

"Fun—yes! It will be fun." Mr Perl beamed, to indicate
he loved sport. He looked at his notes.

"It is *a tragedy*, you have been telling me," he said
gravely. "A tragedy. The villain of your piece, Vincent, is
class. I am right? Tell me if I am not right."

Vincent nodded. "Yup!" he said. "That's allright."

"And you are the hero. *Nicht wahr?* That is already a mistake. You are not a hero, Vincent."

"No," said Vincent. "Not to my valet."

"Ach, Vincent, there you are! You shouldn't *have* a valet. I have no valet. What do you want with a valet?"

"That's advertisement," said Vincent. "That's all my 'man' is."

"Advertisement for what?"

"Just advertisement. Like a big posh doorkeeper outside a hotel or theatre."

"All right," said Mr Perl, conceding him that point. "But it is in terms of *class* that you should think, or not think at all about social injustice."

"Of class?"

"Of class. The sweat—the *smell*: the cheap, ill-fitting clothes: the coarse and incorrect speech, are all inseparable from the life of manual work. You attach too much importance to the *dropping of an aitch*, Vincent, or to an offensive smell. Do you know that?"

"Everybody *does* in England."

"Class is so bad here—in England—because there is no class. I explain my paradox. You are all *one* class—but the poor members of it drop their aitches. *Nicht wahr?*"

"I get you, Mr Perl."

"Humbert. Please!"

"Humbert!" said Vincent, grinning in friendly fashion. He liked this Viennese exile, placidly analysing away, with his inquisitive brown eye, while social systems were crashing all about them. It was because he had liked him he had been so frank.

"You were born among artisans and labourers, Vincent. And you have *willed* yourself a gentleman."

"To *look* like one," Vincent corrected. "To *speak* like one. I am not such a snob as you think, Humbert. Aitches don't matter to *me*."

"I do not underestimate your intelligence, Vincent, believe

me. What I said was that you are not a class-hero." He paused before returning to his exposition. "The effort demanded of you, however, consumed all your energies. You are rather *empty*, Vincent. You do not mind my saying this?"

"No. I like it," Vincent smiled. "I often feel empty."

"The thing you have been so careful to imitate is empty too. There is that. Very empty. A *gentleman!* What is a gentleman? It is a word. It is an accent. You identify yourself with something that is not very important."

"I do. I have."

"Something that is even a little ridiculous. Why did you take so much trouble?" Mr Perl asked him in soft guttural sing-song. "Why?"

"You've got that wrong. It was quite easy really," Vincent answered. "I am naturally rather like this. I'm a good actor, too!"

"Yes, but the trouble of which I spoke was not in the technical problems of imitation—of manner, speech, and so *weiter*. The effort to which I referred, was . . . well psychological, to use that old word."

"I see. Yes, the strain is there. There is strain."

"The strain *is* there indeed. Why otherwise did you come to me?"

Vincent shook his head. "That was for something else," he said.

"Ach, so?" Mr Perl interrogated him with a quick eye, but, as Vincent was unresponsive, continued. "But this thing that had the power over you that it had—to *compel* you to imitate it, is a very un-im-por-tant, *stupid* thing."

"My dear Humbert," the other protested, "If a thug were sitting on your chest, and had his fingers round your windpipe, it would be immaterial to you if he was a bird-brain or a great philosophical intelligence! *To get on top* would be your problem—if the struggle lasted twenty years. A plug-ugly or Plato look much the same, when they have you by the throat."

"Of course. But did you *get on top*? No. You identified yourself with the oppressor."

Vincent roused himself sportingly to reply to this.

"I should have stuck to my class, what!—No, Humbert, I'm not the stuff of which martyrs are made."

"You will be a worse martyr yet, Vincent, if you do not take care!" Perl told him with a rather minatory waggle of his head.

"I may be. But I shall have had a run for my money," Vincent laughed. "But look here, I'm *arguing* too much, Humbert. You go ahead and do your stuff. I won't interfere."

"As you please." Mr Humbert Perl looked at the self-confessed underdog mildly but firmly. "Well, then, you should have ignored *class* (since you are not a 'martyr'—a fighter). You could have done so. Your brother Harry ignores it, as you have explained. But . . . no, let me go on . . . because he ignores it he is debarred from all the good things of life (that is what you were about to say?)—all the free things. Harry condemns himself to a status almost like that of the American negro, who is debarred from entering the hotels, restaurants, or clubs white people frequent—who is a pariah because he is *coloured*. That was your reasoning. But your brother is a completely different man to you. He is a brute. Why think of him at all?"

Vincent waited politely for him to proceed: but as he did not do so, but sat watching him out of one eye—an eye of great shrewdness and great tolerance—he spoke himself.

"How long have you been in England, Humbert?"

"I? Two years."

"Two years. That's too short."

"Too short! I sometimes feel that it is too long."

"No, but you are quite unable to fathom the intensity of the religion of class, which in England restricts the personal development of any man or woman born outside the genteel pale. It *denies expansion* to him or to her as much as the shoes formerly worn by Chinese ladies denied normal development to the feet. It stops you from breathing freely—indeed from existing in freedom at all. If you are born one of the poor, you *must* go about disguised. It is the only way."

"If you had a hunchback, Vincent, would you try to disguise it?"

Vincent looked almost surprised.

"Of course I should—in every way I could."

Mr Perl smiled at Vincent.

"You are a strange case, Vincent! But just now in telling me I was a foreigner and therefore incompetent to deal with purely British problems, you were trying, Vincent, to put *me* outside the pale." Mr Perl smiled reproachfully.

"No," said Vincent.

"You were making use of a similar machinery to that utilized to keep the underdog in his place, were you not?"

"I didn't mean to do that, Humbert."

"That is all right. But as a foreigner I grasp many things more clearly than is possible for a native of England."

"All except the class set-up. That's a closed book to you."

"You are wrong, Vincent. That is the simplest thing of all to master. There is no real class in England proper. I have told you. You are all in a conspiracy to defeat class. *Real class.* Your relatives dislike you because you threaten the conspiracy. You are not snob *enough*, Vincent, for them! Or you are too cynical a snob."

"Thank you for that. There's a great deal to be said for you, Humbert. Mary Mallow was right."

Mr Perl bowed, with staid irony.

"You would *create* class in England, my friend," he said, "if you had your way. But yourself you would float in a genteel no-man's-land. Because you are so egotist."

"I take back what I said just now!" laughed Vincent. "What class do you stem from, Humbert?"

"*Haute bourgeoisie*," said the unruffled Mr Perl succinctly, his single eye mocking Vincent, as he bent down towards his notes upon the table.

"Well, I'll tell you, Humbert. I see no reason for *so much* injustice and misery as one finds here."

"What are you going to do about it?" Mr Perl countered.

"I said I was not a martyr. I've taken unto myself a valet, a wife with money . . . a psychiatrist."

"You are egotist," smiled Mr Perl. His manner changed to a very business-like earnestness, however. "Let us forget *class*. That is not the whole picture. Whatever station in life you had appeared in, it would have been the same. There is something about you (it is very *interesting*) that is proper to you, and independent of education. It is obvious, Vincent, that you suffer to a morbid degree from . . . I wonder if you know it, you who have the analytic mind? From an *excess of Will*."

"Ah!"

"Your will is so powerful that it drives you along like a relentless tyrant. You have a sort of *personal dictator* (to parody 'personal devil') inside you. It drives you on to do this, and to do that: something very distasteful and difficult of course. You have an English expression: he 'steeled his will.' Well, Vincent, your will is *steeled* almost out of human semblance."

"That is very interesting," said Vincent, sitting back and staring thoughtfully at Mr Perl.

"Very," said Mr Perl. "Well—and it's first cousin, 'action'—is the bane of the modern European—and North American."

"Ah!" said Vincent—the monosyllable seemed to serve for applause. "You come from Germany. You should know."

"Of course. Mussolini and Hitler what are they, but extreme, and curiously disagreeable, expressions of this morbid Will. Devils they are not, so much as diabolical machines of empty *will*."

"I think that describes them," Vincent approved. "I have

always thought to call them *devils* was an insult to old Nick."

"Indeed it is. Will, in isolation, is a very peculiar thing. Strangely meaningless and barren. The oriental peoples may, on the whole, possess too little will. However that may be, the European certainly has *too much*."

Vincent stood up.

"I have too much," he said. "You are absolutely right. Thank you for explaining that to me: this has been a very worthwhile visit."

"Please!" said Mr Perl rising. "I am your debtor. You have given me very much to think about. Never have I encountered so much crude Will. And so *aimless*."

Vincent laughed.

"You're all wrong there," he told the analyst. "You think I am an outsize snob. That is bad judgment on your part. It was because I was cold-blooded about class, and saw through the snob, that I was able to play the part I have. I was just—oh, ambitious. That's all. I wanted money. So I took the necessary steps. It seems absurd to you to take so much trouble, because you have not taken the measure of the class-snobbery in this little island."

"But I *have*!" protested Mr Perl. "Who with eyes in his head could miss it? But it is a dementia—these people are *mad* . . . And you, Vincent," he added softly, smiling, "you . . . are a little mad, too!"

They both laughed, as they shook hands.

"Oh, well," said Vincent. "I've been told I'm mad often enough! There you have said nothing new."

"If you imitate—if you ape—someone who is mad for a long time, you are bound to *appear* mad yourself," Mr Perl conceded. "But I think you *are* mad too."

"Anyway, I suffer from an excess of *will*. That was a bullseye, Humbert. I will try and do something about that."

"Do that. And come and see me again. I wish you would."

"I will, Humbert." Vincent paused at the door. "You will

not betray my confidence? Do not tell Mary Mallow . . ."
He laughed.

Mr Perl shook his head.

"You may rely on me," he said. "My code as a professional man."

CHAPTER XXI

REPORT OF A MURDER

A BOVE the 'throne-room' or studio were the sleeping-quarters: and a kind of sun-parlour—furnishings of Alto workmanship—used by Vincent as a breakfast-room, stood above the river, as the larger room below enjoyed an almost horizontal view of its oily tide. From the windows of this airy, sky-lit room, the breakfaster could survey a good stretch of brown waterway, and black and brown waterfront, in either direction.

Water, as the dominant feature of a landscape, loses it's point when a leaking reservoir in the sky fills the air with it as well, Vincent would remark, as he looked at this ugly river of his: for it usually was raining. And as he and his wife sat above the Thames upon this Sunday, drinking their morning coffee, rain in oyster-coloured bands endlessly passed into the moving brown liquid underneath without imparting to the latter any of its filmy transparency.

"It will do this all day, I think," Vincent said as he looked out. He had put his paper down to help himself to a second cup of coffee.

"Probably," said April.

"The seasons have been pulled back a month."

"How do you mean, Vincent?" she asked, looking sleepily up.

"Hadn't you noticed? 'April showers' come in March. 'May flowers' come in April, We have all the so-called 'March winds' in *this* month."

"It certainly has been on the blowy side," she agreed.

"Then in August of course, we have beautiful autumn weather as a rule."

186

April laughed lazily. It was nearly six months now since her pregnancy began, and this fact conferred upon this Sunday morning scene a pleasant air of domestic maturity. Their marriage seemed to be rounding itself out and taking on a mellow fullness already, and in her lazy eyes was the primitive contentment of motherhood.

Vincent had a slightly drawn look which perhaps was emphasized by the presence of a small budding moustache, dark like his hair. He fingered this novelty, once or twice.

"I seem to recall," she said, "an *extremely* windy February last year . . . I'm trying to remember if March was full of showers. Was it?"

"Sure to have been," he said dogmatically. "It was really April."

"I was born in April," she said smiling. "Mother always said when I had fits of crying that had something to do with it. That I was April's child."

"Ah, but that was a good time ago . . . it was before all this started I mean," Vincent corrected himself. "The displacement occurred more recently than thir-twenty-five years."

"Twenty-eight. You *know* it's twenty-eight!" she laughed sheepishly.

"Do I?"

"Of course. I believe you want to flatter me. But I didn't know you were a weather expert, Vincent."

"I'm not, darling," he answered patting her knee, with a few jolly raps. "I got it out of a mystery story. Nothing if not unoriginal!" he laughed, and picked up the paper he had laid down.

The rain altered its trajectory, and tested the stoutness of the window panes with a sharp salvo or two. April was delivered of a faint exclamation, and Vincent looked quickly up.

"Vincent," she said slowly, "there can't be *two* men named Dougal Tandish surely. Can there?"

"I hope there are not *two* of them!" Vincent answered 'Why?"

"It seems he has been found dead in the river."

"Dougal?" Vincent sounded incredulous.

"Yes. Shot . . . Murdered. Look!"

She passed her paper across to him. He took it from her with a frown, and read the news-item she showed him with her finger.

"Well, I'll be damned!" he said. "Yes, that's Dougal all right. Well, well, well."

"How extraordinary isn't it!"

"No, I wouldn't say that," Vincent said, handing the paper back to her. "I am not particularly surprised—though I should have expected it to occur on the Bosphorus or the Red Sea."

"Oh. Why the Red Sea rather than the Thames?"

"Because our Secret Service personnel are usually bumped off in foreign parts. It was always my belief that Dougal was connected with the Secret Service."

"Oh, was he? . . . Ah, I see."

"I thought so. It's a Secret Service crime, I expect."

"I shouldn't be surprised."

"Probably lured to his doom by some agent of another Power. Phillips Oppenheim sort of a show."

"You knew him well, didn't you, Vincent?" she asked, a little timidly, without looking at him.

"Well! I knew him far too well, for my liking."

"You didn't like him did you?"

Vincent laughed disagreeably.

"I wasn't awfully drawn towards him," he said. "I do not wish to speak ill of the dead. But Dougal was a strangely unattractive man."

"Most Secret Service *are*. At least I think so. Mother has always had a perfect *passion* for men in the Secret Service. I always found them very dull."

"Dougal's the only one I have ever known—if he was one."

"I feel sure he must have been. All this," she patted the newspaper—"sounds so like the *sticky ends* that all Mother's

Secret Service friends always seemed to have hanging over them."

"Mary Mallow is wonderful." Vincent laughed. "She really is a great old girl."

April Mallow gave a violent, gleeful, nod—which was quite a passable imitation of Mary Mallow's—and resumed the reading of her paper.

"Mr Chamberlain is still . . . appeasing!" she said, in a few minutes, out of the midst of the *Sunday Times*—this time appearing as a follower of Vincent's, from whom she had picked up the word 'appeaser,' without quite knowing what it meant.

Vincent sighed and nodded. A silence of some minutes fell upon the breakfasting married couple, the rain continued to fill the room with the sound of angry water, obeying peevishly the law of gravitation. The telephone upon the window ledge started to ring. Vincent steered his chair over to it, and took off the receiver.

"Ah, good morning, Martin," he said into the talking-end. "Yes, April and I are both up . . . yes, she's feeling fine, thank you. . . . About Dougal? . . . What do I make of it? Well, it is a most appropriate end for a louse—couldn't have thought of a better one myself."

"Vincent!" said April reproachfully. "I think you're horrible."

"Sorry, I missed that—April is protesting at my realistic attitude! . . . No, Martin, I haven't set eyes on the bastard since our encounter with him in the West End. . . . Oh, you did, did you! No, I might have blacked his eye one of these days, but I certainly wouldn't have thought him worth swinging for! . . . Almost any night next week. . . . That would be heavenly. Tuesday. Come to dinner. . . . Oh, sevenish. That suit you? . . . Of course not—gay togs absolutely *verboten* . . . good-bye, old man."

He put the telephone back on its prong.

"Martin seemed to think I might have done a job on

Dougal Tandish!" Vincent laughed. "It's odd how I strike my friends, as a born man of action."

"What made Mr Penny-Smythe think that? Why should you . . .?"

"I had a row with him," Vincent said.

"Did you? I didn't know you ever had rows with people. I think it's horrid of Mr Penny-Smythe . . ."

The telephone rang again. Vincent slid over to it.

"Who?" he shouted into it. "Mad, darling!—sorry. I thought you were the operator. . . . Yes, she's here . . . she's feeling fine thank you, darling. Dick o-kay? . . . I'm sure he does . . . I will . . . I wish we could have got out of it, too. But we are rather broke just now. It isn't really so damp as all that . . . no, I like a spot of water. We even thought of buying a barge like A. P. Herbert. If London was bombed we could pull out into midstream and anchor there . . . found floating in it? . . . oh, yes, April showed me that. . . . A good riddance I can't help feeling . . . why not? I really can't sentimentalize about Dougal! Don't ask me to do that . . . that's what April says. Look, Mad—April wants to speak to you. . . ."

April got up and took the telephone from him.

"Good morning, Maddie darling," she cooed a deep caress; "are you better now? . . . that's good. . . ."

"Oh, ask Mad to drop in for tea, darling, if she has nothing better to do," said Vincent over his shoulder, as he went through the curtains into the inner room. "I must shave. I have to go somewhere."

"All right, darling . . . *do* cut off the moustache!" April, turned to the telephone again. "Vincent says, Mad darling, could you manage to get round about tea-time, if not otherwise engaged . . . yes, this afternoon . . ."

CHAPTER XXII

AT THE SCENE OF THE CRIME

" S IR VINCENT!"

Without answering, Vincent passed into the small hall, lit by an anæmic bulb. Halvorsen carefully shut the door, and put up the chain. Vincent entered a small office, with three chairs and a roll-top desk. He opened a door that led out of it, and passed with a rapid step into the room beyond.

This was apparently an engraver's workshop. It contained a large and small press: a chest of shallow drawers for the storage of paper; two workbenches and several stools, with powerful cable-joined lights, and a rack full of tools. There were shelves holding a multiplicity of bottles. The buff linoleum was stained all the colours of the rainbow—but a rainbow that had been trampled on a good deal.

Vincent turned about and looked up at Halvorsen.

"For Christ's sake stop fumbling with that budding Blimp on your lip!" the latter said irritably to him.

The blood left Vincent's lips, beneath the young moustache. His eyes fixed themselves in a steady stare upon Halvorsen's face.

"Try and bear in mind, you stupid brute, how much more you have to lose than I have," he observed.

The blazing blue eyes of Halvorsen bathed the other in an unhealthy glare, as they stood looking at each other.

"'Stupid brute,'" Halvorsen mimicked him. "Swelp me bob, Sir Vincent, sir, you are hard on us lower forms of animal life aren't you!"

"Who, but a brute," Vincent asked coldly, "and a pretty stupid one at that, would go blazing away with a gun. . . .

191

An excited kid now, and I could understand it! Did you fancy you were in the Wild West—Mister Buffalo Bill Halvorsen?"

This taunt got home. To be called *Buffalo Bill* appeared to annoy Bill Halvorsen even more than the constant iteration of *Sir Vincent* did Penhale: The salmon pink began to leave his cheeks, and the big blue blaze of his eyes died down. These two alterations, of light and of colour, left him a less pleasant personality altogether. The eyes were still blue, but the big bluff violent gaze was gone, and a good deal of cold malice was discovered at the bottom of them.

"*Stupid* I must have been, Vin—that is the word all right," he said contemptuously, "when I took up with one of the Upper Ten. This wouldn't have happened would it, if I'd not done that?"

"Let's forget about the Upper Ten, Bill."

"All right, but wasn't it one of *your* fine friends who came snooping round here—very la-di-da and *Kiss-me-Hardy*— and *Bless-my-soul, wherever have I strayed-to?* kind of, when I caught him picking a greenback out of that drawer over there. I haven't got friends like that who let themselves in and out of places, with pockets full of phoney keys!" He stirred with his fingers a metal bundle upon the table and Vincent bent over and examined them. "That's what I took out of my fine gentleman's pocket. Isn't it thanks to *you* that all this has come about?"

"Dougal," answered Vincent indifferently, "was no friend of mine. . . ."

"No, gentlemen fall out don't they, like other people! There was a dust-up over Mad."

"Stop talking about Maddie!"

"Pardon milord. But you *was* friends you and him before you had your tiff. He's the sort of friend you've always had —you lounge lizard! I should have tumbled to it sooner that that wouldn't work."

Vincent broke into a nervous laugh, which he mastered and extinguished at once.

"Because he had it in for you he came poking his lousy nose in here and got what he didn't bargain for." Halvorsen glanced at the floor. There was a different stain upon it to, that produced by the ingravure inks.

Vincent demonstrated his scorn and rage at such methods as Halvorsen's for coping with snoopers, by an expressive gesture of appeal.

"Of course he didn't bargain for it!" he cried. "Could he have supposed that I would be associated with such a fool as all that—who was 'quick on the trigger' as I suppose you think of it, in your wild and woolly mind! Couldn't you *tie him up* or something and do a bunk? Have you *grey matter* in that fat head of yours! Were you the village idiot where you come from?"

"I don't appreciate that way of talking of yours, Vin. I don't like the tone. I should stop it. You're not my boss, although you've always acted as if you was."

"Buffalo Bill climbs on his high horse!" laughed Vincent. "*And* he doesn't like his exploits belittled."

Halvorsen squinted at him, a struggle going on behind the black-out in his dull blue eyes.

"You do ask for it, Vin—you don't half fancy yourself since you've married milady!"

"I have no more time to waste," said Vincent impatiently. "I helped you dispose of your . . . victim—for my own sake not for yours. Now what do you want me to do? Help you destroy your counterfeiting plant—or transplant it elsewhere. Or hide it in my cellar? Well, I can tell you right off I'll have no more to do with it."

"No?"

"No. I recommend you to skedaddle just as quickly as possible—and evacuate your plant, if you can manage it. Dougal Tandish may have *talked*. To somebody. You never know. I ought not to be here now as a matter of fact."

"Stout fellow—brave words of a toff at bay and in a spot. But that won't *wash*. We've been too closely associated. . . ."

"Not in your homicidal exploits!"

Halvorsen gave an ugly smile.

"No?" You're an *accessory*. Have you forgotten? . . . *There's* a nice thing for a West-end clubman to be. 'Clubman and Ex-Public School Boy involved in Murder of rich socialite.' That would look well, wouldn't it, at the top of the page in your morning paper?"

He stepped nearer to Vincent.

"You have to do just what I tell you, see?" he said. "You have no choice."

"Why?" Vincent asked.

"Because you have more to lose than I have. Get me?"

"I get you, Buffalo Bill."

Halvorsen scowled.

"You're not funny. It's the way you wear your hair—on your upper lip."

"Well, I don't know what it feels like to be a murderer, but it doesn't improve your reasoning powers. You sent me a telegram didn't you?"

Halvorsen glared at him.

"That's my alibi," said Vincent, "for the blasted silly *murder* anyhow. Then the gentleman you so intelligently and obligingly bumped off was the only person who has ever caught me red-handed passing a phoney note. . . . He flourished one in my face the other day. For *he* was not over-burdened with brains either."

"You didn't tell me that! So you were cagey with me, were you?" Halvorsen snarled. "I thought you was."

"Let me go on. You saved my life, didn't you?"

"Saved your bloody life?" Halvorsen flourished an angry arm.

"You can prove you *didn't*, Bill! I swore eternal gratitude for that. Remember? I deplored your strange methods of procuring a livelihood *of course*. But I am an artist . . ."

"A *what*? A damned pro. A damned double-faced play-actor!"

Vincent drew himself up, and stared haughtily at Halvorsen.

"And you a plain, blunt man," he scornfully retorted, "who when he gets himself into a spot through his own foolishness goes all to pieces, and tries to drag his pals in ... but is *not* double-faced, oh, no!"

"Look here, Vin ..."

"Let me finish what I was saying. The artistic temperament is a damned convenient thing. No one should be without one. It is, as everyone knows, romantic. And amoral. That's a good word too. It finds the coiners-den a rather thrilling place to visit, does the artistic temperament. Consequently it gets itself sometimes into *all sorts* of scrapes, poor harmless little thing! It keeps strange company: and Vincent Penhale was no exception to the rule, as is proved by his friendship with that desperado Halvorsen. You get me?"

"I get you—a very pretty story. Very pretty indeed. There's only one thing about it ..."

A loud knocking at the front door echoed through the small flat. Halvorsen, sweat starting out on his forehead, sprang towards a drawer in the work bench. Seizing a revolver that lay in it, he turned furiously towards the door, his hair ruffled, his eye wild. Vincent stepped in front of the door.

Pointing back towards the empty drawer, Vincent said, matter-of-factly,

"Put it back in the drawer."

Halvorsen eyed him with a little sneer that came and went: every time the will-to-action surged up and was frustrated, the little sneer came out.

"Have you lost your wits entirely?" Vincent asked him, in a rapid undertone. "Listen to what I tell you. You have a perfectly sound plea of self-defence, if the worst came to the worst. You are not a *murderer*—understand?—any more than a man who shoots a trespasser or a housebreaker."

"I know that," Halvorsen muttered. "I don't need you to tell me."

"What are you brandishing that gun for then? You discovered an unknown man upon your premises. He had been drinking, he picked up something to throw at you. You lost your head and fired on him. Understand?"

There was a volley of knocks.

"That *is* the police!"

Vincent took the gun from Halvorsen and returned it to the drawer, wiping the place where he had held it with his handkerchief, turning it over in the drawer to wipe each side. Halvorsen watched him: he returned to the door.

"We don't want to murder the police do we, exactly? That wouldn't be so intelligent either."

Speaking very quickly, as if to get as much said as possible in the time available, Vincent started, in galloping undertone. "Bill, please listen to me, as a friend—we're probably both for it and this is our last chance to talk. You shall have the best Counsel, Bill, money can buy. If I manage to keep outside all this, I can promise that. Otherwise, if you drag me in, we are both sunk for I can't help you then. You understand that? Deny the shooting. If they pin it on you, say o-kay!—you lost your head, that was all there was to it. You found a stranger in your dump. He threatened you. Even if you get a manslaughter sentence, we can have it whittled down. We could appeal."

"I don't give a coot's backside what they do to me, the lousy bastards!" Halvorsen answered violently.

"Are you a half-wit—or only resolved to rat on your pal? I thought better of you than that, Bill. So long as I'm free, I'll work for you . . ."

"You'll work for yourself, you mean . . ."

Rolling rat-tats broke in from the other side of the door.

"All right, I won't argue with you. No time to waste. Here is the dope. . . . You saved my life . . ."

"Blast you . . . I'd save your bloody life for you!"

"Don't be pernickety, Bill.—It would sound swell you old fool! Be a lifeguard! What better alibi? It would go down with the jury like one o'clock. Twelve good men and true would go allmushy, Bill, when they'd heard what you'd done. I was on a holiday wasn't I—in the Lakes, that's the best place for a lifeguard. See? I fall in. Awfully damn, clumsy of me! You, Bill, happen to be passing. You observe a fellow-man in distress. Do you hesitate? Not you, Bill! Not a bit of it. You plunge in! You bring me safely to terra firma. Very heroic. Very unlike a *murderer*, what! Now, Bill, don't be a silly ass. Underwrite that story—back me up through thick and thin. I'm sixty times more use to you outside, than inside a jail. Get that in your head. Let me work for you outside, as your friend, the toff. (I'm not a toff—but let that ride.) I will do my damndest for you—we'll get you off as lightly as we can." There was a thunderous assault upon the door. The Law was obviously in no mood to wait any longer. "Now go to the door and let that nasty crowd in. Leave it to me to deal with them, as far as you are able."

He pushed Halvorsen towards the door into the office, opened it, and Halvorsen passed through, cursing as he went, as the knocking continued. Vincent followed him.

"What noisy visitors you do have, Bill!" Vincent exclaimed in a high-pitched cissified stage voice. "That's the worst of being such a *popular* boy!"

Bill scowled at his drawling, smiling mate, and went out into the passage.

"Who's that!" he called roughly. "Stop making that bloody noise."

Then he took the chain down and opened the door.

Three men came briskly in, one of them a uniformed police-constable.

"Mr William Halvorsen?" one of the plain-clothes men inquired, looking from Vincent to Halvorsen.

Halvorsen nodded.

"That's my name. What's this all about? What can I do for you?"

"Hard of hearing aren't you, Mr Halvorsen? Only just heard us?" inquired the detective with ironic politeness. He was a well-washed, stoutish, pale-faced police-dog. He had one eye larger than the other. The small one had much more expression than the large one.

"No. I heard you before," Halvorsen answered disagreeably. "I wondered what the hell it was. I thought someone had gone mad."

"No, we are not mad," the man said quietly. "I am a detective-inspector. I should like to ask you a few questions, Mr Halvorsen."

"All right. Ask away." Halvorsen took out a packet of cigarettes and put one in his mouth.

Vincent, who had kept in the background, standing in the doorway that led into the workshop, stepped forward.

"Well, I think I'll be moving along, Bill. These gentlemen wish to talk to you in private I expect. Give me a call later on. About five."

The detective stared at him rudely, but with the circumspection that his 'educated' accent imposed.

"No, you stop here, too," he said. "I shall have some questions to put to you as well. May I have your name, please?"

"My name," said Vincent, with a kind of bashful hesitation, and in a low voice, "is Vincent Penhale."

The second plain-clothes man, who had taken a note-book out of his pocket, said, "P-i-n-h-a-i-l?"

Vincent gave him, politely and soberly, the correct spelling.

"Sir Vincent Penhale," Halvorsen, supplemented, leering disagreeably at Vincent.

"Sir Vincent?" repeated the second detective. "I am sorry sir, we have to take your name like this.

"We are investigating the murder, Sir Vincent, of Mr Dougal Tandish," said the detective-inspector.

Vincent started; so naturally that Halvorsen looked quickly up at him in astonishment.

"Dougal Tandish!" Vincent exclaimed incredulously. "Did you say, the *murder* . . .?"

The detective-inspector nodded, grim and short.

"Yes, the murder. That's right," he said. "Why, did you know him, sir?"

"Oh, yes. I knew him," said Vincent briefly, looking away. "It's news to me though that he's dead. Was he really . . . bumped off?"

The detective-inspector looked offended.

"If that's the way you wish to express it, Sir Vincent—yes, he was," he coughed, "brutally done to death." This, he felt, was how a knight *ought* to think of such an unseemly occurrence: though his experience told him that a rakish young knight, like this one, might favour a more racy expression. "But, let's have a look in here." The inspector advanced into the inner workshop. He glanced quickly round and whistled. "What's all this?" he said, turning towards Halvorsen.

Looking sullenly away, Halvorsen shrugged his shoulders. "What do you mean, what's all this?" he said.

"What sort of a dump have you here?"

"I am an engraver," Halvorsen told him. "This is where I work."

"Very interesting," observed the inspector. He said something under his breath to the other detective, who returned his note-book to his pocket, closed the door into the office, and stood in front of it.

"What sort of engraving do you do, Mr Halvorsen?" enquired the inspector.

"All sorts," said Halvorsen thickly. "But, mostly ten-spots."

The inspector looked at him quickly.

"Ten-spots. Ten dollar bills," Halvorsen said, shrugging, with a contemptuous smile.

Frowning, Vincent broke his silence.

"Do you mean, Bill, you *forged* . . .?"

"That's what they call it, Sir Vincent: when other people do it," Halvorsen grinned. "When a bank does it, they have a different name. I call this my *mint*. In my small way, I have just as much right to have a mint, as the government has." The detectives exchanged glances.

"Bill, you fool, you don't mean to say you've been doing

that! I think you ought to have told me!" Vincent expostulated, in a low and distressed voice. "But, if you're not having a joke, Bill—as I hope you are—I'll stand by you."

"Thank you, milord!" sneered Halvorsen.

The detective-inspector consulted in low tones with his colleague in front of the door.

"How dreadful this is, Bill!" Vincent said, with a gesture of great discouragement. "This is perfectly awful! Why, oh, why, didn't you ask *me*, Bill, if you were in need of money!"

"Didn't like to somehow!" Halvorsen said. "Pride, I suppose it was. You know how it is. I'm not a good borrower. I preferred minting a bit myself." He laughed coarsely at the detectives.

"Oh, Bill, you *fool*!" Vincent wailed, in his deepest contralto. "You great big fool!"

Halvorsen flushed.

"I'm not the *only* fool in this room." He began darkly fuming. "I may *look* the biggest, just for the moment . . ."

The inspector wheeled towards him sharply.

"Halvorsen!" he barked. "Do you know anything about the murder of Dougal Tandish?"

"No more than you do," Halvorsen answered. "I read about it in the papers this morning."

"You had no hand in it, yourself?"

"I?" Halvorsen pointed at himself. "Why should *I* have had anything to do with it?"

The inspector went up to him.

"I am going to arrest you, Halvorsen, pending investigations here. You must come with me."

He grasped one of Halvorsen's wrists and slipped the handcuffs on him.

"O-kay," said Halvorsen staring down at his hands. "I suppose you know what you're doing. . . ."

"Bill!" Vincent stopped him in an urgent voice. "I will immediately obtain a lawyer for you. Refuse to make any statement until you are legally represented. . . . There is some dreadful mistake here, Inspector. I insist on my friend,

Mr Halvorsen, being properly represented. I am quite sure he is no criminal. . . . Remember, Bill, you must at once have the advice of a lawyer, and refuse to be questioned, do you hear, until you have seen him."

"Very well, Sir Vincent," said the inspector frowning. "Your *friend*, Mr Halvorsen, is in his rights to have legal advice of course. If he *wishes* to make a statement . . ."

"My friend—and if a man had saved your life, inspector, I think you would call him your *friend*, unless you were lost to all sense of common gratitude—my friend, William Halvorsen, if he has been guilty of anything, has, I am convinced, done so without fully realizing the nature of the crime he was . . . er perpetrating. As I know, he is a simple soul . . ."

"Very well, sir. That remains to be seen."

"Quite. But I am determined to see that he is properly represented."

"Very well, sir." The other detective opened the door, and the uniformed constable appeared in the doorway.

"You will accompany us, Sir Vincent, to the police station," said the Inspector.

"That is as you please, inspector," Vincent answered coldly.

Placing his hat upon his head at the angle affected by Admirals of the Fleet, he passed the plain-clothes men, swept round the hulking city constable, and stepping haughtily, headed the exodus from the apartment, followed by the dejected and handcuffed, Halvorsen, and the somewhat abashed police-officers. There was a professional glitter in his frowning eye. It was a most creditable exit.

PART III

ONE LAW FOR THE RICH

CHAPTER XXIII

FALSUM IN UNO, FALSUM IN OMNIBUS

A PRIL heard steps and put up her head to listen. But it was the discreet domestic step of Willis: it had none of the crisp vitality of Vincent's footfall. She was sitting by herself in the 'throne-room.' The towering easel that served no purpose, except to impress, threw a giant shadow: a rectangular black skeleton sprawled upon the opposite wall and the painted ceiling. A silver-handled tray with tea was on the table before her. Covered dishes of scones and toast were echelonned upon the tiers of a tea-stand.

It was the rich, quiet, tea-hour—with the servant's dutiful footsteps again dying away outside: and April sat motionless, as if in mourning, in a plain black frock, gazing at an open evening newspaper. Its headlines shouted in the stillness—

"POOR BOY PASSES HIMSELF OFF
AS BARONET."

Vincent was to be released on bail, in Mrs Mallow's recognizances. April awaited his arrival.

Since that terrible moment, three days before, when the police had arrived with a search warrant, and, after turning everything upside down—even to the extent of ripping up floorboards and examining the lining of her quilted handkerchief bag—had arrested Vincent, she had learned very little of what was really happening, except that it appeared from the papers that Halvorsen—invited to dinner, by Vincent, and treated as a friend—was a criminal. *That* didn't surprise her! But it did surprise her that Vincent hadn't guessed something of the sort himself.

Then Vincent had been found by the police with Halvor-

sen, in the place where the latter forged his notes. Why had
not Vincent realized what was going on there? She supposed
the police asked that question too. They did not know
Vincent as well as she did, or understand how unworldly
he really was!

It seemed that as yet, they had formulated no specific
charges against him. (How could they, since Vincent had
obviously done nothing, except—for silly, romantic reasons
—known Halvorsen?) But the bail was heavy. The police
were very unpleasant about him, it seemed—in spite of the
fact they had nothing against him. And here was this strange
report that Vincent had tried to impersonate a *baronet* of all
ridiculous things: and was, in reality, a coster or something
equally fantastic!

In the firelight, which painted her face a lurid peach, she
let her mind drift back to the beginnings of her life of love,
to their holiday in Venice: brooding, she saw the handsome,
strange, young man again, as she first had caught sight of
him. It was in the lounge of the hotel. She recalled their golden days upon the Lido. She caught her breath as she remembered his wonderful high spirits. His seemed a life
without a cloud. Her life, as it moved to mingle more and
more with his, appeared to be passing into an unruffled
golden age in which children—her children—would disport
themselves, far from all threats except the gallant martial
one of war. How absolutely she had lost her heart, in
a manner that she could not have believed possible. And now
all this—like fate unmasking itself, with hideous insults.

Her gentle mind, of which the gentle contours of her face
were the outward expression, was not shaped to receive a
content such as this. Even to find a place in her consciousness at all, such events must civilize themselves, be toned
down. Such a drama as had begun to be played all round
her—with herself forcibly recruited as one of the cast—
could only be seriously entertained by her inside an asylum.
Outside, it just could not be true: such things simply did
not happen. It was a dream from which she would wake up

—put her arms round Vincent's neck and cry a little, then forget about it. This was not *real*—she refused belief to it.

Could it be true, she wondered, however, what the newspapers said about Vincent's family? It could not be—*Poor*, they might be, yes; but not poor *like that*. He could not possibly be like he was, had they been really . . . well, common working people. She looked down at the newspaper again, which described a visit to Vincent's mother's home. But, Vincent had lost his mother ages ago—therefore that was a palpable lie! His sister a 'charlady'! Preposterous! All that he had told her would be then a tissue of lies, which was utterly unthinkable.

She could imagine his father being . . . oh, a very fashionable *dentist* . . . horrid, as that would be. But not a . . . railway porter. She shuddered at the vistas this line of thought opened up.

She had been talking to her mother on the telephone, just before Willis had brought in the tea. Mary Mallow seemed inclined to place some credence in the newspaper story— which was just like her!

"*I* don't see why his mother shouldn't be a charwoman!" she had declared. "Why not? He's quite capable of it. He is capable of hiding up almost *anything*. I'm afraid, my dear, we have been fools, both of us. It's too late crying over spilt milk. But we've been *sold a pup* it seems to me! . . . It was all my fault."

Sir Lionel Mallow, her mother had informed April, was furious. He was in Cannes. Reporters had been on his track. He had refused to see them. But he was speechless with rage. Oh, dear, what a mess it all was! April sighed, a resigned and worried little sigh.

In a few minutes Vincent would be here, anyhow. He would clear all this up—and some action ought to be taken against this horrid newspaper. That they could discuss when he arrived. These papers must be stopped!

That abominable man Halvorsen! Nothing surprised her about *him*. She had always known no good would come of

Vincent's friendship with such a person as that. Even if the beastly man *had* saved his life! Vincent's nature was too loyal, too generous, that was the truth of the matter.

April had just lifted the lid of the toast-dish to see if it was any use keeping the tea things there any longer, when there was a step in the hall outside—an ominous step, like that of a heavier man than Vincent: but the door opened, and it was Vincent that stood there.

She rose dazed and smiling. She saw how much he had changed and her heart sank. His vitality seemed entirely to have deserted him. Without a greeting, without a smile, he walked over to her, and took her sadly in his arms. It was more like a farewell than a reunion.

"My darling," he said, "*forgive* me! I have made a mess of everything. You are *so* kind. I have not been kind to you, April, my love. I have been a brute. But that's what I *am*. I am—just a brute."

"Please don't, darling Vincent . . . say such horrible things. Everything will come all right. It *must*. Of course it will."

The wilful, watchful, mask, its eyes closed, against which he pressed her head as he spoke, started to writhe and to break up. He took his arms away from her and hid his face in his hands. "Just a brute," he muttered. "Just a brute."

He sank down beside her. There he was huddled beneath her, upon the sofa from which she had risen to greet him. His shoulders shook, dry strangled sounds came from beneath his hands. He had surrendered to his misery for a moment, at the contacts of this gentle love which he knew he had betrayed. But this was a situation she found as difficult to cope with as she would, if a man sank upon his knees and asked for her 'hand.'

April placed herself beside him. How could she comfort him. She felt so frightened she scarcely knew what she was saying.

"Vincent, darling, *why* are you upset like this?" She asked. "What has happened, darling? I believe in you, whatever people say in the papers." Suddenly the shaking stopped. "When this is over, Vincent, we will go away—to the other end of the world. We won't ever think of this, again."

He shook his head in his hands.

"Why not, darling!" she asked, dismayed.

"Because!" he said. He uncovered his face and turned it towards her. It was so gloomy and empty that she recoiled from him. He took her face in his hands and kissed her.

"You are so sweet, April. You are so *kind* a girl—far too good for me, you know!" He threw himself back. "Why do you stick to me? You oughtn't to. You ought to leave me."

"Vincent! I will not listen. . . .!"

He got up from beside her.

"It's all the worse for me, too," he said. "It makes me feel a more rotten egg even than I am! You ought to have cleared out. Why aren't you a brute, too? Why can't we all be brutes? Life would be simpler that way."

He sat down facing her. Catching sight of the newspaper open at the account of his humble backgrounds, his face hardened up. Toughness seemed at once to return. He looked coldly at its headlines.

"Ah, you have seen that?" he said, pointing at the paper.

"Yes, isn't it *horrid*. All those lies. I do think the news-papers are the most disgusting things. I have told Willis to discontinue *that* one, anyway. I refuse to have it in the house."

"Smart work!" Vincent laughed. "But unfortunately, what they say there happens to be true."

"True! But have you read it?"

"Yes, I read it on the way back . . . from prison. Yes. It's fairly accurate. I didn't try to pass myself off as a knight. That was *their* mistake. Halvorsen called me 'Sir Vincent.' That's one of his tricks. But all allowance made for the technique of reporting, it is true enough."

"I knew it couldn't be true. Of course, if you made allow-ances *enough*, then anything. . . .!"

"Well!" He shrugged. "My father and mother were

working people," he said quietly. "I am pukka *working-class*. It was born, as they say, in the gutter. I had intended to tell you. But not *like this*." He laughed and shrugged.

"But, why on earth didn't you tell me, Vincent? I shouldn't have minded. Why should I? It would make no odds to me, if you father was a sweep."

Vincent laughed—it sounded like a happy laugh, that lost itself halfway and turned unhappy. He got up, went over to her, and kissed her on the side of he head. Then he went and stood with his back to the fire. He was warming his fingers, which felt like icicles.

"You're a swell girl, April. I wish we had met . . . oh, long ago. Though it may make no difference to *you*, if my parents were working people, it makes a hell of a lot of difference to the Law. The fact that these lads have ferreted out my 'humble origin' will tell very much against me, with some old snob of a judge."

"I don't believe that, Vincent. I only know *one* judge."

"One Law for the Rich—One for the Poor. You can't escape from facts. It is the *Law of the Poor*, that now I am up against."

He had a swift, restrained, gesture of despairing finality.

"I tried to escape," he cried.

April sat up, in anguished alarm.

"*When*, Vincent . . . just now, do you mean? Not from . . . from the prison?"

"No," he laughed. "It was a much more terrible prison from which I tried to make my getaway. I was *born* in a prison. . . . I tried to escape from my Class."

He hung his head.

"But now," he went on, "they have set their bloodhounds on me. Their Press. And I shall be brought back and punished bitterly for *that*. . . . My punishment has already begun."

Relief had shown itself in her face while he was speaking.

"Vincent, you *exaggerate*. That will make no difference at all. What does it matter what your people were? Besides, you have *done nothing*, Vincent. All this is beastly—all this in the Press. But, they can't do anything to you, if you have done nothing . . . criminal!"

Vincent stroked his chin wearily. Then his fingers strayed to his new moustache. He began tugging at it, as if he would pull it out.

"I wish you'd shave that off!" April said. "It makes you look . . . I don't know how to put it . . . *Villains* always have moustaches!"

He laughed. "And this hardly is the moment to make myself look more of a villain than is necessary, what! Well, look here. There is something I ought to tell you, without delay. It would be unjust to you, not to tell you. . . . Besides, you'll find out."

April became flushed. She looked at him for a moment with the dumb appeal of animals—as if she would have stopped him, understanding he was about to hurt her. Then, she put down her head. At least she would not *look*.

"Well, here it is," he said, with a touch of his old arrogant competence. "They may not succeed in fastening it on me. It depends mainly on the line Halvorsen takes. And he cannot be depended on, I'm afraid. When he learns I am a slum-product like himself, that will influence him. It will make him angry. My supposed aristocratic education was always admired, believe it or not, by this rugged radical. It is perfectly extraordinary how snobbish most *radicals* are!"

"I suppose they must be," she mumbled.

"Well, you wouldn't exactly expect a Red to attach any importance to Haileybury! But that is of no importance. . . . I don't know why I'm talking about that now. April, I have, for eighteen• months or more, passed forged notes for Halvorsen." April slumped a little forward, and stared at the rug at her feet. "I inherited no money. That was a lie. I have no property in Canada or anywhere else. I was only able to take this place, transport myself to Venice, and all the rest, on the passing of counterfeit money."

April became very pale. She looked up at him. She now

saw the reality standing in front of her. A man, who, six months ago, had been a stranger, who was now her husband, and who . . . subsisted by criminal means. The very sofa she sat on had been purchased with forged notes.

Horror riveted her mild grey eyes upon this handsome face, confessing itself a cheat—this ever so vaguely wolfish face, now ornamented with a half-grown black moustache, so gravely examining her, as if it were a doctor reporting the results of a diagnosis. She could not have taken her eyes off him, if she had wanted to. But she did not want to. She wished to familiarize herself with what she now saw for the first time. The original stranger she had met in Venice, and the greatly loved man, that was her husband, whose child she was carrying, struggled for mastery. It would depend upon *which* of these two men she found herself looking at, when she stopped gazing at Vincent, what her subsequent attitude towards him would be.

"I am not a criminal," he said, very dejectedly, as if the reflection was not a very stimulating one. "At least I'm not certain any longer *what* I am: but I don't believe I was cut out to be a rogue."

"Don't say such absolutely dreadful things, Vincent!" she implored. April was seeing now standing before her, only her lover, driven to the wall, in need of her help. The battle had been won over the dark stranger, with the disreputable black moustache that gave a wolfish prominence to the cheekbones.

"They *are* dreadful things," he agreed. "But, they have to be said." He took a cigarette out of a silver box upon the table, and lit it slowly. "Halvorsen used to talk to me about . . . oh, capitalist society, the usual thing: but also more particularly the theory of money. I didn't understand much about money when I met up with him. I didn't, for instance, regard notes as *credit slips*, for food, or as rent-tickets. As they in fact are. Didn't know that Banks had no gold capital to back up the so-called *cheques* they issue to us with such lighthearted prodigality. Do you know anything about all

that stuff? Don't suppose you do. Nor did I, till Bill Halvorsen explained all the doings to me. It is really *very* demoral-
izing. Money-theory is much more subversive than straight,
emotional, radical stuff. To learn that a Bank is really a
licensed *forger* of paper-money was a new one on me. I had
always thought, that if people were *poor*, it was because there
wasn't enough wealth (gold) to go round: so some had to go
short. Something simple-hearted like that. This really did
sap my resistance to temptation—Bill is, as you know, a very
turbulent *have-not* indeed . . ."

"Turbulent! Ugh!" April shuddered belligerently.

"Yes, well. Bill hates the social order as it exists to-day,
and regards it as something like a highly moral act to defraud
it. He is a moralist, is old Bill. In his view, the modern state
is based upon organized—*legalized*—Fraud. See? Consequently, to counterfeit its fraudulent and oppressively administered currency appears to him, an act of poetic justice.
. . . I know it must sound screwy to you. But that's how he
feels."

"But *you* don't believe that, do you, Vincent?" she asked
very uneasily.

"Never mind, for the moment," he laughed, "what I
think, what I think *now*. I am not such a moralist as Bill.
But this is a historical sketch. We are speaking of the past.
It is sufficient to say that these . . . sophistries, call them,
fitted in with my rather bitter mood of those days. I was in-
credibly broke. One day he told me somebody had made him
a present of a packet of phoney notes, for a joke. He said he
was going to try and pass them. He would just say, if caught,
that some unscrupulous tradesman had passed on the bad
note to him. I took one, and said I would see what I could
do with it. It was a ten-spot. A ten-dollar bill. I got two quid
and something for it at a Cook's Office. That was the first
step. The same imaginary bloke (for of course it was old
Bill himself manufacturing the beastly things), gave him
another packet of greenbacks, and fivers too. I tried my hand
again. I scooped a hundred and fifty pounds at one blow. I

had never *seen* so much money, all at once. Bill gave me that back. He said—*No old man. You stick to that.*—When I had spent it, I felt the need of *more*. When I learnt I could have as many of these things as I wanted, provided I returned a specified proportion of the proceeds to Bill, I was started upon the downward path, I am afraid. I was terribly afraid at first. But it became like a drug. It was a habit that was all the more difficult to break, because I had always been so poor. Now I could put my fingers to my nose at people and keep them there. But I knew that the pitcher that goes often to the well, and so forth. I knew that *one* day I should be caught, and I should have to pay the price of this miraculous freedom. When you and I met, I was by way of curing myself of this insidious habit. Had all this not happened with Tandish, I should never have touched one of Halvorsen's *phoney's* again. I really was through, for good with that. I had told him so . . . He was exceedingly annoyed."

April gave vent to a sound of suppressed rage.

"That horrible, evil, man. I *knew* he was something to avoid—I loathed him, from the first time I saw him. Oh, Vincent, why did you ever have anything to do with that beast!"

"Partly," Vincent answered, "just to get even with the world. Halvorsen was the enemy of society, and society had not treated me too well. I am not a Red, like Bill. But I do not like being kicked around."

"But, you and Halvorsen—how can you mention yourself in the same breath with that brute!"

"Halvorsen and I *have* things in common, I am sorry, April. I am *terribly* sorry for the part that you have been forced to play in this story. But there it is. I mustn't tell you any more lies. Bill and I have things in common that you and I have not got."

"Oh, dear," she said. "That monstrous man! It was *he* who led you into all this. That is plain enough—what you have told me, shows it. Nothing you can say will convince me to the contrary."

Vincent passed his hand over his face. He felt so tired now that he had to make a great effort to go on.

"Well, let that pass. What does that matter? Nothing can be taken back—nothing be done, differently. All that happens according to some plan. To the great Architect of the Universe, I am a necessary flourish—at the foot of some column, or to elaborate some roof-gutter."

April looked up at him, with frightened eyes.

"I do not apologize. Or, I only apologize to *you*, April, whom I have played a very sorry trick upon, without really intending it. (I was too much of a brute to understand.) I have passed a lot of counterfeit stuff on *you*. A pack of lies, to trap you, my poor darling. That was a far greater offence, than any circulating of phoney notes I have ever engaged in."

She shook her head, vigorously, but hopelessly.

"But, it all hangs together," he said. "*Falsum in uno, falsum in omnibus*. That is about all the Latin that I know. That's fearfully true: one falsity leads to another, it is all of a piece. I am just as sham as the sham notes I lived on. The more I lived upon them, the more sham I became."

April went on staring at him, now too numbed and dismayed to make any more response at all. She tried to speak, but though her lips moved, they were so dry, no words came. At last she whispered,

"Vincent."

"Darling? Yes?"

"They can . . . *prove* nothing against you!"

At the reflection of what these words implied, she shrank back into herself. She, too, was conniving to defeat the ends of justice. Now she had, however indirectly, joined the Halvorsen gang! But she did not care! So long as Vincent, her love, should be spared, it did not matter about *her*.

But Vincent sadly shook his head.

"I shall keep it up," he said. "I shall keep playing my part —with a great deal of panache—a great deal of clatter. There is nothing else for me to do. But this parole is an interlude, no more than that. You see, there's the question of Dougal."

April's face whitened, her nails dug into the stuff of the sofa upon which she sat.

"Dougal?" she asked, weakly panting out the words. "You mean . . . the man—murdered? You don't mean that!"

Vincent nodded.

"That's right. Halvorsen shot him."

April clapped her hand up on her mouth, as if to stop a sudden cry. Then she lifted it to her hair, which she patted.

"For some reason, best known to himself," Vincent proceeded to inform her, "Tandish went snooping round the place where Halvorsen engraved his notes. He was a romantic idiot: it is just the sort of thing he *would* do. Bill found him there and killed him. . . . Where I come in as an *accessory*. Bill asked me to go and see him. I had no idea what had happened and like a fool, I *went*. He showed me the body of Tandish. He asked me to help him get rid of it. Like a fool, I did so. He may not *always* keep his mouth shut about that."

April swayed a little, then she slid down sideways, rolling onto the floor. Vincent rushed forward but was too late to catch her. Running to the door, shouting as he went for Willis, he made for their sleeping-quarters above.

"Ah, Willis," he said, pausing at the head of the stairs, as Willis appeared below. "Mrs Penhale has fainted. Fetch a jug of water. Quick!"

Chapter XXIV

"SKIP THE MIDDLE-CLASS!"

"SHE died last night," Vincent said.

For two mornings he had breakfasted here, alone like this, since April had been removed to the hospital, and this was the third. He sat bathed in cold London sunlight, in his Thames-side sun-trap, a yellow Daily propped against the coffee-pot.

He resented the festive light, battering his person without warmth. The poor woman who had died—and the fault was his, it was he who had caused her death—haunted, with her gestures, her soft and friendly voice, this lonely, sunny, cell.

This was a cell of his own making: full of cold, hard, sunlight, like a symbol of his mind. The cheerless glitter meant nothing. It was like the frosty smile of a deaths-head. He felt uneasy in his exposed position—like a parrot up in a cage, making loud remarks he did not understand, but *knowing* he did not understand them. A most luckless sort of parrot.

He did not want to kiss his hand any more to passing tug-captains. Tug-captains had lost their meaning. He hated tug-captains. He hated gulls.—He detested Willis.

Willis stood at a respectful distance, halfway between his master and the curtained arch that led into the room, of which this was an offshoot—April and Vincent's bedroom.

As the man said nothing, Vincent observed shortly—

"Mrs Penhale is dead."

He frowned at his nails, like a teacher waiting for the boy at the bottom of the class to find the answer to *What are ten times ten?*

217

"Has Madame passed away, sir?" The man at last had got it. "It doesn't hardly sound possible. Poor lady . . . I, indeed, am very sorry, sir. I am, indeed, sir."

Vincent lifted up his face to gaze bleakly at his servant. "She died from a haemorrhage. Loss of blood. She was, as you know, going to have a child."

"Indeed, sir. No, I was not aware that madam . . ."

Vincent's face darkened, but he restrained himself.

"Yes," he said. "I wish to see no one to-day, Willis. I am out. You understand?"

"Yes, sir."

"Except Mrs Mallow. She may come in. Or my sister, of course."

"Yes, sir."

As Willis was withdrawing, Vincent called after him.

"Willis. Come here a moment."

"Sir?"

"I suppose you've seen all this stuff in the newspapers? About myself. You don't believe all you read in the newspapers, I hope, Willis?"

Vincent lay back, thrusting his hands in his dressing-gown pockets, and looking up at the ceiling.

"I should be very sorry to believe all I read in the newspapers, sir," said Willis.

"It would be a pity to do that," Vincent agreed evenly. "Give one a pretty lousy view of life, wouldn't it!"

"You're right, it would, sir."

"That's all, Willis."

Willis inclined his head, and, with a minimum of sound, withdrew.

Vincent smiled to himself, under his musketeer moustache, a scornful and angry smile. "Blast!" he said, as the thick glass cap of the coffee-pot shot off, when he inclined it towards his cup.

Willis, he reflected, must go! This ceremonious life must end at once. He could not go on any longer in this way. He would supply Willis with a first-class reference, (not that it

would be of much use to him!). He would say he was a good
housedog and cleanly in his habits. "The English are like
nice dogs." A good saying of somebody's. What a genius for
servitude—and they a supposedly 'free' people! Sayings of
the English themselves about the English. Sturdy and unreal
sayings. That one for instance: 'You may lead an Englishman. You cannot drive him.' There, if you like, is a damn-
fool proverb! S'not a question of leading or driving. An
Englishman just follows you around, if you've got an Oxford
Accent. You don't have to do any *leading*. All you have to
do, is to open your mouth, and allow a few words to escape,
with that magical inflection, hall-marked Cam or Isis, and
it's all right. You are his Leader by virtue of your accent.
(Hence the bankruptcy, of leadership.)

Mr Perl was perfectly right, Vincent sullenly mused: the
class-nuisance in England is not the fault of any one class.
(He would like to see Humbert again, Vincent told himself).
'Tis the *nice-dog* mind, that does it. Vincent left it at that,
with an aggressive shrug.

He gave the newspaper in front of him a disobliging poke.
"New Names Every Morning," was the column he had
under his eyes. Now that dirty, mud-slinging gossip-writer
had got after him. What was this? Her poor hands were
hardly cold, but already she was being turned into sausage
meat. Gossip fodder. Poor April!

"The attractive niece of Sir Lionel Mallow . . . colonial
administrator . . . brilliant record . . . Mesopotamia . . . often
to be seen Klan Box Club . . . Princess Merdinsky . . . husband the versatile, Vincent Penhale . . . bogus baronet . . .
Richard the Second . . . the Dougal Tandish case . . . out on
bail."—Great balls of fire! he inwardly burst forth. *Spies in
the hospital!* Ten-thirty, life is pronounced extinct. A nurse's
mouth at the telephone at thirty-one. Ten-forty, the gossip-
machine gets it. Started on the spot to mash into gossip-
meat. Poor April! Poor, poor, poor, poor, poor, *poor*,
April!

He gazed at a gull. The identical bird, very likely, that

April had fed with bread last week, from the window. It seemed anchored there, so very likely it was. Thought there was a gull-lover up above it, in the window, instead of just another tough-guy, as was the case.

He took up the telephone, which was ringing, and said "Yes . . . Vincent Penhale . . . good morning . . . certainly —when? . . . all right, I shall expect you."

His mail and April's lay in a neat pile beside the tray. He picked up a letter with a Canadian postmark. He opened it slowly and unwillingly. A letter from his sister, Victoria, was not what he wanted. He did not want to hear about Victoria's coloured butler just now, or the Japanese gardener. He never wanted to hear them mentioned again! He read half a page with brooding eyes.

"We had a perfectly swell time, down at Cedar Springs. The Brabazons came along—Bob Brabazon, I don't know if I've told you, Vincent dear, he is the President of the Western Canada Canners Co., and his wife is a distant cousin of Mackenzie King—our Premier, you know. Lady Beazeley-Brown was there, too—she's a great old dear is Emily B-B . . ."

He threw the letter into the waste-basket, without proceeding any farther with the boastful catalogue of personalities. He *never* would open a letter of Victoria's again, lest Lady Beazeley-Brown should be waiting for him inside it. He would go mad if he ever heard the name of Lady Beazeley-Brown again!

On the back of the envelope of one of the letters addressed to April, was a coronet. Also it smelt. It had the Mayfair postmark—it had the Mayfair stink! He tore it in four pieces and threw it in after the Beastly-Brown letter, among the cigar-ends and other trash. All much of a muchness— Meltingbrooks or Beazeley-Browns. All part of the same catafalque. Big and little fleas certainly, there were. But all were parasites—they all had *that* in common.

April, however, had transcended her Meltingbrooks, in a way that Victoria could never emancipate herself from her

Beazeley-Browns. Victoria made him see what he had lost—April, the first human being ever to say to him, and what was more, *to mean it*, that it would be all the same to her if his father was a sweep. He had not known till yesterday, that there was anything stronger than Class. In marrying April he had thought he was marrying Class. Love was a thing he had not so much as suspected. And all this was having terrible effects.

The telephone bell shook him—he reached over and took the little sky-blue dumb-bell off its prong. Pleasure lit up his face, but it died out, almost at once.

"Maddie, darling—how are you, my sweet?. . . No, she is —she is dead . . . yes, darling, I feel the world has come to an end—I don't know what's happened, darling. I don't know what has happened—it's no use trying. All I know is that even *your* voice does not sound so sweet . . . no, no, I'm pretty poor company, but do drop up, my dear . . . what? *Left*—how do you mean, *left*! . . . Dick *not coming back?* Do you mean to say the unspeakable howling cad has *left you*, because of *my* . . . no one could be such a louse! I can't believe it. Where has he gone to—did he say?. . . at a lawyer's—my god—a lawyer! . . . come at once . . . Mrs Mallow may be here but that makes no difference . . . Good-bye."

He put the telephone down with a bang and crouched back in his chair, as if expecting something to spring on him out of the sunlight—something *else* to come rushing up out of nowhere at his throat. Now Maddie must suffer because of him! There was no question of ill-luck—these were effects of which his actions were the cause.

He had driven Dick (the skunk, to be driven) from Maddie's side. Poor April had seen the abyss at her feet. She had seen the end of all her dreams. That abyss was his handiwork. April had not wanted to live. In her eyes, in those last hours of hers on earth, poor child, he had read that too plainly to be mistaken. Even Halvorsen would not be where he was . . .! Bill's charge against him had something to it.

He was guilty there as well: Dougal was *his* mistake. His . . . client.

He sprang up out of the chair and began pacing about in what he had thought of as his *cell*. Soon probably he would have a less pleasant cell than this to pace up and down in— of an evening. For fourteen or fifteen years!

Willis appeared from the side of the curtain.

"Mrs Mallow is in the studio, sir," he said.

Vincent quickly descended the stairs. Maud, Mrs Mallow's old housemaid, was sitting in the hall.

"'Morning, Maud," he said, as he passed her.

"Good morning," she answered stiffly.

No "sir" this time! He smiled. Let her keep her "sir," the silly old Victorian skivvy, for some crooked company-promoter who had enough jack to keep his name out of the Press.

He entered the "throne-room" and closed the door. Mrs Mallow, who looked very frail, he thought, and dark about the eyes, stood by the fireplace. He walked over to her and bowed, moving his lips, then stood waiting for her to speak.

"Well!" she said, gazing blankly and bleakly straight into his eyes, in intelligent communion (on heart-to-heart lines). "You've made a pretty mess of things, haven't you!"

"I have," he said humbly. "I know that."

"If you could only have refrained from dramatizing yourself! . . ."

"I am an actor," he said, and shrugged. "But I am not acting when I say I would give . . . oh, whatever was demanded that I *have* . . . if April could have been spared."

Mrs Mallow wiped tears from her eyes.

"Oh, well . . . I do not wish to censure you! I blame myself. But you are not a very wise young man, are you!"

"Not very smart, I am afraid," he agreed quietly.

"It would seem not," she said. "You appear to have got yourself into such an outsize *spot*, that I don't see how you're ever going to get out of it."

He shook his head sadly.

"I'm finished," he answered. "Life is over for me."

"I don't know about *that* . . ." she mumbled.

"I do. April was my last chance of happiness. But I don't want any other chances. April is gone. I am content to leave it at that."

"You *are* an actor," she said, with a tight, tired smile. "I ought to have spotted that right away. I am *gaga*. That's what's the matter with me. . . . Well, look here, Vincent. Have all that poor child's things packed up . . ." she dabbed at her eyes, and said, "oh, dear!"

He stared at her with terrible fixity, and a large and heavy tear plunged down his cheek, which in carrying his hand up involuntarily, he caught in his palm, in the neighbourhood of his waist.

"I am an old woman," she whimpered. "A selfish old woman. *I* did all this!"

"*We* did all this," he corrected her. "Between us. But you are senile. It is *I* who alone am really responsible."

She began to totter towards the door. He went to her side and took her arm, and led her across the room. She stopped before passing out of the door, and stood, as if collecting her wits, staring through the wall, away at a point in some limbo beyond.

"Mr Hackett wants to see you. The lawyer," she said.

"Certainly, I will go and see him."

"Well, good-bye. And . . . good luck." She grabbed at his wrist and squeezed it in her small gloved hand for a moment.

"Thank you," he answered.

As they entered the hall, Willis was opening the front door. Maddie was there. She came in, tall and black and pale. Mrs Mallow passed her without greeting, followed by the scowling old housemaid, Maud.

Vincent and Maddie went back into the great pillared room.

"What have I done to Mrs Mallow?" Maddie said, sitting down.

"I don't expect she saw you. But it doesn't matter."

Maddie held up her beautiful head, scornful and white. She was confronting offence, as she felt it to be, with that strangely unavailing thing, her beauty.

"I suppose not," she said.

Vincent made an impatient gesture.

"All that's over!" he told her quickly.

"All what, Vincent? I don't understand."

"We're sunk, you and I. We sink or swim together, don't we, sister mine? Well, I am sunk. So there it is. But look, Mad, I have been all wrong. I put you up to a lot of things that are . . . oh, *unsound*. Forget about all that."

The girl's eyes were wide open with amazement, the mask began to writhe at the lips. He saw the sister he had loved so much and worked on like a sculptor with his clay, breaking up beneath his eyes, as a result of his assault upon her dream. He remembered how he had seen the same thing occurring with April, prior to her crashing to the floor, almost on the same spot now occupied by Maddie's feet. Hastily he turned away and pointed at the windows.

"But what a splendid day, Mad, you've brought with you! Thank God the sun is not affected by our little problems. And thank God you are *young*. . . . Now, tell us, before anything else, what that louse Dick has been doing to you."

She smiled doubtfully at him, only half-deceived by his precipitate optimism and appeals to solar detachment.

"Well, Vincent, Dick was very upset by . . . well, what he read in the newspapers."

"Naturally. The little middle-class fool. Well?"

"He said I must stop seeing you, that you were a 'bad hat'. . . . We had words about you, Vincent."

"And then?"

"And then, Vincent, he said I must be . . ."

She began to blush; an angry pale blush.

"What?" he asked. "What did the rat say—before he left the sinking ship?"

"Dick said . . . It is absurd, Vincent. He said, I must be in love with you."

"Ah!" Vincent intoned deeply. "Incest—on top of all my other crimes! Well, what a sneaking double-faced little person. What is that you have in your hand?"

Maddie looked down interrogatively at her hand, in which she held a piece of blue paper.

"His note," she said. "This is what Dick wrote. He left it on the kitchen table."

Vincent held out his hand. He took the note, flung himself against the wall, propping his shoulders, crossing his legs, and frowned down at the sheet of blue paper. His face became sallower and more drawn. He plucked, as he read, with a thumb and finger at his moustache. Still gazing at the document, he said,

"He charges you with unfaithfulness with Dougal?"

Maddie nodded.

"So I had a rival, it seems, for your affections, in the person of the murdered 'clubman'? Almost an insinuation isn't it, that I had a hand in the murder of Dougal? Quite a new angle on the crime, isn't it! . . . What an unspeakable louse."

He launched himself off the wall, stalked over to his desk, and thrust the note into an envelope.

"Look. I will keep this. This is important." He put the envelope in his pocket. "I will see a lawyer immediately. We must do something about Mr Morse without delay. To shut his mouth, and see he supplies you with money."

Maddie shook her head.

"I don't want money!" Maddie said. "I shall go back to modelling."

"He suggests you return to your mother's . . . You *can't* do that."

Maddie began to cry, holding a gloved hand over her eyes.

"You shall not," Vincent banged his fist into his palm. "So long as I have a penny left to my name. Look here, Mad, don't cry about *Dick*. That's nothing to cry about. You are well rid of him. It is damned good news that the little sneak has taken himself off. It was humiliating for you to have such a husband . . . and *that* was my doing too, since I found the little rat. I apologize for allowing you to contemplate such a marriage."

He threw his head up and his eyes were illumined with all his old arrogance. "Now, Mad, go find a proper man. And don't worry, Mad, my sweet, if he jettisons a few silly old aitches. Forget about all that. Anything—*anything* is better than some dirty little middle-class fellow. Pick a duke or a dustman. Take my advice and *skip the Middle-class*."

CHAPTER XXV

SUPPER WITH A PAROLED PRISONER

WHEN Martin Penny-Smythe and Vincent rose from the table, a sense of well-being had been induced in Martin, which he was far from feeling, when he had sat down. The champagne and the Armagnac had removed the sensation of chill and desolation.

The cold meal of canned foods; the gloom of the large pillared room: the great futile easel, like the skeleton of a pre-historic bird, stuck up in the half-lit backgrounds bare of furniture, projecting its menacing shadow; the consciousness that they were alone in this house by the river—for Willis was no longer there—all contributed to make this one of the most unpleasant experiences of his life. To sup with a friend who was out on bail, over whom a formidable charge was hanging (though how far Vincent was involved he did not know), was bad enough. But when that friend admitted you to a dark and untidy hall, and you sat down to eat in one corner of this ill-lit room, the size of a concert-hall—with no whisky, only gin (which he hated), beforehand, because, presumably, the twelve shillings had not been forthcoming to provide a bottle of Scotch—then things indeed, had reached a pass where the pleasure of passing an evening with a friend was a stern ordeal.

Vincent also had undergone a subtle change. This, perhaps, was the worst feature of the situation. He had always been in the habit of feeding upon Vincent's vitality. At the first suck that he took, with his stammering lips, he found the source was dry. Vincent made no effort to dazzle him, or to assert what he had once described as his 'mastery' over him. Like a party at which each guest has to bring his own drink,

227

Martin realized at once that he would have to supply his own vitality. It would even not have been amiss, if he had in very fact brought his own whisky.

Of course, Vincent had disclaimed distress. Now he was a "char-man," but what of that? Did his own butlering too. But he was a damn sight better servant than Willis. He had to give Willis a reference to-morrow, he said. Willis was coming round to fetch it. He was going to say that Willis was the best servant in his experience, after himself. Ha, ha, ha!

They got going during dinner—or rather, Vincent did. He became more like his old self. And now as Martin and he rose and walked over towards the fire—Vincent carrying the Armagnač bottle, and when they sat down filling up his glass—a fairly rosy glow had been shed over the proceedings. Martin sighed. He felt in his pocket for his Peterson pipe and placed it on the table beside him. Then he folded his hands upon his stomach.

Vincent placed two rugged sections of wood upon the smouldering remains of the logs, which had produced such a manly fireworks before they had moved over to the dinner table.

"Thank god, I still have *wood*," Vincent said, standing up. "We have enough . . . I have enough here to build a log-cabin."

"Is it as b-b-bad as all that, Vincent! I mean are you really ber-ber-broke?"

Vincent looked over quickly at him.

"I'm hard up naturally. But it's a hard-up world we live in."

"Why don't you let me l-l-lend you something, Vincent. Jer-jer-just to tide you over old man? If a . . . hundred pounds . . ."

"My dear fellow!"

"No, but if it would bub-bub-be of any *use*."

"You'll want that, my, boy for your new kit when you join the Archies. As a matter of fact, I don't need money."

"But you mus-mus-must . . ."

Vincent laughed.

"Oddly enough, no. For the first time in my life!" he said. "But it's jolly nice of you, Martin, to offer to loan it to me."

"You're qu-quite sure, Vincent? I should be der-der-delighted if you . . . would."

"Really not, old man! I can't tell you how touched I am, that you should stand by me. I haven't deserved it." He sighed. "I have been a dreadful fool."

Vincent emptied, slowly and reflectively, his glass of Armagnac.

"One lives and l-l-learns," said Martin.

"One doesn't always *live* . . . if one learns too much. That's the trouble."

"To learn too much is . . . im-im-impossible."

"I am in a pretty tight corner, Martin. I may have to pay a prohibitive price for experience."

"*Really*, Vincent? I didn't know . . ."

"Yes. I may be in for such a long spell of prison, if they convince themselves I am an accomplice of Halvorsen's, that when I come out I shall be an old man."

"Oh, *n-n-no*, Vincent. You'll get through this all right. I'm . . . positive."

"Hope so. Still, don't let me depress you. I am more interested myself by what is behind it all, Martin. All the problems of Class, for instance, positively seethe and bubble around my sad case. I am a blasted object-lesson in how *not* to conduct one's life, if one starts from scratch, as I did."

"I can see what you mean, Vincent. You made m-m-mistakes. We all do."

"Made mistakes! I have made nothing but mistakes. Every man is allowed one or two mistakes. But I have made mistake my principle."

"We all think that, at c-c-certain mo-mo-moments."

"I systematized a great initial blunder, so that anything I touched was absolutely guaranteed to go wrong."

Vincent leant forward eagerly. His face was irradiated with the joy of the discoverer.

"Picture yourself," he said, "in the bottom drawer. Born in it, educated in it."

"That I c-c-can do quite easily."

"That is such a handicap that when you find out what sort of drawer you are in, it takes your breath away. Now, what do you do about it? That's the next point. When first we talked about this, you saw how *I* was meeting it."

"I dud-dud-did indeed."

"Well, *that's* not the way!"

"Ner-ner-no . . . perhaps not," Martin agreed. "I can see it m-mightn't be."

"No. What you *mustn't* do is to try to *bluff* your way out, as I thought I could. You can't escape by *fraud*—I thought I was a kind of Houdini. There was a stupid thing *to be* to start off with! Life is a big, pompous, exclusive Mayfair party, let us put it that way. Well, if you are born outside the party, it is no use gate-crashing it, is it? If you can't bear the thought of the party—with you outside it—you should do what Guy Fawkes did. Blow it up! Dynamite it. Don't *gate-crash* it."

"That's the road the Red t-takes?" Martin observed. "To blow it up."

"Exactly. The Red is better than the gate-crasher. But there is something better still. Or *is* it better, and can it work?"

"What is that, Vincent?"

"Oh, to arrive at a healthy understanding of how dull the party is. Then forget all about it."

"And leave the per-per-party people in un-un-undisturbed possession of all the fer-fine dresses, the . . . splendid houses, the good food and sham-sham-sham . . ."

"Champagne?" Vincent suggested. "Yes. To take one's ease is not everything."

"No, but there *is* ser-ser-such a thing, as social . . . justice."

"Social justice is *my* province, old man, not yours," laughed Vincent.

"I beg your pardon! We all h-h-have a stake in that!" Martin smiled. "I l-l-like champagne, too." He wiped his lips.

"All right. I should, I know, anyhow, have considered life less. I am a good actor. I should have thought more about my acting, and less of living."

"It is, after all, a very ker-ker-common fault . . . in actors and actresses," the pocket Belloc chuckled.

"Ah," cried Vincent, "that again is my province."

"I know. Still, I h-h-have met a good few Stage folks."

"Oh, you're perfectly right. The Stage is choked with deadly snobs. They no longer try to act anything but the part of their perfect gentleman, or perfect lady. But what a really fearful thought, Martin. I don't think I can bear it!"

He clapped his hand to his forehead—very much in the Adelphi tradition.

"What is the matter, Vincent?" Martin asked, smiling.

"Have I," Vincent asked in hollow tones, "have I all the time been just a very typical actor-man . . .? Nothing but that? Oh, dear."

Martin laughed.

"I should say that that would be ver-ver-very unjust."

"Thank you, Martin, for those kind words!" Vincent pushed the Armagnac towards his friend.

Vincent discarded the Adelphi manner abruptly. His unmannered self was back—and he did not even seem to be thinking of the dramatic value of the unmannered, that was the disturbing part of it. Martin had the feeling that there was something Vincent had to say that could not be said by his routine self. But as Martin had more than his share of the Englishman's aversion to exhibitions of the self, with the veils of 'humour' laid aside, he became watchful and uneasy.

"I try to think clearly about myself," Vincent began, after

a pause. "It is very difficult. I have arrived at the stock-taking. It is hard work; and of course not very pleasant. Am I this sort of man? Am I that sort of man? Why did I act like that? Why have I always acted like this? It is like taking up an unfamiliar and difficult subject. Like studying counterpoint or Arabic."

Martin sipped his Armagnac, allowing each burning velvet sip to call in the nose to complicate the pleasure.

"Wer-why worry?" he asked, putting down his glass.

"Haven't you ever tried to get a dispassionate peep at yourself?" Vincent asked him.

Martin shook his head firmly.

"I'm not interesting enough," he answered. "to m-make it wer-wer-worthwhile. I t-t-take myself for granted."

"Try some day, all the same. Stick your self up and pot at it, with your mind. Capital mental exercise."

"My religion . . ."

"Oh, yes, of course," Vincent interrupted. "The self-satisfaction of the catholic!"

"On the con-contrary," Martin contented himself with saying. "The catholic is ner-not encouraged t-t-t-wards inflations of the ego. That is a per-per-protestant trait."

"But I know what is the matter with me," Vincent assured him earnestly. "I have discovered the flaw. I know all about it. I have no . . . *protestant conceit* left."

Vincent was informing him of this with an unaccustomed earnestness, and a rather stupid expression in his face, but Martin felt relieved all the same at finding them upon this speculative plane. There he felt at home. He had anticipated something . . . oh, like that awful "confession" business in Venice, only probably worse.

"G-g-glad to hear it, old man," he said approvingly.

"I've got all the dope," Vincent assured him in a confidential undertone. "I can never fool myself again. I have the name for my trouble even. I suffer from the *mal du siècle*, wasn't it called?"

"Mal du siècle," nodded Martin, in a less good French accent, but with great authority.

"I've been going about with this *mal du siècle* for years. But now I know the worst. I know I've got it! As a matter of fact, I know so much about Vincent Penhale that it makes me quite uncomfortable to be here any longer, right inside the fellow!"

He gave a strained, sneering bark of a laugh, and stretched his arm out convulsively for the Armagnac.

"I th-th-thought you seemed a little un-un-uncomfortable," Martin said, peering critically up at him, under shaggy brows.

Vincent shrugged off nervously the suggestion of any *visible* embarrassment.

"My main trouble," he told Martin, with finality, "is that I am all made up of *action*."

"That's true, Vincent, I think," Martin gave his heavy endorsement. "Y-y-you *are*."

"The arch-type of that sort of man who is all *action*," Vincent continued, "is to be found in Berlin—or that bloody little Jack-in-the-box up in his balcony, at the Palazzo Venezia. That is obvious enough. Our epoch finds its highest expressions in those dynamical puppets—with little names full of a stupid percussion, like *Hitler*. Our time will go down branded with those six letters."

"There was *another* time," said Martin, "also dominated by a mer-mer-man who was made up entirely of *action*."

"Which was that?"

"The Napoleonic. A great writer, wer-wer-one of Bonaparte's commissars, wrote a ber-ber-book. It was called *Le Rouge et le Noir*."

Vincent nodded.

"That wer-was all about *action*. The theory of action—à la-la-la Bub-bub-bub-bonaparte. . . . Der-did you ever happen to read it . . . V-vincent?"

"Always wanted to . . . language difficulty."

"It is tr-tr-translated," Martin said. "And I am sure Julien Sorel woo-woo-would interest you."

"But that was not a mechanical age was it, like ours."

"Napoleon won his battles with s-s-superior artillery. It s-s-seemed mechanical *to them.*"

"Anyhow, it wasn't full of Napoleons, as ours is full of Hitlers. . . . I know hundreds of Hitlers. I have always felt a hearty dislike for the empty little colourless emperors! And now . . .!"

Martin chuckled good-humouredly.

"But I have the imperialist mind!" Vincent challenged him, before he had time to contribute a remark or two as he wanted to, on the subject of sub-Hitlers: but the stylistic stutter slowed him up. "You are observant enough, Martin, to understand what I mean. I have been overweening in my belief that all can be achieved, by *action.* No one has believed more in action than I have. Arrogant have-not action-and-damn-the-consequences."

Martin had for some time been engaged, intermittently, in lighting his pipe. Smoke now burst forth from his lips. The damp peat-like tobacco at last had ignited.

"But you are, Vincent," he objected, "a mer-mer-man-of-action. . . . Aren't you! It is a faculty. You her-have it. The hero of Stendhal ab-ab-bout whom I wer-wer-was talking . . . *hadn't.* You mer-must *act*—or *die.*"

Vincent, aloof and sombre, observed him for a moment.

"You've got it," he said lighting a cigarette. "If I stop acting . . . I die."

He threw the cigarette into the fireplace and filled his glass from the bottle.

"That, after all is wer-why you have bub-been an *actor.* You cannot her-help . . . *acting.*"

"That's an obvious crack. But there's more in that than you think. It is not just a pun."

"Of-of-course it isn't," Martin insisted that he understood that.

"No. My acting is a form of *action*—not of make-believe.

I have attempted, haven't I, to act my way out of a predicament. . . . I have never been a real actor. It would have been better if I had been more of an artist. I am not an artist, Martin. I am always too much in earnest. I am a very solemn fellow indeed, really."

"Are you, Vincent?" Martin rumbled sceptically, twinking gloomily at him.

"Oh, yes. Really. I'm always acting and throwing myself about, and wisecracking, so you think I'm not, but I'm always in dead earnest, really. Remember, I have been gambling with my life. Only solemn fellows do that. You have been taken in by the gambler's mask. I am a very solemn fellow, like all *actionists*. For what is the driving-power that kept me in such incessant activity? Answer: a sensation of life-and-death importance attached to whatever I had in hand. The will to *change* something: all will-to-action (and-damn-the-consequences), is that. But with that goes the belief that it will be better different. See?"

"A p-p-perfect definition of the protestant mind," gurgled Martin, giving an impromptu impersonation of a jolly monk, taking things very much as they come, and pursuing the static way of life, with suitable conviviality.

"All this is a bug——an infection," Vincent insisted. "Europe has run amok. In my little way, I reflect—I have reflected—what is biting Europe. *Look how I went on!* Just think of it! You must have seen. You ought to have told me."

"Why the past tense, old man?"

"Because . . . I am cured."

Vincent got up.

"I have proved," he said, looking down at Martin, "upon my little personal stage, that force is barren. Conceived in those hard terms of action-for-action's-sake nothing can be achieved, except for too short a period to matter. I have *proved* that, have I not?"

"Perhaps. I der-don't know."

"The demonstration has been plain enough, I am afraid, to satisfy the most particular."

He stood ˙ brooding over Martin, who shuffled his feet and cleared his throat—disinclined, himself, at the moment, to action of any sort, yet feeling it was expected of him.

"You cer-cer-certainly seem out of conceit with yourself to-night, old man," Martin grumbled, taking up his pipe and reaching for a match-box.

"I have some reason to be," Vincent answered, "And now, Martin, I fear I shall have to be very inhospitable and turn you out."

Martin looked up at his friend in uneasy astonishment.

"I have a lot of things to do," said Vincent. "In connexion with my case, you know."

"Can I h-h-help . . . in any way?" Martin asked, as he organized himself, and began the sluggish evacuation of his armchair. He got himself on his feet, his trouser-knees bagging, his waistcoat untidily crowding-up, high upon his stomach. He blinked gloomily at his friend. "I do hope, Vincent, this business wer-won't involve you . . . in more trouble!"

"I don't think so," Vincent answered dully. "They will treat me like a dog, of course, after all that stuff in the papers—about the poor boy that lived in style, and married the niece of the baronet. They will feel I was trying to steal a march on the privileged classes, and will be correspondingly severe. It will take on a political colour in their minds —it always does when the accused is *working-class*. Something like a one-man insurrection. A dangerous slave in revolt, kicking over the traces. And you know how merciless they are, where their beastly little food-and-rent tickets are concerned. *Money* is sacrosanct! So there you are. It will be tough, Martin. It will be pitiless."

Martin knocked out his pipe in the fireplace.

"But they have," he objected, "to p-p-prove old man . . . after all, they must show that you h-h-have . . ."

"I know. Well, anyhow we shall see. And now . . . good-bye."

He held out his hand, which, when Martin took it, was icy cold.

"Well . . . not g-g-good-bye, Vincent." Martin stared in his face almost angrily. He privately considered that *the actor* was uppermost for the moment in this most "difficult" of friends. But he was very worried about him. "Look, I want to t-t-take you out to dinner. To some night-spot. W-w-what do you say? This place," he looked round frown-ingly at the cheerless vastness, "is not calculated to r-r-relieve depression. Damn!"

He tripped, having kicked his foot up under a rug in the semi-darkness, away from the reading lamps, by the fire.

"It's all right," said Vincent, dismissing brusquely that angle of the matter. "This is a good place."

In slow-time they approached the door.

"I should get the h-h-hump . . . in here."

"Oh, no you wouldn't. If you were me."

"Why don't you st-stop . . . at a *hotel*?" Vincent helped Martin into his overcoat. "Just for . . . a week or so?"

Martin shook his head.

"That would be very grim," he declared. "Rich people. Lots of expensive luggage. Commissionaires administering servility, to gouge out a tip. Couldn't stand it!"

Vincent stood in the doorway.

"I wish I could have got you a taxi," he apologized. "But they have cut off my telephone. They are great newspaper readers, the Telephone Company. 'Poor boys' impersonating their betters oughtn't to have telephones."

Martin shook himself. He turned back slowly towards Vincent, who had stepped down into the path.

"Vincent," he said severely, "you ought to let me l-l-lend you . . . a l-l-little money."

"Quite unnecessary," Vincent told him, shivering a little.

"It is unfriendly of you. Wer-wer-whatever you say, when I get back . . . I shall der-der-do so!"

"I have told you, Martin, I don't want it. I have all I want," Vincent answered. He waved his hand a little, and smiled, as Martin passed through the gate. Martin threw up his hand in a clumsy salute—half-wave, half oath of allegiance.

Chapter XXVI

VINCENT IN THE HALL

THE next morning, when Willis arrived at ten o'clock he found the front door about two inches ajar. He did not touch it. Mr Penhale had perhaps gone out to telephone—since the service he knew, had been discontinued. He pressed his finger civilly and not too hard, upon the bell-button, and left it there for not too long. A quiet little sub-servient ring. Then he waited.

In five minutes, Willis rang again. Then he relapsed into the waiting position. In four minutes, he placed his finger upon the bell-button, firmly, but respectfully, and ventured to leave it there for a somewhat longer period. He withdrew it a fraction of an inch, and, greatly daring, drove it home again. Then, looking more deeply respectful than ever, he stood back from the door and disposed himself for a further period of expectant inactivity.

It was only after a quarter of an hour that Willis, first looking up and down the street, very gently pushed the front door inwards a few inches, obtaining a view of the hall. There, hanging from the disused gas-suspension in the middle of it, was Mr Penhale, his tongue protruding, and his face black. A piece of white paper, in the manner of a placard, was attached to his chest.

Willis stared at his dead master fixedly, for a matter of thirty seconds. He then stepped back, carefully restored the door to its former ajarness, and left the premises with a brisk step. Seeing a motionless policeman, a block away, he stood outside the gate, placed his hollowed hands to his mouth, and allowed his voice—which when given full rein, was of considerable volume—to issue in a hoarse and urgent cry.

The constable considered him, without moving. Willis then semaphored with his arms. Thereupon the constable set himself in cumbrous motion; looking up and down the street, passed with great deliberation from one side to the other; and at length arrived where Willis was patiently awaiting him.

Entering the house together, they stood looking at Vincent Penhale for a short while without speaking.

"Wots all this?" the constable asked in a suspicious voice at last.

"It is Mr Vincent Penhale, officer," said Willis—in a tone that suggested the officer was wanting in knowledgeableness.

The constable whistled—a low blast of understanding. He then turned upon Willis, a dull censorious eye.

"'Oo 'er you?"

"I was Mr Penhale's servant," Willis informed him modestly.

The police constable stepped nearer to the hanging figure.

"Wot's this 'ere?" he asked, pointing to the paper pinned upon its chest. In block letters were written the words:

"Whoever finds this body, may do what they like with it. *I* don't want it.

Signed. Its former inhabitant."

The policeman prowled round behind to see if there was anything unusual at the back. One of the hands was curled up, the hem of the jacket twisted into the vice-like fingers. The policeman felt the other hand. He took his own away quickly.

Willis regarded fixedly the hideous mask of his former master with fear and curiosity. This blackened object was not more remote than had been the everyday face of the man he had served. This was a strange form for his employer's wilfulness to take certainly; but little stranger than many other manifestations, of which Willis had been the impassive spectator for a considerable period.

"The gentleman may have left a message," Willis suggested, stepping forward. "Probably in the studio, it would be—the door is just be'ind you."

He came beside the constable and opened the studio door. There upon the floor, just inside, were several letters.

Willis went in and picked one up, addressed to himself. He tore it open.

"'Ere wot do you think you're doin', eh? All this 'ere 'as to be left like we find it. 'And me that, *if* you please. And don't you go touchin' nothing else."

Willis handed him the letter.

"That's my reference that is," he said, in an offended voice to the policeman. "No, that one. '*To 'oom it may concern,*' Ah, that's it."

The policeman without answering, drew a letter from an unsealed envelope, which had been inside the first. He looked down at the notepaper.

"Is this 'ere, your bloomin' character?" he asked, handing the sheet to Willis, with an eye of dignified derision.

Willis read—

"Dear Sir, or Madam. James Willis, the manservant, has asked me for a reference. He has a suitably low opinion of himself. He is so unobtrusive as to be alarming, at times. He often makes you jump, if you don't know he's there. Should your heart be at all dicky it would be best to insist upon the heaviest footwear. He is honest. He is too stupid to be anything else. As to the jargon of etiquette: I believe he could cope with a duke, or a marquis, though I believe a knight's widow is as high as he's gone so far. Is moderately clean. (Needs watching). Is lazy and slow. Not over fond of whisky, but needs watching with rum. Disguises his inebriety, when that occurs, under a cloak of sanctimonious rheumatism. ('Rheumatics' is his stand-by whenever in a spot.) His great handicap is that his feet smell. (As none of his teeth are his own, his mouth's all right). You will have to be firm about *the feet*. It's a sickly smell, like decaying flowers. You should never ask him to cook. He can't do it. But if you *do*, the result is so unpleasant you'll never ask him again."

Willis was quite inscrutable as he handed this back to the constable, who had collected the other letters, one of which was addressed to Mrs Madeleine Morse, 29 Linlithgow Terrace, Harrow Road.

"Now, where's the telephone?" asked the constable.

"The telephone service was discontinued officer," Willis answered, studying a floor-board dispassionately.

The constable snorted.

"O-kay," said he, as if Willis had been concealing the telephone on his person. "You come alonger me."

"It's as you wish, officer."

They passed singly the rigid figure suspended in the middle of the hall. Willis threw a reproachful look at the black profile, with its tongue out. The perusal of the reference had imbued with a new life for him these sardonic remains. He took his eyes away quickly from the face, for he had the sensation that it might speak. He hastened his step. He did not like to have it at his back. He suddenly felt it might kick him as he passed in front of it. He ran into the constable, who drew up in the doorway, assailed by an afterthought.

"'Ow did you get 'ere? 'Oo opened this blinkin' door?"

Willis hesitated, and became a little red in the face.

"I came here, officer, to fetch that letter you 'as in your hand."

"Your blinkin' character?"

"That is so, officer. . . ."

Three hours later, Maddie sat beside the fire, in Mrs Penhale's sitting-room, knitting a black and white jumper. Her mother was ironing a petticoat. Minnie sat, her hands folded in her lap, by the window, in such a position as to be able to command the entrance to Linlithgow Terrace, which at the other end was sealed with a blank brick wall.

Mrs Penhale was in action, in defence of Vincent, and she thudded with her iron to accompany her defensive barrage. Minnie (the attacking force), was tight-lipped. She listened to the thudding iron, and stared stonily out of the window.

"I don't care wot you say," she answered, "I say 'e's disgraced all of us. The young man wot come 'ere to do the write-up told me 'e'd be 'ung."

"Oh, Minnie!"

"Yes. 'Ung!"

"I don't believe a word of it!" Maddie burst out. "You've invented it, you know you have, Minnie. You ought to be *ashamed* of yourself. You're a very wicked woman!"

"Oh, 'ark at Lady Maddy-line!" screamed Minnie, swivelling her hand in that direction.

"And so you *are*. Right down wicked!" Mrs Penhale thumped home the iron upon the petticoat. "Pity, they don't 'ang *you*, Minnie, for all your wicked thoughts. You *poison-pen!*"

Mrs Penhale threw a great deal of venom into "poison-pen."

"I! A poison-pen?"

"Yes. A poison-pen—wot sends anomalous letters," her mother reminded her, in barbed tones, "to people about 'oo their 'usbands sees, time they're away."

"It's a pity you 'asn't anything better to do, mother, than listen to people like that Mrs Baines. You'd sooner listen to 'er than wot you would to your own daughter . . ."

"Ah, that I would!" Mrs Penhale assured her heartily, delivering a terrific thump at the ironing board. She shuffled round the table casting sideways glances at her antagonists, and sat down heavily in a chair opposite Maddie. "It catches me there," she told her youngest daughter, placing her hand upon the lumbar regions. "Me backs opening and shutting."

"I told you, mother, not to do the ironing this morning," Maddie scolded her. "I'd have done it for you, this evening . . . . I had to finish this, before I did anything else."

"I know you 'ad, dear."

"Just *in case*. I must have some clothes if I'm going modelling again."

"Why don't your husband support you?" Minnie broke

in bitterly. "Anyone would think you wasn't married to 'im, the way you goes on!"

"Minnie! That's quite sufficient!" Mrs Penhale commanded, classily hissing "sufficient." "There's no call for you to give your advice, where nobody 'asn't asked for it!"

Minnie bridled darkly, sat in silence, and glared out of the window.

"There's a policeman coming here!" she exclaimed in a moment.

"'Ow do you know 'e's coming 'ere, Minnie?" Mrs Penhale demanded.

"I'm sure of it!" Minnie answered with sinister triumph.

Maddie put her work down. As she could get no paler than she was at normal times, Maddie tended to flush when alarmed; and now a slight pinkish bloom had come into her face. Her eyes seemed enormously dark and large. All three women sat in silence. Then came the heavy bullying knock upon the outer door.

"You was right, Minnie!" gasped her mother.

Minnie had already flown to answer the summons. The door into the miniature hall half-closed behind her. The gruff voice of the Law came through, to Maddie and her mother, alternating with Minnie's rapid tones.

"'E's 'anged 'isself, I tell yer!" Quite distinctly both women heard the gruff voice swell angrily to say.

"Mother!" Maddie clung to Mrs Penhale staring into her face in demented interrogation, as if this ignorant old woman, the domestic goddess of her childhood, were an all-wise sphinx. But the mother's eyes had a wild staring look as well, and her old hands began to tremble.

Minnie returned into the room, closing the door behind her.

"A letter for you, Madeleine," she said solemnly, handing her sister a letter.

"What is it, Minnie?" her mother asked the inexorable Minnie, almost cajolingly. "Nothing as 'appened, dear, 'as it?"

Maddie had opened the letter and was staring at its contents. It comprised a few lines only.

"I am leaving you, Maddie, darling. I am blotting myself out to-night and you will see me and hear me no more, but remember me as one who loved you very dearly. Kiss mother for me, and ask her forgiveness. Do what you can to take care of her. Good-bye, Maddie, my sweet."

A piercing cry rose from the writhing lips, now whiter than the cheeks. Vincent's sister flung herself back in a violent swoon. Mrs Penhale hung her head like a contrite child and whimpered. Minnie picked up Vincent's letter, put it on the table, and returned to the front door. Half the helmet, half the moustache, the sullen eye, of a police constable appeared and disappeared, as she opened and closed the door into the living-room.

CONCLUSION

TWENTY young men were looking closely at Madeleine Penhale. They screwed their eyes up; they struck their arms out at her and roughly computed the distance between her haughty and pathetic eyebrow and the tip of her chin; they sat hunched up, staring at her, as if she were a sphinx and they were awaiting her answer to their eternal question: Were they duds, or had they the makings of a Picasso or a Paul Cézanne?

Maddie was back upon her throne. It was the portrait class at the St George's School of Fine Arts, and Maddie sat unblinking—with more pins and needles in her legs than she used to have, and dizziness sometimes at the end of the day, but still the most immobile as well as the most beautiful of London models. And those students even who started with a prejudice against her, because she was not ugly, like Madame Cézanne, were soon reconciled to her beauty— because at least she was as motionless as a plate of Cézanne's apples.

A young man who bore a distant resemblance to Vincent Penhale, had, as he squinted at her, other thoughts. As he mixed his paints upon his palette, attempting to discover the equivalent for the warm pallor of her face, he saw other possibilities in this beautiful young woman, beside those appropriate to a hired dummy. He played with the thought of carrying his investigations into nature still farther, and reflected that a visit to the movies in her company might as a first step tend to break the ice. For that there was a good deal of ice to break was obvious to anyone.

At the next rest, when Maddie got down from the "throne," he was smiling at her.

"Tired?" he asked.

246

"No," she smiled. "Only a little stiff."

"Have a chocolate?" he invited, holding out a box he had just opened.

"A chocolate?" she repeated, looking, a little confused, down at the pretty box. "Thanks, I don't mind if I do."